DRAGON'S STORM

DRAGON'S STORM

Legion of Angels: Book 4

www.ellasummers.com/dragons-storm

ISBN 978-1-5455-6070-9

DRAGON'S STORM

Legion of Angels: Book 4

Ella Summers

Books by Ella Summers

Legion of Angels

1   Vampire's Kiss

2   Witch's Cauldron

3   Siren's Song

4   Dragon's Storm

Dragon Born Serafina

1   Mercenary Magic

2   Magic Games

3   Magic Nights

4   Rival Magic

Dragon Born Shadow World

The Complete Trilogy

Dragon Born Alexandria

1   Magic Edge

2   Blood Magic

3   Magic Kingdom

4   Shadow Magic [2017]

Dragon Born Awakening

1   Fairy Magic

2   Spirit Magic [2017]

More Books by Ella Summers

Sorcery & Science
Coming soon…

Read more at
www.ellasummers.com

Chapters

CHAPTER ONE
The Interrogators

I STOOD ON a high balcony, the sort you'd expect to see at an opera house. But the horror scene playing out on the stage below was not a dramatic rendition for the entertainment of me and my fellow Legion soldiers. It was just another day at the office.

A single beam of light punctuated the dark room, casting the vampire in a pale halo. He sat on a hard metal chair bolted to the floor. It looked like a cross between a dentist's chair and a medieval torture device. Tools and levers protruded from the arms of the chair like porcupine quills. Shackles locked the vampire's ankles to the footrest just as smooth metal cuffs bound his hands to the armrests.

The vampire's gaze darted in quick, nervous movements across the room. I didn't blame him. If I'd been in his place, I'd have been scared too. The Legion of Angels didn't take kindly to misbehaving supernaturals.

The door groaned like a dragon awoken early from a long nap. It wasn't old or broken. It groaned for the same reason the vampire had been left alone in the room for the past hour: the Legion's Interrogators wanted to scare him out of his wits. So far, they were doing a pretty amazing job, not surprising since breaking people was their job.

A man and a woman, each one dressed in a bright white uniform, stepped through the door, and the vampire's agitation escalated into all-out panic. He thrashed and pulled at his restraints, trying desperately to free himself. The shackles and cuffs moved just enough for him to hurt himself without giving him any chance of escape.

The Interrogators moved forward like two white ribbons of silk, smooth and elegant. The color of their uniforms was also significant. The standard Legion uniform was black, a practical color for a soldier. It hid bloodstains well. Which was precisely why the Interrogators wore white. They weren't soldiers on a battlefield here. They were fighting a different sort of battle, a mental battle. Interrogators were mind-breakers and soul-crushers. They wanted their prisoners to see the blood, down to the very last drop.

The vampire let out a quiet moan of despair. On my right side, my roommate Ivy shifted her weight uncomfortably and looked away. She possessed the sort of unwavering empathy that made her an excellent counselor for the Legion's traumatized soldiers—but a terrible witness to the Legion's atrocities. On my left side, my other roommate Drake continued to watch the Interrogators advance on the shackled vampire. His eyes had glazed over, taking on a distant, distracted look. We were required to observe this interrogation as part of our training, so he was watching, but he was trying really hard not to see. The rest of the soldiers standing with us fell somewhere on the spectrum between Ivy and Drake.

Except for Jace. He stood perfectly still, his eyes

following the vampire's every movement, his brain processing every twitch. I wasn't surprised. Jace was the son of Colonel Fireswift, the cruelest angel I'd ever met. His father had probably been taking him to witness prisoner interrogations since he was a toddler.

"Mr. Farrows," the male Interrogator said, standing over the vampire like a great white shark.

His name was Captain Alexander Norton. Most Legion Interrogators didn't have a home office. They went where they were needed, when they were needed. Captain Norton had visited the New York office several times since I'd joined the Legion. He always sat alone, or with other Interrogators. They didn't like to fraternize with the other soldiers in the Legion—you know, just in case someday they had to torture one of us. Immortals had long memories. Interrogators viewed personal connections to other people as a liability. I preferred to see friends as a perk of life.

"You have been seen in the company of Charles Rune and the other members of the so-called House Rune," Captain Norton continued.

"House Rune is not an officially-recognized body of the vampire kingdom," the female Interrogator said in a low, eerie whisper.

The vampire's whole body shook.

"That's Selena Singh," Jace said behind me. "She's one of the best Interrogators at the Legion. My father speaks highly of her."

Which was reason enough for concern. I'd never heard Colonel Fireswift speak highly of anyone, the other angels included. Major Singh must have been a cruel beast for him to admire her. I looked at her. She'd have been taller than her male colleague even without the massively high heels she wore. With them, she towered over him—and over the whimpering vampire bolted to the chair.

"The vampires of House Rune are rogues," she told the vampire. "Rogues are dangerous creatures, Mr. Farrows. They turn humans into vampires whenever they feel like it, without the approval of the vampire king or the Legion of Angels. Rogue vampires believe themselves above the laws of this Earth. Above the laws of the gods." She leaned in, her face stopping only inches from his. "Do you believe yourself above the laws of the gods?"

The vampire shook his head.

"And yet you are one of the vampires made by House Rune," said Captain Norton. "You knew they were a rogue group and yet you willingly joined them."

"Please," the vampire croaked. "Have mercy."

"The Legion of Angels offers mercy and protection to all loyal, rule-abiding citizens, Mr. Farrows," Major Singh declared, braiding her fingers together. "We show no mercy to traitors who spit on the gods' laws."

The vampire sagged against his restraints.

"Do you know why the transformation of vampires is so highly regulated, Mr. Farrows?" she asked him.

The vampire said nothing. He didn't even look at her.

"Because vampires are dangerous beings," she said. "Every vampire is a potential bloodbath. They are strong, fast, and have an insatiable appetite for human blood. Candidates must be thoroughly screened to weed out individuals with a weak constitution. And all candidates who pass the rigorous screening and become vampires are carefully observed by the vampire house that made them. For one whole year, they cannot go anywhere alone. A guard from their house is always with them, ready to execute them if they cross the line. This procedure is for everyone's protection. It's how we keep people safe." She grabbed the vampire's face between her thumb and index finger, tilting it up until his gaze met hers. "Do you know how rogue vampires keep people safe?"

He swallowed hard.

"They don't," she hissed. "They create vampires whenever it suits them, which is usually when they need more bodies to fight for them. They make vampires out of murderers, rapists, and other criminals. Becoming a vampire doesn't change who you are inside. It only magnifies your most defining personality traits."

Captain Norton stood behind his colleague, his face quiet, almost serene. "Before Charles Rune turned you into a vampire and you changed your name, you were Julian Kane."

The vampire looked up at the mention of his former name.

"You lived a respectable life as a member of the Kane Coven, one of New York's most prestigious witch covens," Captain Norton continued. "Though your parents are both witches of great power, you inherited none of their gift. You had no significant magic of your own, so the coven offered you the position of their accountant."

"Forced me."

Captain Norton looked at the vampire.

"They *forced* me to be their accountant," he ground out. "My parents forced me to take it. It was the only job that didn't require magic, the only way for me to be part of the coven. The great Henry and Alexa Kane were too proud to admit to the other covens that they had spawned a magical dud."

"The Kanes have another child, your younger sister Marina, a magical genius," said Major Singh.

The vampire frowned at them. "If you're trying to rub my face in my wretched inadequacy, you're twenty years too late."

Major Singh gave him a cool smile. "Mr. Farrows, what do you know about how a Legion Interrogator works?"

"You torture people until they break."

"Torture is such a crass word," she said. "Haven't we been having a very pleasant conversation?"

The vampire shot her a cautious look, like he didn't like where this was headed.

"It isn't our job to hurt you."

"But you'll do it to save the world, huh?"

"What if I were to tell you that neither my colleague nor I will harm you?" she said.

The vampire wriggled inside his restraints. Yep, he definitely didn't like where this was headed.

"What are the Interrogators up to?" Ivy whispered to me.

I shook my head. Her guess was as good as mine. The Legion's Interrogators weren't known for their hands-off approach to questioning prisoners.

"Mr. Farrows, when you decided to take matters into your own hands to gain the magic fate had denied you, why did you not come to the Legion?" Major Singh asked him.

The vampire blinked in surprise. "What?"

"The Legion of Angels welcomes candidates of all backgrounds, whether or not you possess magical powers. We would have given you the magic you desired and more.

There was no need to break the gods' laws. It's as simple as that."

Actually, it wasn't quite that simple. Legion soldiers gained their supernatural abilities by drinking the gods' Nectar in progressively stronger doses. The first sip primed your magic, unlocking your potential. The next dose gave you the physical powers of a vampire. The next bestowed the abilities of a witch. And then the powers of a siren. One by one, you gained more and more magic.

If it didn't kill you. That was the catch. If your will wasn't strong enough, if you hadn't trained hard enough, then the Nectar killed you. The mortality rate of the first sip was over fifty percent. Half the people who drank it died a horrible, excruciating death.

Fear was the reason the vampire hadn't come to the Legion. Fear of death. Fear of pain beyond imagination. I could see it in his eyes. Fear ruled him, even now. He didn't think he would survive the Nectar. And that was the reason he wouldn't survive. The mind was a powerful thing. It could be your greatest ally—or your worst enemy.

Major Singh pressed a button on her watch. A floodlight high above clicked on, shining down on a hole that had just opened in the floor. From that hole rose a pedestal, a white platform bathed in ethereal light. And on the pedestal sat a clear bottle of Nectar.

It was pale, diluted. There were only a few drops of pure Nectar in there, mixed thoroughly with water. I'd drunk this same Nectar on my first day at the Legion. This was the Nectar that had unlocked my magical potential, the same Nectar that had killed half of my fellow initiates.

Major Singh opened the bottle. A warm rush of pure longing swept over me like a tidal wave. The Nectar sang to me. It wanted me to come to it, to drain that bottle down to the last delicious drop. I slid my tongue slowly across my mouth, wetting my lips in anticipation of the sweet ecstasy that awaited me down below. All I had to do was take it.

"Leda, stop," Ivy whispered beside me.

One of my legs was already over the balcony rail. Another second, and I would have jumped down there. Another two seconds, and it would have taken a small army to pry the bottle of Nectar from my mouth. The Interrogators would have loved that.

I backed up, swinging my leg back onto the balcony. I shot my comrades an embarrassed look. Most of them chuckled. Many people found my uncommon reaction to Nectar amusing. I couldn't really blame them. Despite its magic-bestowing qualities, Nectar was essentially poison. I craved poison. That was pretty messed up.

Sure, soldiers of the Legion drank heavily diluted drops of Nectar when they wanted to unwind, but that was something entirely different. Those drops were soft Nectar. They contained a tiny fraction of the Nectar present in that bottle below, which itself was the weakest Nectar the Legion used in its magic ceremonies. There was someone else who craved hard Nectar: Nero Windstriker, the only person ever born to two angel parents. Angel magic was in his blood, so of course he craved Nectar. What was my excuse?

I'd never known my parents, but Nero didn't think they were angels. Before joining the Legion, I'd never shown signs of having any significant magic, as was common of people with an angel parent. All I had was my weird hair, which for some reason mesmerized vampires. Considering those mesmerized vampires almost universally tried to tear my throat out, I wasn't calling my pale shiny hair an ability. It was more like a curse.

"Mr. Farrows," Captain Norton said with perfect calmness, completely unaware that I'd just nearly ruined their interrogation. "This is Nectar." He picked up the bottle and filled a small goblet. "We thought you'd enjoy an opportunity to remedy your past mistakes. Empty this cup, swear your undying allegiance to the Legion of Angels, and all will be forgiven."

The vampire pressed his lips together, sealing his mouth. His eyes never left the goblet.

Captain Norton sighed. "How disappointing."

"But not unexpected. Which is why we have invited Ms. Kane to join us today." Major Singh flicked her hand, and the door groaned open once again.

A woman about twenty years old stepped into the room. She wore a dark blue corset top with wide bell sleeves made of periwinkle chiffon. Her black skirt fitted her curves, its smooth lower hem kissing the tops of her knee-high leather boots. The long golden coil of her braided hair was pinned to the top of her head, and a tiny black hat sat at the center. A small piece of dark lace spilled out of the hat, covering one side of her face.

I knew that witch. Marina Kane went to school with my sister Bella. They were both students at the New York University of Witchcraft. Just last week, I'd sat at the same table as Marina and Bella, eating cheesecake and drinking tea. My sister said Marina was a talented witch, but it was her sense of humor that I'd found most interesting. Witches were usually too prim and proper to tell a joke, let alone tell one joke after the other for over two hours. Her hilarious tales of growing up in one of New York's premier witch covens had kept us thoroughly entertained. At the time, I'd thought she'd left no stone unturned about her life, but I'd been wrong. She'd never mentioned she had a brother.

When Marina looked at her brother now, there was no pity in her eyes, only sadness. She kept her hands folded tightly in front of her body, never reaching for him. The two Interrogators moved to either side of her.

"The universe requires balance, Mr. Farrows," Captain Norton said. "Some call it karma. Some say it's justice. I simply like to think of it as 'balance'. Every act of evil must be countered by at least one act of goodness. Otherwise, the Earth swings out of kilter. If darkness reigns, the demons gain a foothold into our world again. I don't think anyone wants that."

"We're giving you a precious gift: the chance to right your wrongs. The chance to help us save the world." Major Singh offered him the goblet. When the vampire didn't jump at the opportunity to drink it, she sighed. "The funny thing about the universe, Mr. Farrows, is it's not particularly picky about who rights the wrongs. As long as humanity's acts of goodness outweigh their acts of evil." She handed Marina the goblet.

The vampire screamed, thrashing against his restraints. The chair shook but held. It had been designed to withstand beings with supernatural strength far beyond his. It could even hold an angel.

"You leave her out of this!"

His eyes glowed silver-blue. Despite the fact that she represented everything he could never be, the vampire clearly loved his sister. He didn't want her to die.

"Drink the Nectar, and she may go home."

The vampire growled in frustration, fear burning

through the eerie glow of his eyes. I saw it then. His desire to live was stronger than his love for his sister. He wouldn't drink the Nectar.

The Interrogators must have seen it too. They shook their heads in silent disapproval.

"By order of the gods, I command you to drink," Major Singh told the witch.

Marina slowly lifted the goblet to her mouth, her hands trembling. The vampire watched in horror, tears streaming down his face.

"Wait." Captain Norton stayed her hand before the goblet touched her lips. He looked at the vampire. "There is another way. A way to balance your dark act without anyone swearing their life to the Legion, without anyone drinking the Nectar."

The vampire's eyes lit up with hope. "What is it?"

"The vampires of House Rune are responsible for countless acts of terror against humanity. But you, Mr. Farrows, are uniquely equipped to help us put an end to their campaign of extortion, fear, and death. All you have to do is tell us where to find Charles Rune's base of operations."

"You want me to betray the Butcher of New York?" The vampire shivered. "You might as well kill me yourself."

"The Legion of Angels is perfectly capable of protecting you from a few rogue vampires," Major Singh said, her nose turning up at his suggestion of incompetence. "But if you don't wish to help us, there are other ways for justice to be served."

"Justice? I thought you called it balance," the vampire said drily.

"My colleague calls it balance. He is an incorrigible

romantic. I've tried to cure him of it, but he remains stubbornly idealistic," she replied. "But I do not share his romantic notions of cosmic balance. I subscribe to the eye-for-an-eye school of thought. Blood will be spilled, Mr. Farrows. You will decide whether it's yours, your sister's, or the blood of the murdering traitorous vampires you call friends. Choose quickly, or I will choose for you. And I can guarantee you won't be happy with my choice."

Indecision crinkled the vampire's forehead. His gaze shifted to his sister, and then, just like that, the indecision melted away. His eyes hardened with the look of a man who had chosen his fate.

"Rune's base is in an old castle in the Wilds," he said.

Every band, belt, and chain on the chair simultaneously popped open.

"Show me." Captain Norton pulled up a magical projection that displayed a map of the Wilds.

The vampire's eyes darted to the restraints, as though he expected them to slam shut the moment he stood. He rose slowly, cautiously. The chair let him go. He crossed the room to stand before the shining dots and lines floating in the air, ruled by the Interrogators' magic and will.

"There." He pointed at a spot in the northern Wilds, a few hours' drive from Montreal. The projection shifted and jiggled like liquid silk, then the contours of the map reformed. "That's where it is."

Captain Norton glanced at his colleague.

She looked up from the readings on her tablet and nodded. "He's telling the truth."

Vampires were mostly immune to telepathy and truth serums, and compulsion only worked on them if they weren't fighting it. But the Legion possessed sophisticated

Magitech that could pretty accurately determine whether someone was lying by reading various bodily signs, keyed by supernatural species. It took a pretty hard-boiled person, typically a soldier with advanced training in resisting interrogation, to fool the machine. This vampire was untrained. I could decipher every emotion that surged through him just by reading the expressions on his face. I didn't need a fancy magic machine for that.

"The Legion thanks you for your cooperation," Major Singh told Marina. "One of our soldiers will return you to the university."

Marina's eyes flickered to her brother, who was wringing out his hands like he didn't know what to do with them. "What will happen to him?"

"As soon as House Rune has been destroyed, we will release him into the custody of House Vermillion, who will oversee his long journey toward integration into civilized vampire society."

"How long will it take for him to atone? How long before the black mark is cleared from his name?"

"That depends on him—and on his new vampire house. House Vermillion is quite adept at reforming rogue vampires. Their average time is just under fifty years."

"Fifty years?" A gasp broke Marina's refined facade. "This taint will be on our family for fifty years?"

Amongst supernaturals, the entire family bore any dishonor incurred by its members. For witches, that dishonor extended to their coven. The other covens of New York would shun the Kanes. Their alliances would crumble, their wealth and influence evaporate. Fifty years was a long time to bear that black mark. It was very unlikely the Kane coven would ever recover from that.

The vampire frowned. He clearly hadn't thought this through. When you dealt with the Legion of Angels, you had to be very, very careful. By betraying Charles Rune, he'd spared himself and his sister from the Nectar that killed half the people who drank it, but he had not spared them the dishonor of his previous crimes.

"The mark will be lifted as soon as your brother's reformation is complete," Major Singh told Marina. "*If* he is able to reform. As I said before, House Vermillion is quiet adept at reforming rogue vampires. But even they do not succeed every time. One-third of their reform candidates have to be put down. Not everyone can be reformed, so their success rate is quite remarkable actually. It is the highest in the world."

"So what you're telling me is that everyone in my family and coven will live with a black mark for half a century."

"Yes, everyone now and those born in the years to come," Major Singh added with dubious helpfulness.

"And that there's anyway only a two-in-three chance that he will survive to be redeemed. So my coven could live with this mark forever."

"Yes."

A worry line crinkled the delicate, smooth skin between Marina's eyebrows.

"It's best not to worry about things you cannot change," Major Singh said, turning toward her colleague.

"What if I could," Marina said, and the Major stopped and met her eyes. "Change it."

"You may petition the Legion for mercy," Major Singh said.

A small smile cut Marina's lips. She hadn't been here earlier to witness the Major's soliloquy on mercy, but everyone knew the Legion's reputation as the merciless enforcers of the gods' will.

"The gods reward great acts of heroism and piety," the Major told her.

Some Pilgrims, the voice of the gods' teachings, had been granted immortality in exchange for acts of uncommon piety. Soldiers of the Legion, the hand of the gods' will, were granted magic and favors for their acts of bravery and self-sacrifice.

"Oh, gods," Ivy gasped as she reached the same conclusion I just had: Major Singh was as ruthless as she was intelligent. There had only ever been one possible conclusion to this interrogation. It was all a game, a game designed to turn out exactly as Major Singh had designed it. It was no wonder Colonel Fireswift spoke highly of her. She was his sort of person.

Marina looked down at the goblet in her hands. Fear ignited her eyes. She'd gotten there too. She knew there was only one way out.

"If I join the Legion, will the black mark on my coven be lifted?" she asked.

"If you survive the first sip of Nectar, yes," the Major promised.

Marina stared into the depths of the goblet. She lifted it to her mouth.

"No, Marina!" the vampire shouted.

Major Singh waved her hand at him, her eyes never leaving his sister. An invisible blast of telekinetic magic hit the vampire hard, shooting him across the room. He slammed against the back wall and stuck there, four feet off the ground.

Marina tipped back her head and emptied the goblet in

a single go. The convulsions hit her immediately, rocking her whole body. The goblet slipped from her shaking hands and clinked against the hard floor. Her knees hit the floor next. Her hands followed, her palms smacking against the white marble, a surface so glossy that her harrowed eyes shone in it. Marina crouched on her hands and knees, barely holding herself up. The beautiful ribbons and stitches of her corset were just inches from the ground. The Nectar was dragging her under, its song of shattered dreams crushing her spirit as the poison led her to an early grave.

A sudden, heavy wheeze heaved out of her. Her chest rose another inch off the ground. Her legs and arms shook with vicious tremors, but she didn't let go. She was fighting. The power of her will was pushing back the pain. She stubbornly rose another inch. And another. Her hands pushed off. She rocked back from her knees. Her feet hit the ground. She was in a deep crouch now, like a tiger rising from the bushes. Slowly, she rose to standing. The aftershocks of the spasms twitched across her body, but she stood her ground. She propped her hands up on her hips and met the Major's eyes with cold triumph.

"Congratulations, initiate. You have survived the Nectar of the gods." Major Singh waved her hand at the magical projection, and a wall of text replaced the map of the Wilds. "By the power invested in me by the Legion of Angels, I hereby remove the mark of dishonor on your family and coven in appreciation of your bravery and sacrifice." She twirled her finger in a few loops, signing 'Major Selena Singh' to the bottom of the projected document. The text glowed once, then dissolved. "Welcome to the Legion of Angels."

The vampire came unstuck from the wall and tumbled

down. "No, Marina," he wailed. "My poor, sweet sister."

She pivoted around, her face lit up with fury. "You are not my brother. My brother would have drunk the Nectar himself and spared our coven the shame of his dishonor."

"I am not strong like you."

"No, you're not strong. You are a *coward*," she spat. "Fear rules your life. Fear drove you to the rogue vampires, the fear of living without magic in a world of magic. And fear prevented you from trying your luck with the Legion."

"I would not have survived."

"Then at least you would have died my brother. Instead of living on as this...thing."

"I will atone. I'll be better. I promise."

She shot him a look of pure loathing. "You are no longer my concern. If you survive House Vermillion's efforts to reform your black soul, do not seek me out. Do not seek out anyone in our coven. Julian Kane is dead."

With that said, she turned and followed Captain Norton toward the door. It groaned open, spitting out two Legion soldiers dressed in black leather uniforms. Marina and Captain Norton left the room. The two new arrivals pulled the vampire off the ground and followed them out. Only Major Singh remained. She looked up at the balcony, her dark eyes watching us. She didn't blink. Neither did I. I could feel my comrades' micro movements as they resisted the urge to fidget under her penetrating stare. Finally, after what felt like a hundred years, she turned crisply on her heel and left the room.

"That sure was eerie," Ivy commented. "I have this unsettling feeling she could reach deep inside of me and yank out my soul."

"Selena Singh has many grim talents, but soul-snatching is not one of them," Captain Somerset declared.

I turned around in surprise. How long had she been standing there, observing us? She moved like a ninja.

"Pandora, a word," Captain Somerset said, using my nickname. "The rest of you, head down to Hall Three for evening training."

They filed out without a word.

"Pack your winter wear. The perfect mission just came up," Captain Somerset said.

"This perfect mission wouldn't have anything to do with the Wicked Wilds and a band of rogue vampires, would it?"

She grinned at me. "Indeed it would. We're going vampire hunting tomorrow morning."

CHAPTER TWO

Wicked Winter Wilds

"WHEN I JOINED the Legion of Angels, no one said anything about Abominable Snowmen," I said, looking down at the heap of dead monsters at my feet. Sometime during the battle, the sky had split open like a punctured balloon. It was now dumping an entire winter's quota of snowflakes down on us.

"It was in the fine print." Captain Somerset stabbed her sword through a twitching monster arm. It stopped twitching. "But these creatures hardly qualify as Abominable Snowmen. They're just plain old snowmen."

"Yeah, except for the steel-trap jaws, razor claws, spiky fur, and their appreciation for the taste of human flesh, they are *exactly* like snowmen," I said drily.

I gave the pile of dead monsters a wide berth as we continued up the snowy mountain path. Monsters were nothing new to me. I'd faced a few in my days as a bounty hunter, and I'd fought even more of them since joining the Legion of Angels, the supernatural army that served the gods. The Legion's job was to protect the Earth and its people from supernatural threats and to uphold the gods' laws—not necessarily in that order.

As a soldier in the Legion, I'd fought everything from dinosaurs, to carnivorous plants, to misbehaving vampires and witches. I'd had to kill more living beings than I cared to think about. The first kill had been a shock. Each following one was getting easier—and that's what I was worried about. The gods' gifts of Nectar bestowed us with new powers, but it also changed us. It changed who we were inside, at our very core.

Nectar was a double-edged sword, a brutal ally. You were either strong enough to gain the new power or it killed you. Most people thought that this dance with death was the true price of power.

They were wrong. The Nectar's price came in the subtle ways it changed you, sip by sip, week after week, until one day you realized you were no longer the same person who'd set down this path. *That* was the price of power. Each time I drank the gods' Nectar, I could feel the change penetrate me deeper.

I was fighting that change with everything I had. I'd joined the Legion to gain the magic I needed to save my brother. I had no intention of gaining that magic only to find that I had become a heartless monster who didn't care about saving anyone I wasn't ordered to help.

"How do you do it?" I asked Captain Somerset.

Her dark brows, frosted with snowflakes, arched. "How do I do what?"

"Hold onto who you are. You've been serving the Legion for over a century, and you are still so human."

Her mouth twisted into a wry smile. "None of us are human anymore."

"And yet you have held onto your humanity."

I'd never have ventured the subject if we'd been out here with a full team. Badass Legion soldiers did not wax poetic about their feelings. And they certainly didn't talk about their humanity. Angels were supposed to be too perfect to be human, and we were supposed to aspire to become angels.

But it was just the two of us here. The Legion's scouts had determined that Charles Rune's base was in fact made up of six castles spread across the mountainside, connected to one another by a massive underground tunnel system. So we'd broken up into groups to hit the castles from every direction—well, as much as you could hit six castles from every direction with a team of sixteen soldiers. Yeah, we might have underestimated the size of House Rune just a bit. Captain Somerset and I were taking the south castle.

"Yes, I've held onto my humanity," Captain Somerset finally said. "The angels are beautiful, powerful, seductive. It's easy to be swept away by them, so easy to lose yourself. It happens to us all. It happened to me too. I was starting to think exactly like them. The day I realized that was a major wake-up call."

"What did you do?"

"I couldn't leave the Legion, but I could hold onto who I was."

When you joined the Legion, you joined for life.

"I gathered the shreds of my humanity and wove them around me like a cloak," she said. "And I've worn that cloak of humanity ever since."

"That's beautiful. You're a real poet," I told her.

"Yeah, well this poet can still kick your ass."

I knew she could. Two weeks ago, the First Angel had served notice that Nero would not be returning to his post commanding the New York Legion office and all its underlings, myself included. I'd thought my early-morning one-on-one training sessions with Nero would fall to the wayside, but Captain Somerset had taken them over. Though it didn't hurt as much when she kicked my ass as when Nero had done it, it hurt more than enough.

"How much further?" I asked Captain Somerset, looking up the steep and snowy mountain trail.

The path was hardly wide enough for a person, let alone one of the gigantic off-road vehicles the Legion used to cross the world's wildernesses. So we'd parked our trucks at the base of the mountain. At the rate the snow was coming down, we might have to dig them out.

"Tired already?" Captain Somerset's mouth quirked.

"Of course not. I just want to know when to pull out my big, ferocious sword and wave it about in the air."

"You can do that now if it makes you feel better."

"Only if you light the blade on fire," I replied.

"You try."

I pulled out my sword and stared at the blade. Nothing happened. I stared harder. The sword remained stubbornly mundane.

"Leda," Captain Somerset said.

"Just another few moments," I said stubbornly, willing that accursed blade to catch on fire. "I think I'm almost there."

It was a lie. I wasn't there. Not even close. I was just too stubborn to admit defeat.

I wasn't yet a master of elemental magic. It was called Dragon's Storm, the magic to cast fire, water, earth, and wind. The perfect storm of the four elements. It was a fourth level Legion ability, which meant I was supposed to be working on it. Unfortunately, the elements had proven completely unresponsive to my efforts.

I was trapped. I couldn't use elemental magic until drinking the Nectar that bestowed the gods' fourth gift. And without some affinity for elemental magic, I wouldn't survive that same Nectar. Some people had a natural power over one or more magical abilities. For me, that was Siren's Song, the power to compel people.

Legion brats, those with an angel parent, could do a little bit of every kind of magic. For that reason, they were the soldiers most likely to survive the Legion's promotion ceremonies—and to become angels. The rest of us had to train twice as hard for half the results. It sucked and was completely unfair, but such was life. My foster mother Calli had told me often as a kid that life was pitilessly unfair. And that you could either give up and be life's bitch, or you could grab it by the horns and make it yours. I'd chosen the latter. There was nothing worse than feeling helpless.

"We have to keep going," Captain Somerset said after a while.

"Right." I sheathed my sword.

We had a job to do. There was a difference between being determined and being hardheaded. Hardheaded soldiers got themselves—and their comrades—killed. The rogue vampires of House Rune wouldn't catch themselves while I stood here in silence, glaring at my sword. I could always glare at my sword later.

The trail was thick with snow. It was halfway to my knees by now. Every step felt more like swimming than walking. The vampires hadn't selected the Wilds by accident. No one was crazy enough to come out here to this frozen, monster-infested wasteland. Not even the Legion sent soldiers out here unless there was a damn good reason. Criminals knew that. That's why so many of them hid within the dangerous lands beyond the wall. Of course, most criminals hiding in the world's wildernesses didn't survive the first month. There were too many hungry monsters hunting for their next snack.

A generous pile of snow dropped into my path. If I hadn't hopped aside in time, it would have landed on my head.

"I know I can't set my sword on fire, but *you* can," I told Captain Somerset. "We could melt the way to the vampires' castle."

"I'm not going to waste magic on that."

I sighed. The snow was so high it was pouring into my boots.

"Suffering builds character," Captain Somerset said.

That was easy for her to say. She was several inches taller than I was. The snow hadn't yet reached the inside of her boots.

"Good one. But let's not forget 'what doesn't kill you, only makes you stronger' and 'if you can complain, it doesn't hurt enough'," I said, reciting some of Nero's favorite sayings. My relationship with Nero was… complicated. Yeah, that was it. Complicated.

Captain Somerset nodded, her eyes twinkling with amusement. "Exactly."

"I didn't think you were a disciple of the Nero Windstriker school of thought."

"I'm not. But with him gone, someone has to whip you into shape." She shot me a grin that would have sent a shiver down my spine—if I weren't already frozen solid from the inside out.

"I'm sure Nero wishes he were here trudging through this snow with us," I said. "He loves torturing himself to build his character. He'd happily push himself to the breaking point, all the while bearing it with angelic demeanor."

Which meant bearing it without betraying a hint of emotion on his face.

"He always was an overachiever," Captain Somerset said fondly. She and Nero were best friends. How she managed to be friends with an angel while remaining perfectly human was nothing short of a miracle.

"Yes, he really is," I agreed. "Which is why he's being promoted."

"Nero is being promoted because the First Angel wants him in a different office than you. You two are too much trouble together. You're a bad influence." She said it like it wasn't a bad thing.

I pointed at myself and formed my face into an expression of pure innocence. "Who me?"

"Yes, you, Pandora," she chuckled.

Nero had come up with my nickname, and it had stuck. Nowadays, everyone at the Legion was calling me Pandora. It's almost as though they thought I was the official herald of the second apocalypse, the bringer of chaos.

"During your recent adventure to the Lost City, you and Nero broke fifteen separate regulations."

"Only fifteen? I always aim for at least twenty."

"I'm glad you find this so funny."

Not really. Humor was the bandage I was sticking over that awful experience in the Lost City. I'd been captured, tortured, forced to see visions, and shot with an immortal weapon. No magic could completely heal the mark of an immortal weapon. I'd carry the scar for the rest of my life. If it would just hurry up and scar over already. It had been two weeks, and the wound was still not closed. I had to keep a bandage on it when training or going out on missions. All it took was my body moving the wrong way, and the delicate threads of my skin popped open and I bled out all over.

The wound in my stomach, coupled with Nero's continued absence, was a constant reminder that breaking the rules had a price. But sometimes the price for toeing the line was even worse. If I'd played the good little soldier, the immortal weapons of heaven and hell would have fallen into the hands of a psychopath on a mission to kill each and every supernatural in the world.

Nyx, the First Angel of the Legion, the most powerful angel of them all, was well aware of the fact that my and Nero's rule-breaking had saved the supernatural world. She hadn't wanted to punish us. Nyx liked our rule-breaking as much as she liked rules. The First Angel was a dichotomy like that. She was cool. I liked her—when I forgot to be afraid of her.

"Actually, you helped me and Nero break quite a few of those rules," I said, keeping the smile planted on my face. Just keep smiling. Keep smiling. No matter what.

She winked at me. "Shush. Don't tell anyone. I want to keep my bad behavior under the table."

"Aspiring for a promotion yourself?"

She snorted. "I'm too busy covering your asses to worry about a promotion. But it might come knocking just the same. Our new leader Colonel Fireswift doesn't care if someone is ready for a promotion," she added grimly.

Colonel Fireswift had stepped in to take charge of the Legion's New York office, filling the power void Nero had left. We all hoped his presence was temporary, but he hadn't yet shown any signs of leaving. He was too busy killing us. The Legion needed high-level soldiers to counter the expected demon activity. Colonel Fireswift's solution to the problem was to promote everyone and see who lived. He'd taken the Legion's level-up-or-die philosophy to the next level.

The Legion was usually cautious, only submitting someone for promotion if they thought the soldier had a good chance of surviving the Nectar. It didn't make sense to kill off perfectly good soldiers.

Colonel Fireswift didn't care about casualties. He only cared about results. If a promotion ceremony resulted in a hundred Legion soldiers with new magic and twenty corpses, he didn't even blink. Those were acceptable losses to him. And Nyx gave him free reign. She was all right with his methods, even though the promotion ceremony death toll at the New York office had exploded. Did I mention Nyx could be inhumanly frightening?

"Wait," Captain Somerset said, indicating tracks in the snow. They looked like boot prints. She crouched down beside them. "Two sets. Spaced far apart, like they were running. But no normal human has that stride. The spacing between them is too large. They must be vampires or someone else with supernatural speed."

I looked from the prints to her. "Wow, I'm impressed. You're brainy. I thought you only knew how to hit people over the head with a hammer."

Captain Somerset smirked at me. "Don't flirt with me, Pandora. You'll make Nero jealous. He'll attack me in a rage."

"He'd never do that. You're his best friend."

"So was Harker," she said, her face suddenly solemn.

Nero and Harker, best friends, had once fought because Harker had given me a little party Nectar. That's the first time I'd seen Nero's hard exterior crack. He'd attacked like a man without conscience or compassion. Like an angel. It had been one of the most terrifying things I'd ever witnessed.

"What's wrong?" I teased her. "Don't think you can handle Nero?"

"Mmm, let me see. A fight against an angel." She pretended to consider her odds. "Of course I can't beat him. Not if I play fair anyway."

"You've beaten him before?" I asked, intrigued.

"Yes."

"How did you do it?"

"I tied his shoelaces together before the fight."

Laughter burst out of my mouth. I didn't even try to hold it back. Nero was as sexy as sin, but Captain Somerset was my hero. She was everything I wanted to be. She was a good soldier who knew the rules better than anyone. She followed them too—well, most of the time. But she also knew how to get her hands dirty when she had to. She was strong, but she often won by outsmarting her opponent.

I'd had to learn the same thing back when I'd lived on the streets: winning by fighting dirty, by using tricks and traps. When you were the smallest kid on the street, you got smart or you got dead.

Nero was not like us. He fought with honor, dignity, and precision. And he won by being a better fighter than anyone else. His presence was overwhelming. You knew when you faced him in battle that he would destroy you—and that there wasn't a damned thing you could do to stop him.

He'd trained my initiate class for that first month after we'd joined the Legion. Everyone had been so afraid that he would call on them when he was demonstrating something. Some of my fellow initiates decided to hide in the back of the crowd. Naturally, that was a surefire way to encourage Nero to call on you. He didn't suffer a coward; he wanted us to confront our fears and to push through them.

One time, I'd had enough. I did the unspeakable: I volunteered. I don't know what possessed me. Maybe I just wanted to prove he didn't scare me. Maybe I wanted to show everyone that they shouldn't be scared of him either. If that was my goal, I failed miserably. Nero didn't take it easy on me because I'd volunteered. If anything, he'd taken it *harder* on me. I'd cursed his name back then, thinking he relished breaking people. But that didn't stop me from volunteering again the next session. The look on his face when I came back for seconds and thirds and fourths… It was priceless. And it was worth every bump, bruise, and broken bone.

I later realized that he didn't enjoy torturing me. He was impressed that I could hold out for so long, that I didn't give up. And he wanted to help me reach my magical potential. The more I could take, the higher my chance of surviving the Nectar. That was the true reason he pushed us so hard. That's why he didn't show mercy and didn't let up.

"If you're done chuckling over my pranks, let's move on," Captain Somerset said to me.

I nodded, swallowing the last laugh. Charles Rune and his house of rogue vampires needed to be stopped. The

Legion had taken out their hideouts in several cities, but they just kept coming back stronger than ever. Not being choosy about what lowlives you turned into vampires was a quick way to build an army, but fear and a twisted sense of loyalty to the man who'd given them supernatural powers would only go so far. It was just a matter of time before someone snitched. Mr. Farrows had been that snitch.

We followed the trail up the mountain. Vampires had run along this path recently, but the heavy snowfall was quickly covering their tracks. In a few minutes, the tracks would be gone completely. The vampires hadn't chosen this location at random. It was easy to be invisible out here, here where snow fell like goose down from the heavens. Here where the cold dulled the vampires' scent trail, and the sweet aroma of fresh needles diluted it further.

The path cut through the rocky forest. I swiped my hand across my scarf, breaking the thick crust of icicles that had glued it to my mouth. A stone castle peeked through the pine trees, tall and imposing. The vampires were living in a castle. They sure had delusions of grandeur.

A cloak of slow, steady decay hung over the castle. Broken bricks jutted out at awkward angles from its weather-warped exterior. We snuck up on the castle, stepping softly. Or at least trying to. It wasn't easy to step softly through a foot of snow. There were no guards keeping watch outside. They thought they were safe, that no one would find them out here on the snowy shores of winter.

Captain Somerset pointed at a passageway into the dungeon blocked by a cage of vertical metal bars. Then she pointed at me. She didn't speak because we didn't want the vampires inside to overhear us, but that simple gesture was clear enough. She wanted me to make an opening for us to pass through. I gripped the bars and heaved. Predictably, they didn't move. They were made of hard, heavy iron.

I shot Captain Somerset an annoyed look.

She waved at the bars.

I pantomimed setting off explosives.

She shook her head. She pointed at me, then flexed her biceps.

I rolled my eyes.

It was amazing the conversations you could have without speaking a single word. She could have broken those bars already five times over, but she'd left it entirely up to me. With Nero gone, she saw it as her job to make me stronger.

I grabbed the bars again and pulled, trying to move them apart. They didn't budge. I tried again, this time thinking warm, liquid thoughts. I'm not sure if it was my burgeoning elemental magic skills or if I'd simply put more muscle into it, but the bars began to separate. I kept pulling, widening the opening until there was just enough space for me to squeeze through. I moved into the dreary castle dungeon. I'd taken only a few steps when the soft clink of metal jingled behind me. I looked back to find Captain Somerset stuck halfway through the opening in the bars.

She motioned for me to draw the bars further apart.

I responded with a series of rapid hand movements.

Her eyebrows drew together in genuine confusion.

I slowed down the hand movements and exaggerated the motion of shoveling one cupcake after the other into my mouth.

Comprehension dawned on her face. She flipped me off.

I laughed under my breath and pulled the bars apart. Truth be told, Captain Somerset's plight wasn't due to her fondness for cupcakes. Our supernatural metabolism almost immediately burned through anything and everything we ate. No, her hours each day of lifting weights in the gym was the reason she couldn't fit through the bars when I had. She was only about ten times stronger than I was. I don't care what people say about magic's ability to distort the rules of the universe. There was only so much strength that magic could buy you. The body's muscles had to pick up some of the slack. Captain Somerset was just buffer than I was. Then again, so were most Legion soldiers. I was more of a runner than a lifter.

The dungeon's ceiling was so low that we had to bend over to avoid bumping our heads. The passageway was colder than winter's kiss, but for once I welcomed the cold. There was no proper ground to this tunnel. We were walking on ice—or, as I suspected, old frozen sewage. Winter had reigned in this part of the Wilds since the monsters overran the Earth two centuries ago, so whatever was frozen beneath our feet must have come from that era. I prayed that it stayed frozen.

In theory, it would. The monsters' magic had dropped the temperature in the whole area, plummeting it into perpetual winter. The monsters and the Wilds were trapped in a never-ending cycle, each affecting the other. It would take an incident of enormous magical power to melt these frozen wastelands, something that could kick this magic ecosystem out of its loop.

As far as I knew, there wasn't a power on Earth that could do it. If the Legion had such a power, sometime in the last two centuries they would have used it to kill the monsters and return the lost lands to civilization. And then we wouldn't be out here in the wilderness, sneaking across a layer of frozen sewage, infiltrating a castle occupied by the vampire mafia. On the bright side, at least the vampires hadn't yet noticed us.

Gunfire erupted from the far end of the tunnel, shattering that fragile illusion.

CHAPTER THREE
Poison

VAMPIRES STREAMED DOWN the tunnel, shooting wildly. But they weren't shooting at us. They were shooting at something behind them. A thick steamy mist flooded the hallway and swallowed the vampires whole. When it cleared a few moments later, all eight vampires lay dead on the ground.

"That's weird," I said, looking down at them.

The vampires' throats were slit. No bullets or cuts marred their bodies. In fact, there wasn't a scratch on them.

"Indeed, it is weird," Captain Somerset agreed, frowning.

"Maybe there's an angry spirit roaming these halls."

She shot me a hard look.

"What? We live in a world ruled by gods, and you're telling me angry spirits don't exist?"

"I've never seen one."

I gave the dead vampires on the ground a pointed look.

"I'm sure there is another explanation." She stepped around the vampires. "Let's keep going."

We made our way through the castle's dungeon. It was

like walking through a metallic jungle. Chains hung from the walls like soggy vines. Levers, wheels, and hooks jutted out from between the bricks. The Legion's Interrogators would have felt right at home here.

A chorus of screams pierced the cold air. It was coming from a room on the right. We ran, but by the time we got there, dark fog was rising from the bodies of three dead vampires.

"I get the feeling we're not the only ones after the vampires of House Rune," I said.

"Except we're not supposed to kill them. The Legion wants to question them."

"Maybe someone doesn't want us to question them," I suggested.

Captain Somerset brushed her hand across the neck of one of the vampires. "The fog could be poison."

"A witch's brew?"

"Perhaps. We should keep our distance from it in any case."

Legion soldiers were pretty resistant to poison, but we weren't immune. After all, Nectar was poison. And so was Venom, the demons' drink of choice. If witches had laced their spell with either, the fog could kill us too. But why would witches come all the way out here, deep into the monster-infested Wilds, to kill a few vampires?

"The Kane coven," I realized. "This is their way of getting back at House Rune for turning one of their own."

Marina had been standing right there when her brother told the Interrogators were to find Charles Rune and his band of rogues. She must have told her parents where the vampires were hiding. And now the witches were taking matters into their own hands.

"Witches," Captain Somerset growled. She pulled out her phone. "Sergeant Vance, have you come across any mysterious fog?"

"No," Claudia Vance's voice came out of the phone. "Morrows?"

"Describe this fog," Alec Morrows's voice clicked.

"Creepy, magical, and poisonous."

"It sounds like Captain Somerset."

Captain Somerset frowned at the phone in her hands. "Try to take this seriously, Sergeant. The fog has already killed at least ten vampires in the south castle."

"All's quiet in the west castle," Claudia told her. "We haven't seen any fog. In fact, we haven't seen a single vampire yet."

"Keep your eyes out for the fog. And for any signs of witches," said Captain Somerset.

"Witches?"

"We believe the Kane coven might be responsible for the poison fog."

"You hear that, Morrows?" Claudia said. "The witches might have cast a storm of poisonous fog on these castles. You'd best hold your breath for the duration of this mission."

"And deprive you of the joy of my witty tongue? I'd never dream of it."

"You keep your tongue to yourself."

Captain Somerset ended the call, and not a moment too soon. I did not need to hear anything more about Alec's tongue. But at least he wasn't talking about his cannon.

"What now?" I asked.

In response, my jacket buzzed. I reached in and pulled out my phone.

"Hey, Leda," Drake spoke, his voice so quiet I could barely hear him.

"Drake? Why are you whispering?"

"I don't want *it* to find us."

'Us' meant Drake and Jace. They were partners on this mission. Neither one had looked particularly pleased when Captain Somerset made the assignment.

"What is *it*?" I asked Drake.

"The fog."

"This wouldn't happen to be the cloud of poison rolling around the castles, killing vampires, would it?" I asked him.

"You've seen it? And survived?"

"It didn't target us. We saw it kill a few vampires and then dissipate. It doesn't seem interested in killing anyone but the rogue vampires."

"Not just vampires," Jace said grimly. "It tried to eat us."

"It nipped Jace's arm before he managed to pull it away," Drake told me. "It ate right through his clothes. Every inch of skin from his wrist up to his elbow is covered in blisters."

Why would the witches target Drake and Jace? Maybe they realized the Legion would not be happy they were killing our prisoners. But if they were just trying to cover their tracks by killing all witnesses, then why hadn't their poison fog attacked me and Captain Somerset?

Captain Somerset grabbed my phone. "Where is the fog now?"

"It's dissipated," Jace said.

"If you see it again, keep your distance. We're coming," she told the guys, then hung up. She handed my phone back to me. "They're in the southwest castle. This passage should lead us there. We're going to find the fog, those witches, and put an end to this nonsense."

"Wait."

We both turned at the sound of that voice, a voice that did not belong in this place.

Nero was behind us, his body framed by a halo of pale light. Magic. No daylight reached this part of the twisting tunnel. Nero's magic, on the other hand, penetrated everything. The angel looked at me with eyes that burned like green fire. His gaze cut through me, right to my raw, naked soul. It burned away everything, until it was just the two of us and no one else. Nothing else.

He stood with his arms folded across his chest, a pose that accentuated the hard, supple muscles of both. The angel was like catnip for any woman with a pulse. I made a concentrated effort not to ogle. As Nero would say, ogling was not becoming of a soldier of the Legion. Sometimes behaving myself was seriously dull.

He wore the usual black leather uniform of the Legion. It was like a second skin to him, a part of him, of who he was. I'd once asked him if he even took off his uniform before he went to bed. He'd replied that I was welcome to come find out.

"What are you doing here?" I asked him. "Are you here to deal with the vampires?"

"No, I'm here to deal with the fog. Or, more specifically, the person behind the fog."

He must have predicted that the Kane coven would go after the vampires.

"Which witch cast the spell?" I asked him.

"It was not a witch who cast the spell. It was my father."

CHAPTER FOUR
Cold to the Last Drop

WE FOLLOWED NERO down the tunnel. I had to run to match the pace he'd set.

"Your father is killing vampires?"

Nero looked at me, his mouth a hard, determined line. "It seems I underestimated Damiel's magic. Early this morning, my security alarms alerted me that he'd broken through the magic field containing him. I tracked him here."

"But why did he come here? And why is he killing vampires?"

"House Rune has turned many vampires. But it has also welcomed other rogue vampires with open arms. Before we met Damiel in the Lost City, he was searching for one of those vampires, a man named Raven Rhodes. Damiel believes Rhodes might be one of the last people who saw my mother before she disappeared."

"And now he's hunting down the vampire in the hopes of finding his wife," I said.

So the Kane coven hadn't come here seeking revenge. That was good for the witches. It wasn't so good for

Damiel. The Legion thought he was dead. They had ordered his execution.

"He's risking exposure," Captain Somerset said, voicing my concerns. "If the Legion finds out he's alive—and that we've been hiding him—we'll be the ones stuck in the Interrogators' chair."

"I won't let that happen," Nero promised her. "Damiel is coming back with me, whether he likes it or not."

"I don't think it will be that easy, Nero," she replied. "If he came all the way out here, he's not going to leave quietly. And if you fight him, there won't be a single person in all six castles who doesn't know he's here."

She had a point. When angels fought, they didn't do it subtly. Nero and Damiel would probably blow up half of the castles on the mountainside.

"I will reason with him."

Captain Somerset snorted. "Reason with an angel? Good luck with that."

He shot her a hard look.

"You're not the most reasonable person, Nero," she told him. "And neither is Damiel Dragonsire."

"Which is why I'm going to make sure we both get what we want. I'll help him find Rhodes, we'll interrogate the vampire, and then he will quietly return to his apartment."

"Now that sounds like a reasonable plan," Damiel said.

A second ago, there hadn't been a soul in this hallway except for the three of us. Now, Damiel stood facing us, his pose reminiscent of Nero's. The two angels faced each other, their eyes alight with fire—one blue, one green.

"So you agree?" I asked Damiel.

"To hunting down and interrogating the last person

who saw my wife? With pleasure." His words dripped dark intentions.

"There was another part to the deal," Nero said with strained patience.

Damiel gave his hand a small, dismissive wave. "Yes, very well, Nero. I will return quietly to my gilded cage afterwards."

"You might want to begin your quiet return to sanity by telling your fog to stop attacking Legion soldiers," I said.

"I assure you, I am only hunting vampires. The fog probes their minds to find the location of Raven Rhodes."

"And that requires killing them?" Captain Somerset asked with quiet skepticism.

"No, I just believe in keeping a clean workspace. The fog unfortunately isn't all that intelligent. It would waste precious time probing the same vampires over and over again. That's simply not an efficient use of time or magic."

That was angel efficiency for you, brutally cold to the last drop.

"You *did* attack a Legion soldier," I told him. "His arm is now covered in blisters."

"Oh, him." If Damiel weren't an angel, I might have described his expression as sheepish. But I knew better than that. "I didn't think you would mind if I gave Colonel Fireswift's son a little scare, considering how his father's been treating you."

"You tried to cover Jace in poisonous fog to give him a 'little scare'?" I said in disbelief.

"Yes."

"Jace is my friend."

"You are friends with the son of the man making your life a living hell?"

"It's not his fault his father is a psychopath."

"I see." Damiel looked at his own son, his mouth twitching with mild amusement.

"Enough," Nero told him. "Stop the fog. The Legion needs those vampires alive."

"Very well." Damiel blinked once. "It's done. I've already located Rhodes anyway. He's headed this way. Conveniently, so are your friends."

The roar of gunfire echoed through the halls.

"Ah, they've found one another," Damiel said casually. "Another group of vampires is coming up on your friends from behind."

"Basanti," Nero said.

"I'm on it," Captain Somerset replied, running off down the hallway.

A few moments after she turned the corner, the gunfire died down.

"Whoa, you came out of nowhere," Drake's voice said.

"The vampires are still alive," Jace said.

"We'll pick them up later. There are more of them headed this way. Let's go," she said.

Their footsteps tapped off in the opposite direction from us. By the time we reached the vampires, they were moving to their feet. Nero raised his hands. A distortion crackled in the air, and then four pairs of handcuffs popped up over his shoulders, bobbing slowly up and down like buoys on the ocean. Flames ignited on the handcuffs. They shot toward the vampires so fast I couldn't even track their flight. One moment the vampires were backing away, and the next the flaming handcuffs had them chained to iron hooks on the walls.

The vampires kicked their legs in hopeless panic, like

fish caught on a fisherman's hook. One of them pushed against her handcuffs, hissing in pain when the restraints bit back. The smell of burning flesh filled the tunnel. They all stopped struggling real fast.

Nero stepped up to the dangling vampires. "Which of you is Raven Rhodes?"

The vampires remained silent.

"You can answer me or a Legion Interrogator. I'm considerably more amiable." Nero's face was granite, his voice ice.

He was playing the bluff well. The Legion wasn't looking for Raven Rhodes, not any more than they were looking for the rest of the rogue vampires.

"That's Raven," the female vampire pointed at one of her comrades.

Nero flicked his hand, and Raven fell to the ground.

"Thank you for your cooperation," Damiel said brightly.

A flash of light flared up, as bright as a star. I shielded my eyes. When I opened them again, all that remained of Raven's companions was a cloud of ash floating slowly down on him like black snow.

I frowned at Damiel. "You weren't supposed to kill any more vampires."

He shrugged. "They were witnesses."

I looked at Nero.

"He's right. They saw him. They had to die."

Nero was a lot more like his father than he cared to admit. He was channeling his inner angel now, watching Raven with the cool patience of a predator stalking its next meal. By the time Nero spoke, the vampire was hyperventilating, impressive considering that vampires didn't need to breathe.

"Tell me about Cadence Lightbringer," Nero said.

"The angel?"

"You saw her nearly two hundred years ago, days after her supposed death."

"I was human back then." The vampire's left eye twitched erratically. "Memory's a bit fuzzy."

A psychic blast shot out of Nero, slamming Raven against the wall. "Where did you see her?"

"I saw her wandering in the Western Wilderness. Dehydrated, starving, and dirty. Her body was covered in cuts caked over with dirt and blood. Her frayed wings dragged on the ground. She didn't have the strength to fly. She didn't even have enough magic left to retract her wings again."

I recognized the calculation in Raven's eyes. I knew his kind. He was the sort of person who built his fortune on the misfortune of others. He had neither morals nor compassion.

"You captured her. You were going to sell her like some animal, weren't you?" I realized, my eyes burning with anger.

"Your hair," he gasped. "What the hell is wrong with your hair?"

I glanced down at my glowing braid. A red light was spreading up from the tips.

"Never mind that. It does that sometimes."

The vampire definitely minded. In fact, he couldn't look away from my glowing hair. His eyes were locked on it, transfixed. It was a good thing Nero's magic had him pinned to the wall, or he'd have probably tried to bite me by now.

"What happened to Cadence Lightbringer?" I asked him.

His eyes were dilated. He didn't blink. "She escaped her cage one night. I followed the trail of blood, but when I reached the end, she was gone. She'd vanished. I never saw her again."

He spoke the words in a dull monotone. There was something weird going on with my hair, and it wasn't just the glow. I felt my magic growing stronger. I'd somehow managed to compel a vampire who didn't want to be compelled. In his situation, he should have fought my mental control every step of the way. I could feel a spark of resistance in him, but it didn't make it through the trance my hair had put him in. I knew he was telling the truth. Right now, I had him so far under my spell that he couldn't have lied to save his life.

"That was remarkable," Damiel told me as the red light faded from my hair.

I swayed to the side, barely staying on my feet. I felt like I'd just run back-to-back marathons. Compelling the vampire had used up every drop of magic in me, and my body was screaming in protest, a hammer pounding inside of my head.

"I must admit I've never seen anything quite like it."

The fact that an angel of Damiel's age had never seen anything like my glowing hair worried me. What was I?

"Well, this was fun." Damiel drew his sword and severed the vampire's head in a single slash of his burning blade. "And now I believe Nero and I must be going. Your friends are on their way."

I caught Nero's hand as he began to lead his father away. "Be safe."

"You too. Try to stay out of trouble." His hand brushed softly across my cheek. "I'll see you in New York."

I couldn't stop the smile that was spreading across my face. "You'll be there?"

"Race you there," he said with a wicked twitch of his mouth.

Then he and Damiel were gone. And not a moment too soon.

"What happened here?" Drake asked as he came around the corner with Captain Somerset and Jace.

"The vampires didn't come willingly," I said.

Drake's brows arched. "So you burned them to ash?"

"Captain Somerset set my sword on fire before she ran off to save your asses," I said.

I hated lying to my friends, but Nero's secret wasn't mine to tell. Besides, if Jace found out about Damiel, I wasn't completely sure he could keep it to himself. He might tell his father. That's what the Legion would want him to do. But doing the right thing in the Legion's eyes would get Nero and Damiel into hot water—not to mention me and Captain Somerset.

"You need to be careful with that sword, or you'll set your pretty hair on fire," Captain Somerset told me with a smirk.

"I'll try to remember that," I replied. "So, how did you fare?"

"The castle is clear. Thirty-two vampires captured, including Charles Rune himself," she told me. "The other teams are also done with the other castles, so let's get these rogues down the mountain."

"How are we going to do that?" I asked.

"You're going to carry them, of course."

My bones groaned at the promise of more pain. "All of us?"

"No, I'm going to observe while the three of you carry them."

I frowned at her. "You're stronger than I am, so you should carry them."

Captain Somerset snorted. "Pandora, you keep forgetting that the Legion of Angels isn't a democracy."

I sighed. So much for not being life's bitch. "Ok, show me these vampires." Only the prospect of seeing Nero again soon kept the despair out of my voice.

CHAPTER FIVE
Precipice

IT WAS WARMER in New York. The weather lay on the precipice of spring, just waiting to take the plunge. Dirty black slush was thick in the streets, and freezing rain fell from the sky, pecking at my face like cold needles. It was considerably less romantic than the fat snowflakes and winter wonderland back in the Wilds. But at least there weren't any monsters here in the city, just crowds. Unlike the monsters, the people split out of my way at the sight of my Legion uniform.

As soon as we'd gotten back to the Legion office, Captain Somerset had run off in search of a hot shower. I would do the same shortly, but first I had a stop to make.

A brick building lay before me, a warehouse that had been converted into an apartment building at some point. I chuckled as I passed the fat naked cherub statutes outside the entrance. Nero owned this building. There was just something too funny about an angel owning a building with cherub statues. The chubby cute angels of mythology had nothing to do with the real thing.

I passed under the entrance arch and followed the

rotating door inside. A grandiose lobby spread out before me. With its majestic water fountain, magically-tinted windows, and gold handrails, the room resembled a cathedral more than the entrance hall of an apartment building. All that was missing were the walls painted with angels and the armies of supernatural soldiers bowing before them, sappy looks of utter devotion pasted on their faces.

As I walked past the bar, I paused for a moment to glance at the rows of colorful alcohol bottles laid out in perfect lines behind a glass closet. The illustration on one of the labels caught my eye: a picture of a witch in a corset, her pale hair tucked around a tiny top hat. I couldn't help but think back to Marina Kane, the witch who'd joined the Legion to save her family's honor. A distant airship floated over the witch's left shoulder. The text bubble coming out of her mouth promised that the drink within the bottle was like a trip up into the heavens.

"No, thanks. I prefer Nectar," I told the fictitious witch.

"I never should have left. You're so lonely that you're talking to yourself."

A smile crept up my lips, threatening to consume my whole body. I turned around to face Nero, and the sight of him took my breath away. His wings were out, spread out behind him in a vibrant tapestry of luminous blue, green, and black feathers that rivaled the most beautiful paintings on Earth. He sure liked to make an entrance.

"Nah," I said with a nonchalant shrug.

Do not stare. Do not stare. Nero knew he was gorgeous, and he used that fact to his advantage.

"I've always talked to myself," I told him.

"That does not befit a soldier of the Legion," he replied,

his lower lip turning downward in disapproval.

I wanted to taste his mouth. I settled for allowing him to taste my sarcasm.

"No." I smirked at him. "It really doesn't."

He watched me for a few silent moments, his eyes burning right through me. Suddenly, he rushed forward, swallowing me in his arms. My heart lifting in joy, I squeezed him to me. I'd missed him so much. I hadn't truly understood that until now. Though we'd seen each other just a few hours ago in the Wilds, that hadn't been the same at all. That had been all business. This was different. It was just the two of us and no one else. Finally.

"What's that smell?" Nero asked, inhaling the scent of my hair.

"My shampoo. It's cherry blossoms."

His mouth dipped to my neck. He kissed me softly. His hands tensed on my shoulders, and he pulled away.

"It's Colonel Fireswift." Nero's voice dropped to a savage whisper. "His scent is all over you."

"We trained with him yesterday evening," I said. "He's made it his newest mission in life to kill me."

"You grappled."

"Technically, he grabbed me and threw me against the wall and broke my arm. It hurt."

Nero's hand traced down my arm. "You should not train with him," he said in a dangerously soft voice.

"I don't have much of a choice."

"He's dangerous."

I arched my eyebrows. "As opposed to the nonthreatening angel before me?"

"I will always keep you safe."

"I can handle Colonel Fireswift. He's mistaken if he

thinks he can kill me off so easily."

Nero pressed lightly against the big, black bruise on my arm, and I winced in pain. How did he even know where the bruise was? It was hidden beneath my clothes.

"Apparently you're not handling him so well," he commented.

"How do you know that's not from my adventure this morning in the Wilds."

Nero gave me a hard look. He knew. It was impossible to lie to him. Every move I made, every glance, every blink, every shift of my body was a dead giveaway. That, plus he could read my mind.

"Ok, fine," I admitted. "It was from my fight with Colonel Fireswift."

"And his son."

"Yes, Jace was there too. The Colonel likes to pit us against each other." I frowned. "Jace isn't all bad, though. We train just fine together when his father isn't around."

"You should find another training partner."

"Well, there was this one guy. Strong, powerful, lethal as all hell, easy on the eyes too. Nice wings." I brushed my fingers against the tip of his wings. "But then he got himself tied up in angel business. I'm lonely, you see. I need someone to keep me warm during these cold winter nights." I was trying hard to keep my face serious, but a smirk was pulling on my lips.

Nero leaned over and took my lower lip between his teeth, drawing it out slowly. "You shouldn't provoke me, Pandora."

My heart thumped against my chest. "Oh, but it's so much fun. Your reaction always makes it worth my while."

"I'm going to make you forget all about your jokes.

And about your friend."

His look was dark, his voice ruthlessly sensual. He was so close—and yet so far away. He took my hand and flipped it over. His thumb massaged slow, deep circles into the inside of my wrist. He was hardly touching me, and my heart was threatening to explode out of my chest. I was so doomed.

Nero dipped his head, his mouth stopping only inches from mine. "There won't be a single word on your lips but my name."

I snorted. "Confident, aren't you?"

"Yes."

His mouth swooped down on mine and he drew me into a deep, all-consuming kiss that overrode all logical thought. There was nothing but the two of us—and that kiss. My hands clawed at his back, trying to pull him in closer. He didn't budge. His hands didn't even touch me. His lips trailed my jaw, dipping to my neck. Nero took my hand in his and kissed the top with gentlemanly grace. Then he flipped it over and kissed the underside of my wrist. Each touch of his lips was a burning brand in my skin, devouring me. It was the most sensual kiss I'd ever experienced, and I wanted more.

His fangs brushed against my neck, so lightly that they didn't break the skin. My blood surged beneath the surface. Why wasn't he biting me?

My lips parted, a soft moan escaping them. "Nero."

He looked up, hitting me with a deliciously dark smile. "There it is."

He grabbed my hips roughly, turning me around. My palms slammed down on the countertop. His chest was hard against my back, his breath hot against my neck. He exhaled slowly, then his fangs sank into me. Liquid fire pierced my skin, cascading through my veins, drowning me in a firestorm of pleasure.

I moaned in protest when his mouth lifted from my neck.

"Leda." His eyes were wide, dilated.

I turned around, clawing at him in sheer desperation, drawing him closer, a silent demand for him to continue drinking from me.

"I have to stop now, or I won't be able to," he whispered against my lips.

His voice rumbled, a sign that he was at the verge of losing control. Like standing at the edge of civilization, just one more step would send him tumbling into the wilderness. I wanted him to tumble. I wanted him to lose all control. And to take me with him.

He kissed me, his tongue sliding across my extended fangs. "Drink from me."

I dipped my mouth to his neck, kissing the skin softly once before sinking in. His blood flooded into my mouth, as sweet as the gods' Nectar—and just as addictive. I pulled him hard against me, drinking deeper. He groaned in approval.

I can hear you two making out down there, an amused voice chimed inside my head. Damiel.

I pulled away from Nero, dizzily plopping onto one of the barstools.

"I am going to kill him," Nero growled.

I touched his face. "You don't mean that."

"I do." And he looked serious.

"Come on," I said, sliding off the stool. "Let's go check on your dad."

CHAPTER SIX
The World of Angels

NERO AND I took the staircase up. Each step was made of glass. Transparent, almost invisible, they seemed to float up to the next floor, where Damiel was staying in his 'gilded cage', as he liked to call it. And he was indeed staying in a very luxurious prison.

The entire floor was a single room with majestic ceilings so high and vast that two teams of angels could comfortably play a game of football in the air. Large windows looked out on the city. Like downstairs, they were made of enchanted glass. Damiel could see out, but no one outside could see in. It was an essential precaution since most of the world, the Legion included, thought Damiel had died long ago.

We passed through the magic barrier that kept Damiel inside the open apartment. It also kept everyone out except for Nero, Captain Somerset, and me. The barrier was completely invisible. Only the low hum of the Magitech generator powering it betrayed its presence.

Damiel stood behind the cooking island of the open kitchen, a spatula in his hand. At first glance, he looked a lot like Nero. He had the same hair as his son, if not a bit more bronze than caramel. And his eyes were blue instead of green. But other than that, the two angels might have been twins. They had the same body type: hard, flexible muscle filling out a set of wide shoulders and a chest cutting down into a narrow V waistline. Their hair was cut short with a little extra length in front. They both wore the same stern expression on their faces—especially when they looked at each other. And they both looked the same age, forever frozen at twenty, when they'd drunk the gods' Nectar for the first time.

Damiel had changed his clothes since his return from the Wilds. Instead of black leather, he now wore a t-shirt and jeans. He wore them comfortably, as though he'd dressed like this every day of his life instead of donning the Legion's battle leather. But there was something that wasn't quite right. Even though Damiel's outfit consisted entirely of egregiously expensive high-end designer clothes—probably stuff of Nero's that he never wore because he preferred to be in uniform—the clothes looked shabby compared to the elegant angel wearing them. He was a king in peasant clothes. The king shone right through. Or in this case, the angel.

"Hello, hello," Damiel said, his stern expression evaporating the moment his eyes met mine.

Thank goodness he was speaking aloud this time. I can't even begin to describe how unsettling it is to have someone poking around inside your head.

"Pancakes?" Damiel asked brightly, flipping a pair of them onto a large plate.

"It's three in the afternoon. It's too late in the day for pancakes," Nero told him.

"It's never too late in the day for pancakes." I watched with morbid fascination as Damiel poured maple syrup all over the pancakes. "There's enough sugar on them to kill a fairy."

"One of the perks of immortality. You can survive most things that kill others." Smiling, he handed me the plate. "Dig in."

"So, sixty-five vampires captured. That's quite an impressive catch. Have any of them spilled their secrets yet?" Damiel asked casually as he poured more pancake batter into the pan.

I pushed a piece of pancake into the pool of maple syrup. "How do you know how many vampires we captured?"

"I eavesdropped."

Of course he had.

"If you're reading my mind, you know everything I know," I said.

"I stopped reading your mind five seconds after you entered the building. That's when you started thinking about my son naked."

I almost choked on my pancake. I coughed, trying to dislodge the piece stuck in my throat. Damiel calmly handed me a glass of water. I glanced at Nero, who had a rather smug expression on his face. Naturally. Angels didn't get embarrassed. Modesty wasn't even in their vocabulary. Things that would make any decent person flash bright red, they just regarded with cool indifference. Or pride. Apparently pride wasn't a sin if it was well-deserved.

"As far as I know, the vampires haven't spilled their secrets yet. We shot them full of sedatives before loading them into the trucks, so they're probably only now waking up in an Interrogator's chair."

Damiel smiled fondly as he flipped a pancake. "I do miss the days of brutal interrogations."

I looked at him in shock. I really shouldn't have been shocked, not after all I'd lived through in the Legion. Angels were not human. When would I finally remember that?

"Have you had any luck activating the armor and weapons of heaven and hell?" Damiel asked me.

"I haven't tried again recently. I've been too busy."

Damiel looked disappointed. He thought the armor, which had once belonged to the Guardians, was the key to contacting them. Since they lived outside our dimension, separated from us, it wasn't easy to get their attention. Damiel believed his wife Cadence was with them. Raven Rhodes was supposed to confirm that, but he'd turned out to be a pretty worthless source of information. All we knew now was that Raven had been a despicable human being long before he'd become a despicable vampire.

There was actually another thing we'd accomplished this morning: Nero now knew his father hadn't killed his mother. Raven had seen Cadence alive after she'd supposedly died in the fight with Damiel. I'd known from the start that Damiel hadn't killed her. The way his eyes lit up when he spoke of her was undeniable. How could Nero, an expert at reading body signs, have missed it? It seemed that even angels had blindspots and Nero's father was his. He was convinced that Damiel was perpetually up to no good.

"I couldn't get the armor and weapons to work when I tried them at Calli's house after our return from the Lost City," I told Damiel. "I think I need to level up my magic more."

"You got them to respond before," Damiel pointed out.

"That was under extreme circumstances, extreme stress." The stress being a psychopath trying to kill me, Nero, and Damiel. "I'm not even sure how I did it. And I can't repeat it."

A calculating gleam slid across Damiel's eyes. I had the sinking suspicion that he was thinking up a plan to recreate the horrible conditions that had allowed me to access the power to control the immortal artifacts. I certainly wouldn't put it past him. He'd done it before, tortured me to force me to unlock the memories that opened the doorway to the armor and weapons.

Damiel was quite possibly the scariest angel I knew, maybe even scarier than Nyx. He seemed like a great guy on the outside, but then he could switch just like that. I saw it in his eyes. He was crueler than Colonel Fireswift, more calculating than Nyx, and darker than Nero. He was fueled by his desperation to find his wife, the love of his immortal life. And that desperation stemmed from his guilt. He'd promised to find her after they'd put on a good fight for the Legion, but he'd never seen her again.

His guilt and desperation had blended together, hardening into a cold shell. It had made him very, very dangerous. He was looking for Cadence with the same chilling brutality that he'd once used to execute the gods' justice.

"Have you had any more visions from the Guardians?" Damiel asked me.

"No, but I have been having nightmares."

Nero looked at me. "How long has this been going on?"

"Pretty much since we got back from the Lost City."

A worry line formed between his eyes. He thought I was cracking under the stress of the trauma I'd experienced in the Lost City. And maybe he was right.

"What happens in these nightmares?" Damiel asked.

"I am stuck in a volcano, being slowly boiled alive."

"You're worried about your training with the Dragons," Nero said.

"I know." It didn't take a degree in psychology for me to understand that.

I was leaving today for Storm Castle to undergo elemental magic training that would prepare me for the next level. I'd heard stories about Storm Castle, stories of being subjected to the elements in extreme, magical conditions far beyond the ordinary. It was the Legion's tried and true way to prime our magic, to build up our resistance, to increase our chances of surviving the gods' fourth gift. The gift of elemental magic.

"But I'll be fine," I said quickly. "What doesn't kill you, only makes you stronger, right?"

I flashed him a big, confident smile to cover up my complete lack of confidence. The wound I'd received from an immortal weapon was interfering with my training. Whenever I pushed myself too hard, it flared up. That meant I was slower and weaker than I needed to be. I wasn't ready for intense training, training that would likely open up old wounds—and create lots of new ones.

Then again, when would I ever be ready? I had to train, to level up my magic so I could gain the power I needed to find Zane. I'd joined the Legion for that single purpose, and I was not about to allow a pesky immortal weapon wound to stop me.

"And how are your preparations for your level ten trials coming along, Nero?" his father asked.

Nero said nothing. His default response to his father was no response.

"The trials will be difficult, like nothing you've ever faced before. The gods—"

Nero lifted his hand, interrupting his father.

"Have you asked Damiel for help?" I asked Nero.

"No."

Damiel flipped the pancakes, a resigned look on his face.

"You really should. He's been through it. He can help you," I said.

"I don't trust him. He's hiding something." He looked at his father. "I can feel it."

Damiel clicked his tongue. "I can feel you trying to break through my mind, Nero. You aren't strong enough. Not yet. You need to grow your magic. You should listen to Leda. I can help you survive the trials."

"The last time you offered to help me, I nearly died. You are not a good teacher."

"That was centuries ago, Nero."

"You haven't changed. You're incapable of changing," said Nero. "No, I will do this alone. You aren't supposed to tell me anything anyway. It's forbidden to speak of the trials."

"The Legion holds no sway over me. Not anymore."

Nero's eyes were as hard as green diamonds. "You might have turned your back on everything we believe in, but I have not. My answer is no."

I didn't want Nero to die. He had to survive, Legion be damned.

"A few tips wouldn't hurt, right?" I said to him.

He shook his head. "I don't break the rules."

"We've broken quite a few rules lately."

Our mission to the Lost City. Keeping the secret about my brother's powers and my ability to control beasts. Hiding the weapons and armor of heaven and hell. The list just went on and on.

"I did what I had to in order to protect you," Nero said. "But I won't cheat on a test for my own personal gain. There's no honor in that."

"Did it ever occur to you that I want to protect you? That I don't want the trials to kill you?"

Dipping his forehead to mine, he wrapped his arms around me.

"You made a good choice. I didn't expect this of you, Nero. So impulsive. So angelic. So incredibly unlike you," Damiel said with an approving nod.

I met Nero's eyes. "What is he talking about? What choice?"

"Nothing." He glowered at his father.

"He's marked you as his, my dear." Damiel inhaled deeply. "I can smell him all over you."

"Marked me? What does that even mean?"

"He's marked you with his scent, his magic. Anyone with supernatural senses can smell it. It's especially potent to other angels. He's broadcasting that you're under his protection. That you belong to him. And that anyone who hurts you will answer to him."

I lifted my arm and sniffed. Damiel was right. I smelled like Nero. But when... Just now, I realized. Those kisses. I brushed my hand across my lips. The blood exchange that had felt better than any we'd had before. I dropped my hand to my neck. He'd marked me. Without asking.

"Why?" I choked out. My shoulders shook with anger.

"Nero gave you a book on angels," Damiel said. "You should know how territorial we are. Why do you think Nyx has only one angel assigned to each territory with a lot of space between us? It's because when we get too close, we start fighting over property."

"And marking your property," I said in a whisper.

"He's telling Colonel Fireswift to piss off and leave you alone."

I looked at Nero.

"I told you Fireswift's scent was all over you. He must have marked you during training."

I shook my head slowly. This was not happening.

"He was sending me a message. I had to respond."

"Why..." No other words came out. Colonel Fireswift had marked me. Just to annoy Nero.

"Angels do this sort of thing all the time," Damiel told me.

This was unbelievable.

"By marking you, Colonel Fireswift was declaring you to be one of his," Damiel said. "Like his children. Under his protection."

I felt sick. I'd seen firsthand just how well Colonel Fireswift treated his son. He'd tortured him to teach him a lesson. I didn't want his so-called protection.

"Nero had to respond," Damiel continued.

That was angel logic at its finest. And thanks to that dubious logic, I was now caught in a power struggle—a mind game—between an angel who wanted to kill me and one who wanted to claim me.

"How does an angel mark someone?" I asked Nero

quietly. If I didn't whisper, I'd scream. I was surprised by how steady my voice was, how calm. Nero looked surprised too. He must have expected me to blow up at him. That might still come. I was so furious.

"Through a blood exchange usually."

Colonel Fireswift had thrown me against the wall. I'd bled from multiple places. And he'd hit those wounds. He could have put his blood into me that way.

"But there are other ways," Nero said.

"Sex," Damiel told me. "He means sex. Plus a blood exchange on top of that. That's the recipe for the strongest mark. A mating mark."

"Your blood is in me," I said to Nero.

"I drank your blood and changed it, giving it back to you when you drank from me."

I knew that blood exchange had felt different than the ones before. Better. No, not better. I didn't want it to be better. Nero had done this without asking me.

"So Colonel Fireswift marked me as his property to piss you off, and you decided to do the same?" I said. "I'm not a bone you can fight over. I'm a person."

"He wanted every person you met to think you belonged to him."

I gritted my teeth. "I don't give a rat's ass about that psychopath and his games. Let him mark me up all he wants. That doesn't make me his property."

"You are naive, Leda. In our world, it means exactly that. If I didn't challenge his claim, I would be accepting it."

"So you just marked me without asking?"

"As your reaction proves, you were not going to be reasonable about this."

"I am no one's property," I snapped. "As soon as I get back to the Legion, I'm going to find a potion to remove this mark."

Damiel chuckled. "There's nothing on this Earth that can remove an angel's mark. Nothing but another angel's mark. Or the mark of a god."

"Then how do I get it off?"

"You can't," Damiel said. "This happens all the time. Angels marking their family, their mate, those they wish to protect. I'm surprised Nero did it, though. He thinks himself above such things."

I frowned at Nero. "Well, it looks like he's not above anything."

"Be silent. You're not helping," Nero told his father.

I jutted my finger in Nero's face. "Remove your mark from me."

Nero glanced down at my finger. "As my father said, it doesn't work that way."

"You're intelligent, creative, and determined. I'm sure you'll think of something."

"There is nothing. And even if I did remove my mark, Fireswift would just mark you again."

Despair stretched my lips into a hard smile. "He's going to do that anyway when he sees me, isn't he?"

"My mark is potent. I was quite thorough."

An involuntary shiver shook my body at the memory of just how thorough he'd been.

"Unless you sleep with Fireswift, he won't be able to cover Nero's mark," Damiel added helpfully.

The thought of sleeping with Colonel Fireswift made me ill. He wasn't a bad-looking guy. Like all angels, he was beautiful. But that beauty could not hide the ugliness inside. He had the personality of an assault rifle.

"This is ridiculous. I'm not some tree to be peed on," I declared.

"Actually, an angel's mark is considered to be a pleasant scent. Some consider it an aphrodisiac," Damiel said.

I scowled at him.

"This is why I won't ever accept your help," Nero told him. "Your help isn't help at all."

"I could mark you myself if you don't want to be caught in the middle of their power struggle," Damiel offered. "My magic is stronger than theirs. It's unlikely either of them will be able to cover my mark."

A gust of magic and feathers shot past me. Nero grabbed his father, hurling him across the room. Damiel somersaulted in the air, slowing down. His wings burst out of him, and he hovered there for a moment. Nero shot straight up into the air, tackling him hard. Damiel's back hit the ceiling with a wretched crunch. The angel didn't seem to notice. As fast as lightning, he slipped out of Nero's grasp, circling around him. He slammed his hand against Nero's shoulder. A sharp crack signaled that Damiel had broken his shoulder. Three more cracks sounded as Damiel snapped three of Nero's ribs.

Nero kept fighting. The two angels flashed across the room, fists flying, feathers falling. Despite the world of pain he must have been in, Nero wasn't holding back. He grabbed Damiel by the foot and slammed his head against the wall. He'd lost all control.

I'd seen him like this before, two weeks ago in the Lost City when he'd seen his father again for the first time in centuries. That same savage ferocity had consumed him then too. No thought, no control. Only instinct.

His father was his trigger. They had a long history of distrust and hatred. As they'd just reminded me, angels were prickly and territorial. Having two of them so close to each other wasn't helping Nero's mood. Especially not after Colonel Fireswift, another angel, had pissed him off by marking me. Not that I was excusing Nero's behavior. There was no excuse for this.

I glared up at the warring angels. I needed a shower and a nap, not this nonsense. Nero hit the ground right in front of me. Damiel dove down after him. I planted myself between them.

"Enough," I snapped, packing that single word with as much magic as I could. "There are more than enough enemies in this world to fight without resorting to hurting each other. You need to start getting along now, or this won't work. You'll never find Cadence."

The blind fury in Nero's eyes went out at the mention of his mother. He was returning to his senses, so I pressed on.

"She wouldn't want you two to fight," I told them.

Nero's fists were still clenched. "Stay away from her," he growled at his father.

Finding Cadence without Damiel might be possible, but it would be easier with an extra angel on our side. Nero had to see that.

"You will never pass the gods' trials like this," his father said. "You need more control when it really matters. When everything is at stake. When they tear you apart from the inside, taking everything you are, everything you have, everything you care about. Nero, you are in control when it doesn't matter, and you lose it when it does. I've been telling you that since you were a child."

I feared Damiel was right. Nero wasn't in control. If his father could make him lose it with just a few words, I could only imagine how easily the gods could break him.

Nero folded his arms across his chest and glared at Damiel. Damiel glared back. Tessa would have fainted if she'd been here to see the two angels with those 'smoldering' looks, as she liked to call angels' battle eyes. My little sister often mistook murderous for smoldering.

"I don't need yet another angel marking me," I told Damiel.

He shrugged. "Suit yourself." He didn't look bothered. If anything, he was amused. The barely perceptible twitch of his lip gave him away. Even angels had weaknesses. Even they had their telltale signs.

"Come with me," I told Nero and turned to take the very long staircase upstairs, not even looking back to check if he was following me.

The stairs spilled into a room that resembled a king's bedchamber. The ornate canopy bed alone, with its gem-studded posts and gold-thread curtains, must have cost as much as a car. It was enormous, large enough for two angels to sleep there side-by-side with their wings extended.

"That was Cadence and Damiel's bed," I realized.

"Yes," Nero said right behind me, making me jump. I needed to outfit myself with a proximity alarm. Though I somehow doubted it would work against angels.

I looked out the window at the city. The cold rainclouds had parted. A rainbow shone over the airship station at the end of the street, setting the station's bronze beams aglow. They reflected the rainbow, sending it into a hundred different directions. There was a innocent beauty to that magical light. But I couldn't enjoy it. Not right now.

"You should have told me that Colonel Fireswift marked me," I said, trying to keep the judgment out of my voice. And the anger. I was so pissed off right now. "But instead you just did whatever you wanted without consulting me."

He looked at me, infuriatingly silent.

"Nero, I want this to work. I want *us* to work," I told him. "But you need to stop making decisions for me."

"Something in me snapped when I smelled him on you. I couldn't help myself."

"You, with all the willpower in the world."

"This goes beyond willpower," he said. "It's instinct. It's the way we are."

"Said every man in the history of the world ever."

"You misunderstand. This isn't about men or women. It's about angels. Both male and female angels mark what is theirs. In fact, the female angel's mark is far more potent. This is what angels are, Leda. It's how we act, how we tick. If you can't accept that, this won't ever work. We can't work."

"So you're saying you will only remove your mark if we stop this…"

Whatever *this* was. We weren't dating. Not really. We hadn't even finished our first date. But the way I felt about him meant something to me. *He* meant something to me. But even if he felt the same way about me, what did it change? He was going to keep acting however his angel programming told him to. I should have known better than to get involved with an angel. They weren't human. They didn't think like we did.

"Fireswift is a dangerous angel, Leda," he said. "Whether or not you accept him, everyone will accept you are his if his mark is on you. If you think you're hurting now under his command, just wait to see how much worse it will get when you are one of his. Like his children."

I shuddered to think of what Fireswift had done to Jace. He'd basically crucified him to the wall to make a point, to teach his son a lesson.

"You are in our world now, Leda. The world of angels. You joined the Legion willingly. You went into this with eyes open."

"Not this," I said, throwing my hands up in frustration. "The work, the magic, the training. The very real possibility of death. Yes, I signed up for that. I didn't sign up to be marked by warring angels."

"It's all part of the same thing," he said with a patient sigh. "I am trying to protect you. The fact that you expected to continue your life in the same manner as you had lived before joining the Legion shows how naive you are. You are no longer human, Leda. You need to stop thinking of yourself as such. You have to make some adjustments to our culture. You won't survive otherwise. And you won't ever be happy."

Loneliness swelled up inside of me. I felt so lost, so out of place. The world of angels, the Legion, the path to becoming an angel myself—it was so different from everything that I'd ever known.

I missed my home. My family. The familiar smells from Calli's kitchen. Waking up next to my sister. Sharing that stupid tiny bathroom between the six of us. Laughing over meals. Teasing each other. I missed it all. It made my heart hurt to think of everything I'd given up.

But there was no going back now. I'd thought the hard part of joining the Legion would be surviving the Nectar.

The trials, the training, the monsters. The constant exhaustion and stress that pushed me to the breaking point.

I'd been wrong. The hardest part of joining the Legion was everything I'd had to leave behind—and this whole new world I'd blindly flung myself into. I'd read a book about angels, but I didn't understand them. I didn't even understand my place in the world anymore. I wanted to bury my head in my knees and rock back and forth, humming loudly until it all went away. But I couldn't do that. It wouldn't all go away. I knew it wouldn't. This was my life now. The best I could hope for was to hold onto as much as my humanity as I could, like Captain Somerset had.

"Please. Remove the mark," I pleaded with Nero. "If you care at all about me, you will."

"I did this *because* I care. Fireswift did it to hurt me by hurting you. I'd rather you hate me and be safe than be a slave to him."

My heart was a twisted clump of joy and pain. "I know why you did it, but you should have asked me."

"We both know you would have refused. And that your refusal would have been a foolish decision. You still don't understand our world, Leda."

He was right. I didn't understand this crazy world of angels and gods. How could I? It was all so alien to me.

He looked at me, his expression softening slightly. "There is a way to remove my mark. It hasn't spread far. I can still drink it out of you."

"Please do it."

I thought I caught a flash of pain—of betrayal—in his eyes, but it was gone so fast that maybe it was just my mind playing tricks on me. I didn't want to hurt him.

Nero lifted his hand to my face. He brushed the hair off my neck, and my pulse sped up in anticipation. I was so hopelessly addicted to him that it was hard to think straight. But I had to. I had to wrap my humanity around myself like a shield, just as Captain Somerset had.

His fangs penetrated my skin, but this time when he drank from me, it didn't feel good. I didn't feel anything in fact, except for a dull pain from the wound. There was nothing sensual about it. He drank carefully, draining his mark from me with surgical precision.

Finally, he pulled back and said, "It is done."

"Thank you." I reached into one of my pouches for my healing powder, which I dabbed over the puncture marks on my neck.

"Fireswift will just mark you again," he warned me.

"I will handle him. Now that I know his game, I can stop him."

Nero didn't respond. His expression proclaimed he knew it wouldn't be that easy. Maybe he was right, but I'd cross that bridge when I came to it.

Nero turned away. "I have to go." His voice was so cold.

I caught his arm. "Removing the mark isn't about you."

He glanced back at me. "Leda, don't insult both of us by lying to yourself. This is entirely about me. And it's about you. You joined the Legion. This is your world now, your culture. You just haven't accepted it. And you haven't accepted me for who I am."

I opened my mouth to argue, but he spoke first. "It's the truth. You want to become an angel, to gain our powers for your own use, but you want nothing to do with who we are. You can't have it both ways, Leda. And you can't have me both ways either. If you want to be with me, you have to accept me for what I am. I'm not going to lie to you. A lot of what angels do isn't pretty. Humans paint us in shining halos, but we aren't that way at all. We are vicious and stubborn and simply don't think the way humans do. We can be cold-hearted bastards, but we always protect those we care about."

"I do care about you, Nero."

"The angel and the man are one person. Intertwined, inseparable. It is who I am. Can you accept that?"

"I…"

I stopped myself. This was important. Could I really accept all of the angel politics, the games, the power plays? Nero was right. It was part of him and his culture. I couldn't ask him to stop being who he was. I wouldn't even respect him if he did.

I took a deep breath. "I need some time to think." To decide if I could really get involved with someone who was so different from me, from someone who would do whatever he had to in order to keep me safe—at the expense of my own freewill.

"Let me know when you've made your decision."

His face was as hard as granite, not a single emotion present on it. He brushed the back of his hand softly across my cheek. A gust of wind shot through the room, and then he was gone, leaving behind a single dark feather.

CHAPTER SEVEN
The Cold Kiss of Vengeance

I HELD THE dark blue angel feather between my thumb and index finger. There was magic in it. Nero's magic. It melted through my skin like a warm snowflake dissolving into my soul. I zipped open my jacket to put it inside, but I stopped.

A skeptical voice inside of me screamed that this was just another angel game. Nero hadn't left the feather there by mistake. He'd wanted me to have something of him with me always. It was just another way of marking me.

What is so bad about taking something of him with me? I asked that voice. That's what people who care about each other do. They give each other mementos. I tucked the feather inside my jacket and invited the skeptical voice to go take a hike.

When I got back downstairs, Damiel was still standing at the kitchen island, making buttermilk pancakes. And eating them. He must have the metabolism of a race horse.

"More pancakes?" he asked, offering me a small stack.

I waved the plate away. I wasn't feeling very hungry anymore.

"Chocolate?"

I looked at the piece of dark chocolate in his hand. Chocolate was different. I was always hungry for chocolate. I took the tiny piece into my mouth, allowing the rich flavor to slowly melt into my tastebuds.

"So Nero figured out how to remove the mark." Damiel dumped a small bowl of strawberries over his pancakes. "I figured he would if sufficiently motivated."

"So, you knew it could be removed?"

"Yes." He looked offended. Of course he knew. He knew everything about angels. Nero really had to put aside his pride and ask his father to help him prepare for his promotion trials.

I plopped down on the barstool across from the stove. "Yes, Nero was sufficiently motivated to remove it."

"I couldn't help but overhear."

I cringed. Somehow the fact that he'd overheard my serious conversation with Nero upset me much more than him eavesdropping when we'd been making out downstairs. What we'd spoken of up there as we bared our hearts and souls was deeply intimate.

"Nero is right, you know," he told me.

"Thanks," I said darkly.

Damiel shrugged. He was an angel and Nero's father. The two of them had a lot of views in common, more than Nero and I had, in fact.

"You have to be sure you can accept the angel and the man," he said. "Best to head this off now before you break his heart."

Break Nero's heart? My heart was in far more danger. Angels took many lovers, but they didn't love. Not easily. Most of them had one true love in their entire immortal life and that was it. Everyone knew that, even the girls who lied to themselves that they would be the one, the love of an angel's life—right before they threw their panties at them. I blushed, recalling that *I* had thrown my panties on the floor of Nero's office. But I'd been high on Nectar. That was different.

I wasn't in this for fun. I wanted something else. But could I even have that with Nero? He'd only been gone a few minutes, and I missed him already. But the thought of that archaic angel tradition of marking whatever you'd deemed to be yours… It just made me mad! How many other bizarre angel traditions were there that I didn't know about?

"A lot of them," Damiel told me.

I looked up sharply. "You need to ask before you intrude on someone's thoughts."

Damiel gave me an unrepentant smile. "I like you, Leda."

I didn't know why that offhand comment made me feel better, but it did. A little anyway. But a little wasn't enough. Not even close.

"You are torturing yourself," Damiel said.

It was a comment, an observation. Not a judgment. An angel would never judge someone for torturing themselves. They believed self-flagellation built character.

I rose from my seat. "I have to go."

"Come back soon. It's horribly dull here."

I left Damiel in his gilded cage. Outside, the clouds were back. There wasn't a rainbow in sight. The frozen rain had slowed to an icy drizzle. It spilled down my neck. My boots squelched against the slushy pavement.

I couldn't run fast enough to the Legion office. When I

got there, the reception area was as full as I'd ever seen it, packed with soldiers hauling in prisoners and bodies. One of the soldiers was arguing with the secretary about whether he was allowed to bring in a werewolf who smelled of garbage. The werewolf had apparently been hiding for weeks. His injuries coupled with the tight security around the city had prevented him from ever making it out of New York. So he'd been eating out of trashcans to survive.

"He smells," the secretary declared. "Colonel Fireswift will hold me personally responsible if I allow that werewolf and his stench past the reception hall. You shouldn't have even brought him inside."

"I cannot leave him unattended. He's very good at escaping his restraints."

"You could have waited with him."

"In that freezing rain?"

"It is the lesser of two evils."

"Only for the person who is standing warm and dry inside."

"You would only have to wait there until the decontamination team arrived."

The Legion took decontamination seriously. As soon as the team smelled the werewolf, they would burn off his clothes and give him a telekinetic shower that fried the muck off of him, down to the last dirty particle.

The secretary and soldier were still arguing over the werewolf when I passed through the door that led past the reception hall. Back here, it was just as full as up front. Soldiers in workout suits, soldiers in uniforms headed to or from missions. Lately, there hadn't been any downtime at the office. Train, work, level up your magic or die. That was pretty routine for the Legion, but there were usually a few bright spots in between. Nights off, drinking Nectar drops, music, and dancing—just a little fun here and there to forget about all the horrible things in the world.

I was passing by my friend Nerissa's lab on the way to my apartment when raised voices attracted my attention. Colonel Fireswift was in there. Ignoring my body's desperate plea for a warm shower, I stopped. The Colonel was a jackass, and he was terrorizing my friend. I couldn't abandon Nerissa now.

"Eight soldiers have come to me, each one with a note signed by you, Dr. Harding. A note that declares them too unwell to participate in the upcoming promotion ceremony."

"It is against the Legion's regulations to force sick soldiers to drink the gods' Nectar," Nerissa said.

"Sick soldiers," Colonel Fireswift repeated with disgust. "There is nothing wrong with them besides their cowardice. And you are covering for them."

Colonel Fireswift was an ass, but he wasn't wrong. He'd made it his mission to level up the magic of as many soldiers as possible, no matter the cost. He considered the people who died in the ceremony to be casualties of war. He was a firm believer of thinning the herd. To him, those people would never have made it to a high enough level to be useful. The problem was Colonel Fireswift had a really narrow view of what constituted as useful.

Nerissa had a mission of her own. She was going to save anyone she thought wouldn't survive the Nectar. She saw it as her duty as both a doctor and a decent human being. Her plan and Colonel Fireswift's were fundamentally opposed.

"I have had enough of your incessant meddling and

rule-breaking, Dr. Harding. The time you waste interfering with the smooth operation of the Legion could be put to far better use. You need to worry about yourself instead." He waved his hand in the air, and a magical projection lit up the space in front of him. "You will head to Storm Castle with the other candidates for level four. Let's just see if the Dragons' training can't cure you of your penchant for pissing me off." He added her name to the end of the list etched in golden light, then swiped the magical projection away.

Nerissa just gaped at him, speechless.

"What's wrong?" he asked smugly. "No snappy comeback?"

"Leave her alone," I told him, putting steel into my voice.

Surprise froze Colonel Fireswift for a moment, but he quickly recovered his arrogance. He turned and walked out of the room, leaving Nerissa to pick up the pieces of her shattered life. I could see it in her eyes. She was sure she was going to die. Well, not if I could help it.

"Your impudence is rubbing off on your friends," Colonel Fireswift told me. He towered over me like an ogre. "The First Angel thinks you're special." He made a derisive noise. He didn't share Nyx's opinion. He'd told me that countless times. "What's this?" His nostrils flared. "Windstriker," he spoke Nero's name as though it were a curse.

He must have smelled Nero on me. Nero's mark was gone, but his scent was still all over me. Colonel Fireswift could probably smell him in every spot he'd kissed me.

"As I thought." His nose crinkled with disgust. "It must be exhilarating for a nobody like you to have an angel

78

enthralled with you. You might think you're filling that sad, hollow hole in him left by his dead parents. But you never will. You are *nothing*. A nice piece of ass, a way to pass some time, but in the end, nothing. Trash is trash." He lifted his hand toward me.

My hand darted down to my whip. The electrically-charged cord hissed, catching his hand before he could make contact with me.

"You won't lay a hand on me," I ground out through clenched teeth.

"This is insubordination."

"By not letting you mark me? Again."

His eyebrows drew together. "So you know."

"Yes," I said. "This isn't insubordination. It is self-defense."

"You are out of line."

"No, you are out of line, Colonel. I am not your property."

"But you are Windstriker's?" A cold smile spread across his lips. "You are nothing. A mere distraction, a tiny *pawn* in a game of giants. A game you do not even understand."

Pawn. He used that word like he knew it would be the one to strike the right cord. He was right.

Colonel Fireswift pushed against my whip, reaching for me. He was going to mark me again. I felt it with every drop of magic in me. And there was no way I was going to let that happen. I stepped back and pulled, tightening the whip's hold around his arm. Lightning sparked, singeing his skin. He didn't wince, didn't blink. Not even a little.

He didn't care about me, neither as a lover nor as property. He hated me. He thought I was trash. He just wanted to mess with Nero. And he knew Nero *did* care about me.

Streams of lightning shot up Colonel Fireswift's arm, swallowing it. The whip was hitting him with more lighting than anyone should be able to take. I hoped it didn't lose its charge. I couldn't cast elemental magic on weapons myself. The electric whip was powered by a tiny Magitech battery. It needed to be recharged by a larger Magitech generator. The whip was powerful, supposed to last the whole day under normal combat. Which meant it might last a couple of minutes against an angel.

"Stop," I warned him. I kept my voice hard and cold, trying to cover up my fear that the magic would go out on the whip. That whip was the only thing standing between me and Colonel Fireswift's plan to send Nero a message by kicking my ass. "I will take off your arm."

"You wouldn't dare."

"That just goes to show that you don't know me at all. I would dare a lot of things."

Colonel Fireswift pushed against the whip's hold. He was going to wait it out until its magic failed. Bastard. The hum of the lightning was growing weaker. It wouldn't last much longer. I had to change tactics. Colonel Fireswift knew he could beat me in a direct fight. He wasn't afraid of me. He wasn't even afraid of Nero. But there was someone he was afraid of.

I pulled out my phone. "Shall we have the First Angel settle this? I have her number saved."

Colonel Fireswift looked at me with those cold, inhuman eyes. Those eyes that had tortured thousands in his centuries as an angel. He was trying to psych me out. I met his eyes and didn't back down.

"The First Angel does not get involved in such trivial

matters as lowly insubordinate sergeants," he finally said.

"Maybe not, but she does get involved in angel disputes." I was showing him I knew exactly what this game was about.

"You have no idea what you're doing."

"I know *exactly* what I'm doing. I'm refusing to be dragged into your spat with Nero."

"Windstriker will eat you alive, you stupid little girl. And he will spit you out in pieces. That's what angels do. You are nothing to us. Playthings, distractions. This is our game, and you don't even know you're playing it."

No. Nero didn't want to be with me unless I knew what I was getting into, unless I accepted the rules of the game. Colonel Fireswift wasn't giving me a choice. Nero was. That was one of the many, many differences between them. If I decided I didn't want to play, Nero wouldn't push me.

"Do you think you're the first naive girl who's caught his eye? There have been hundreds just like you," Colonel Fireswift told me.

I smirked at him. "There's no one like me."

His eyes swept over me. "You're right. The others were prettier."

I resisted the urge to punch him. Firstly, because that wouldn't be self-defense; it would be attacking an angel, a superior, out of anger. And secondly, because he would kick my ass.

When I didn't take the bait, he lowered his hand. I held in a sigh of relief as I slowly retracted my whip. But I wasn't putting it away. I had to be ready in case he attacked. Colonel Fireswift could kill me before I could call Nyx. He must have been thinking the same thing because he started to move toward me again.

"Wow, you sure will be in an awkward position when Nero is promoted and outranks you," I said quickly.

That froze Colonel Fireswift, right down to his icy eyes. "If Nero doesn't survive, *you* will be in the awkward position. And I will be waiting."

He looked me over like I was already dead, then turned and walked down the hall. As soon as he was out of sight, I took a deep, calming breath. I unclenched my fists and went into the lab to speak to Nerissa.

"He really is an ass," she commented.

"No kidding." I set my hand on her back. "Are you all right?"

Nerissa let out a pitiful laugh, then dropped her head to her desk.

I shifted my phone to my right hand. *Colonel Evil put Nerissa on the list,* I typed to Ivy. *Hurry down to her lab. She needs you.*

Be right there, she wrote back immediately.

Ivy had a talent for talking to people. If anyone could cheer up Nerissa, she was the one.

"I should have hit him," I said to Nerissa.

She lifted her face off her desk just far enough to give me a censuring look. "That would have been foolish."

"Probably. But it would have felt really good. Well, at least for the split second before he hit me back."

Nerissa didn't laugh. Clearly, my attempts to distract her weren't working.

"The Colonel is a calculating bastard," she said, leaning heavily against her arms. "The cold kiss of vengeance doesn't come swiftly. It is agonizingly slow. The worst part is watching death come for you, knowing there's nothing you can do to stop it."

"Don't talk like that. You'll be ok."

"Leda, I've spent years doing only the minimum physical and magical training required by someone in my position. It's enough to keep me fit and battle-ready if the apocalypse knocked on our door tomorrow. It isn't enough to push me higher. Nero was fine with me where I am."

"You do a splendid job where you are," I told her.

"Yes, I did, didn't I?"

She was already talking about herself in the past tense. That was not good. Not good at all. Where the blazes was Ivy? I wasn't good at calming people. I was good at inciting them. Maybe I could try to compel Nerissa into a state of calmness, but even if it worked, it wouldn't be real. Ivy could calm people even without magic.

"Hello, ladies," Ivy declared, sweeping into the lab like a beautiful summer butterfly, her long red hair bouncing against her back, her heels clicking like a runway model. "Nerissa, I've asked Soren to mentor you. He's on his way. Everything will be all right."

Captain Soren Diaz was Ivy's former beau. They'd split up just last week after dating for a few months. The breakup had been amiable, just like all of Ivy's breakups. She was friends with all of her former boyfriends. Everyone loved Ivy. She was like sugar-sprinkled strawberries. Everyone loved sugar-sprinkled strawberries.

"I have to go pack," I told Nerissa. "Will you be all right?"

"I'll take good care of her," Ivy promised, wrapping her arm around Nerissa.

I gave them a final wave, then hurried toward my apartment. I checked the time. There was barely enough time to pack—and only if I ran all the way. I sped up. I guess that meant no hot shower for me. The story of my life.

CHAPTER EIGHT
The Elemental Expanse

OUTSIDE MY CAR window, smoke billowed up from the burning trees peppered across the plains. On the other side of the road lay a frozen forest. Overhead, storm clouds rumbled and lightning flashed. Below our wheels, the dusty, cracked earth shook and trembled. And at the center of it all, high above at the peak of Mount Cornerstone, sat the mighty fortress the Legion had dubbed Storm Castle.

Here, within the inner ring of magic that stretched out from the mountain, all four elements blended together in perfect, inexplicable harmony. Hot and cold, wet and dry, mountains and plains, ocean and desert.

Beyond that lay the outer ring, the four lands of the Elemental Expanse: the Fire Mountains, the Sky Plains, the Wetlands, and the Desert Rose. One of the four elements flourished in each realm under the power of its guardian Dragon, a Legion soldier with extraordinary elemental magic.

The Elemental Expanse lay on the west coast, past the monster-infested Western Wilderness that had consumed a larger piece of the continent. There were no monsters here in the Elemental Expanse. There weren't any cities either. And the only people who lived here were the Legion soldiers stationed at Storm Castle or at the Legion base located at the northern border of the expanse, not far from the wall that separated these civil lands from the Western Wilderness.

"What are they like?" I asked Captain Somerset as she brought the truck to a stop at the base of Mount Cornerstone. There were already three other cars parked there.

"The four Dragons?" Captain Somerset guessed. "They are exceptional soldiers and powerful magic-casters. The Legion only asks the best to become a Dragon."

"They ask?" I said with surprise. "They don't command?" That didn't sound like the Legion.

"Living here, protecting the Elemental Expanse, nurturing its magic—it's an enormous responsibility, one you can only give to someone who wants it. Each Dragon links with the castle's magic to protect their designated territory, which in turn boosts their own magic. They are the most powerful elemental spell casters on Earth."

"Stronger than the angels?"

"Stronger even than the First Angel," she told me. "But only inside the Elemental Expanse, where they remain linked to Storm Castle. As soon as they pass the border, they can no longer draw on the castle's magic."

I looked up at the rocky wall that seemed to stretch on forever. "How do we get up there?"

"We climb."

"We didn't bring any climbing gear," I pointed out.

"That was intentional."

"You want me to climb up with nothing but my hands

and feet?" I said.

"And your strength of will." She slapped me hard on the back. "Come on. Get moving, Pandora."

I stared down the mountain and silently promised it I would conquer it. I hoped it was listening.

"This is crazy," I muttered a few minutes later when a loose rock nearly caused me to plummet to my death.

"It's tradition," Captain Somerset told me. "All Legion soldiers who visit the Four Dragons for training must climb this mountain."

"And how many of those soldiers fall to their death?"

"Don't think about that."

Well, wasn't that reassuring? I pushed thoughts of my own mortality out of my head and made a conscious effort not to look down. Looking up wasn't a good idea either. Hearing the deep growl of thunder and the sizzle of lightning was bad enough; I didn't need to see the ominous storm cloud swirling over the castle too. If I made it up this mountain without being struck by lightning, I was going to call that a victory.

"So, why aren't we allowed to use climbing gear?" I asked.

"Because that would be cheating," Captain Somerset told me. It sounded like something Nero would say.

One hour. That's roughly how long I'd gone without thinking about Nero. I didn't know what to do about us. After spending the first few hours of our journey to the Elemental Expanse playing out one scenario after another inside my head, I was no closer to knowing what to do— and I'd come to the conclusion that obsessing over it wasn't good for my sanity.

"So, Nero and Damiel nearly killed each other today," I

told Captain Somerset. Thinking about Nero might not be good for my sanity, but it was a good distraction from thoughts of my impending death, curtesy of a wayward bolt of lightning. What good was sanity if I weren't alive to enjoy it?

"That's nothing new. That's what angels do. They can't stand one another for too long."

"It's more than that. Nero hates his father. And I can't figure out why."

"Nero claims Damiel was a cruel and brutal father," she replied. "But I think the true reason Nero hates him is he sees Damiel's darkness in himself. He fears he will become like Damiel, just as cruel, just as brutal."

"And what do you think?"

"I think that when you choose to become an angel, you invite that cruelty and brutality into you. The magic changes you. It brings you closer to the gods. You gain great power, but you also lose something: empathy for humans. You see them as fleeting moments in the vast expanse of time. You concentrate solely on the bigger picture, and in doing so forget that it is in those moments that we truly live, not in the cold, logical confines of our immortality. There is more to life than duty, honor, and the constant push to the top. There is friendship. And love."

"Can you become an angel and remain yourself?" I asked.

"No. Becoming an angel changes you." She turned her head, glancing sidelong across the rock face at me. "Being with an angel changes you too. As a lover, they are spectacular. But as a partner, they are the stuff of nightmares."

"Are you speaking from personal experience?"

"Yes," she said darkly.

"I have enough nightmares without piling on more. Last night, I dreamt I was drowning in a volcano."

"You're nervous about training with the Dragons." Her words echoed Nero's.

"I've heard the experience isn't pleasant."

"No, it's not, but it will make you stronger. *If* you survive," she added.

"You're not helping."

She continued anyway. "You dreamt you were drowning in a volcano. The reality is far worse."

"You know, I'm suddenly finding myself missing Nero's dark pep talks. I never should have shared my nightmares with you."

"Probably a good idea. Don't be so trusting. Don't expose your weaknesses."

"In other words, don't trust anyone."

"Trust your friends," she said as we finally reached the top of the mountain.

The sun parted the clouds, its glistening beams of light pouring down on the castle, making it shine like a million tiny diamonds. A soft hum, resonating with magic, sang out from the walls, and the expanse below responded. The land and castle were linked, their magic intertwined.

"But be careful who you call a friend," Captain Somerset finished.

She stared across the rocky mountaintop, where Jace and five others stood in front of the castle, waiting. Nero had warned me about Jace too. They were right to warn me. Colonel Fireswift's son was talented, hardworking, and ambitious. That ambition toed the line of cruelty. Jace wanted to be a good person, but that was in complete opposition to his desire to be a powerful one. I often wondered which part of him would win out in the end.

"Who is that standing with Jace?" I asked Captain Somerset.

She looked at the woman, who was wearing a full leather uniform despite the heat. The emblem of a hand, the symbol for telekinesis, marked her as a captain, a soldier of the sixth level.

"That is Kendra Fireswift," Captain Somerset told me, frowning. "Colonel Fireswift's first born."

"Jace has a sister?" He'd never mentioned her.

"Yes, but you'll find her more like her father than her brother."

"So, she is Jace's mentor for this training."

To take part in the Dragons' training, each of us had to bring along a mentor. That right there told me how intense this experience would be.

Kendra Fireswift returned Captain Somerset's gaze with obvious distaste. Her perfect nose turned up with presumed superiority.

"I take it you two know each other," I said.

"I helped train her once," Captain Somerset replied as we approached the castle. "She was arrogant even then, an attitude fueled by her uncanny ability to best her peers at everything. She rose through the ranks quickly. Becoming an angel is her life's mission, and I fear for the world should she ever get her wish."

"Captain Somerset," Kendra Fireswift greeted her. "Still training the poor, underpowered soldiers? You always did have a soft spot for charity cases. How very altruistic of you."

"There's nothing altruistic about it." If Captain

Somerset had smiled any harder, her face would have broken. "I'm just doing my job. At the Legion, we serve. We don't seek glory."

"Yes, you were repeating those tired lines to us when I was initiated. It's interesting how little the non-legacy soldiers really understand of duty and honor."

Translation: your parent isn't an angel, so what you're saying doesn't matter.

"Duty and his brother honor, the perfect shields for sanctioned atrocities," I quoted to Kendra.

Kendra looked at me like mushrooms were growing out of my head. It seemed she didn't appreciate Salas, the philosopher from the last century who'd questioned the acts committed by the world's military bodies, all the way up to the Legion of Angels.

Captain Somerset's hand locked around my arm, and she pulled me away from Kendra. "You should have better sense than to quote Salas to a Legion brat."

"They don't know who he was?" I asked, forming my face into an expression of perfect innocence.

"Of course they know. They grew up hearing his passages derided as heresy and treason."

I'd figured as much.

"You're poking a nest of hornets, Pandora," Captain Somerset told me. "No one talks to angels or their kin the way you do."

"It wouldn't be fun if everyone did it," I laughed. "The look on Kendra's face is too good."

Captain Somerset looked at the outrage burning in Kendra's eyes. "It *is* pretty good." She sighed. "Now look at me, encouraging you. You're a terrible influence. How can you make perfectly sensible people willingly take leave of their senses?"

I grinned at her. "By nature, people want to have fun. Well, most people." I glanced at Kendra. "She really is her father's daughter, isn't she? She looks just like Jace, minus the crisis of conscious."

"That is an accurate description of her. Her methods are cruel, but that doesn't mean they aren't effective. Colonel Fireswift is pulling out all the stops to get his son up the ranks."

"Don't associate with the competition," Kendra scolded Jace.

He dropped the hand he'd waved at me.

"That woman clearly doesn't understand the true meaning of duty or honor," I said. "All she knows are the twisted versions of them tattooed into her consciousness from the time she could speak."

"In Kendra's eyes, it is her duty to beat anyone and everyone from a non-angel family—at everything she does," Captain Somerset replied. "To not be the best at absolutely everything is a grave dishonor."

The castle's great gate swung open. The movement was soundless, without even a hint of a creak. The pleasant aroma of herbs spilled out of the gate. We all entered the castle.

A grand chamber awaited us. Or perhaps 'throne room' would have been a more accurate description. Four thrones made of stone stood tall at the far edge of the hardwood floor. An elemental symbol was etched into the peak of each throne: a flame, a lightning bolt, a tree, and a water drop.

We stopped before the empty thrones and waited. Besides Jace, I recognized Sergeant Alec Morrows, a raunchy fellow who also worked at the New York office. The woman standing beside him, his mentor, was a pretty lieutenant. I'd seen her around but didn't know her name. She was short and slender, almost waifish. She didn't look strong enough to pick up a sword, let alone wield one in battle, but appearances could be deceiving. No soldier at the Legion was weak.

Even so, she looked so tiny next to Alec's massive figure. Bulky, muscular, and tall, he was built like a battering ram. And he liked shooting things with cannons. Despite his unrepentant desire to talk every woman he met into his bed, he was actually a really nice guy.

I felt someone brush against my back, and I turned around to find Nerissa standing with Soren. Ivy had pulled through.

"You're here," I said, giving Nerissa's hand a supportive squeeze.

"I'm here," she replied.

"Better late than never." Morrows swept in and put his arms around both of us. "Doc, I can't tell you how happy I am to see you."

"Are you injured?" she asked.

"If I said yes, would it get me some quality alone time with you?"

"No."

He grinned at her. "It worked last time."

Kendra looked at us like we'd completely lost our minds, like we were freakish beasts in a circus.

The tall, white double doors at the back of the chamber opened, and three soldiers entered. Their clothes were unlike any Legion uniform I'd ever seen, but they wore the standard metallic rank pins, accompanied by a second pin depicting an element. When they took their seats on their thrones, the symbols at the top lit up with a magical glow.

The dark-haired Sea Dragon, who controlled the powers of water and ice, looked stunning in her blue dress accented with white ribbons. The robe flowed around her as though she were underwater. The water drop etched into her throne glowed sapphire blue.

The Sky Dragon, master of wind and lightning, wore a purple and yellow robe. Magic rolled across the fabric like a river of lightning. That same spark of magic lit up his throne's lightning bolt emblem. It shone like liquid gold.

The Earth Dragon was the mistress of trees, quakes, sand, and metal. Her dress was an earthy green, accented by metal jewelry. A dagger hung from her belt. The tree etched into her throne glowed a vibrant green.

The fourth throne, that of the Fire Dragon was empty.

"Trainees," the Earth Dragon said, her voice filling the entire room. The metal flower pin on her dress identified her as a major in the Legion of Angels. "You have come all this way for nothing."

"Early this morning, Colonel Starborn, the Fire Dragon of Storm Castle, was called away on an urgent mission," said the Sky Dragon. He wore the same psychic hand pin as Captain Somerset and Jace's sister.

"Without the Fire Dragon, this training cannot take place," added the Sea Dragon, another captain.

The Earth Dragon held up her hand. "Wait." She was looking at Captain Somerset. "Captain, your reputation as a master of elemental magic is known throughout the Legion. The First Angel once offered to make you a Dragon."

I gawked at Captain Somerset in surprise. So that's how

she knew you could refuse the Legion's offer to make you a Dragon.

"That was long ago," Captain Somerset said.

"Your magic has only grown since then," replied the Sea Dragon.

The Sky Dragon nodded. "You could take the Colonel's place until her return."

Captain Somerset's mouth tightened. "I already have a job as this soldier's mentor." She waved her hand to indicate me.

"If you do not become the Fire Dragon, this training cannot take place," the Earth Dragon said. "And without this training, these soldiers have a much lower chance of surviving their next sip of the gods' Nectar."

Colonel Fireswift would make us go through with the ceremony, with or without the training. The trainees here from other offices might have a more reasonable leader, but those of us from New York weren't so lucky. Without this training, not everyone would survive. Nerissa wouldn't survive.

"You have to do it," I whispered to Captain Somerset.

She glanced at Nerissa. She'd obviously come to the same conclusion as I had. "Very well. I accept," she told the Dragons.

"She can't do it," Kendra declared. "Her trainee would be left without a mentor. The rules of this training state that every trainee must have a mentor."

"Will you be my mentor?" I asked Soren quickly.

"Of course," he agreed.

"A mentor cannot have two students," Kendra said. "It's not allowed."

I turned to face her. "Oh, really? Where does it say

that?"

"Article seventeen, section four."

"Article seventeen, section four. 'Every soldier who participates in the Elemental Trials must have a mentor. This mentor must be an officer in the Legion of Angels'," I quoted the section in question. "Nowhere in there does it say a mentor cannot oversee two trainees."

I could see the wheels turning inside Kendra's head as she pictured that passage. Her mouth dropped in outrage. She knew I was right—and she hated it. Kendra Fireswift was obviously the sort of person who liked to hit people over the head with the Legion's very fat rulebook. She was pissed off as hell that I'd grabbed that book and hit back.

"It's decided. Captain Somerset will serve as the Fire Dragon, and Captain Diaz will take over her student in addition to his own," the Earth Dragon declared. "Trainees, mentors, follow us."

The three Dragons stood and walked toward the white door. The rest of us followed.

"I see you've been spending some quality time with the Legion's rulebook," Captain Somerset said to me as we moved out of the throne room.

"After what happened in Purgatory, I thought it best to be prepared."

A few weeks ago, two gangsters had attacked a woman in my hometown. Purgatory was out on the Frontier of civilization. Things weren't like they were in the cities. Crime lords and cowboy justice was rampant. The innocent suffered, but the Legion didn't care who was running things way out there as long as they remained loyal to the gods.

The gangsters had attacked the woman right in front of my face, but I wasn't allowed to hurt them back. As a soldier of the Legion, I couldn't interfere with how the crime lords and their minions 'kept order' in their territory. I'd been ready to fight them anyway, but Nero stopped me. I'd been furious with him—until he lured the gangsters onto land owned by the Legion, where he was free to do whatever he wanted to them. He'd killed them and strung them up outside the Legion office for me to see.

That was angels for you. Some men wooed you with flowers; angels wooed you with the dead bodies of deranged criminals. I should have been horrified by the gesture. Instead, I appreciated it. That just went to show how much I'd already changed. I couldn't afford to change any more.

I'd learned another thing that day, the importance of knowing the Legion's rulebook by heart. Nero's brutality notwithstanding, his knowledge of the rules had saved that woman's life.

"You recited that passage perfectly," Captain Somerset said.

"Thank you."

"But you neglected to include the related passage in section twenty-six," she continued, her voice a soft whisper. "Which does, in fact, state that a mentor may take on only one student in the Elemental Trials."

"Yes, it does," I agreed. "But Kendra Fireswift doesn't know that. You have to always know the rules better than your nemesis, right?"

Captain Somerset laughed. "You learn fast."

"So I might just survive the Legion?"

"Yes, I think you will," she said. "The real question is whether the Legion can survive you."

CHAPTER NINE
Storm Castle

MAJOR HAILEY VALENTINE, the Earth Dragon, led the tour of Storm Castle. A mix of medieval and modern, the Magitech trimmings blended in beautifully with the cold stone walls of the fairytale fortress. Its tall ceilings were as grandiose as they were practical. The height accommodated the Legions' training sessions—and allowed angels to fly in and out of the castle with ease.

The castle's main hallway was wide enough to drive a truck through. Lanterns hung on the stone walls, glowing with magic, humming like an elemental tune. As we walked past them, the lights changed from orange fire, to blue ice, to gold lightning, to green flowers. The halls echoed with a sweet melody, each change of the elemental lights accompanied by a note of music.

Major Valentine brought us to the brink of darkness, stopping just outside the black room. Though the lanterns continued to pulse and shine in all their magical glory, not a single ray of light made it into the black room. Darkness ate light. But when we stepped into the room, a rush of magic rippled past us. The room's walls changed from opaque to clear. That's when I realized the room was made of glass—a very magical glass. The floor seemed to disappear. It was so transparent that I couldn't even see what I was standing on.

"In addition to our large training hall, Storm Castle has four elemental training areas," Major Valentine said as the floor slowly began to turn.

Far below the rotating glass platform, a red glow illuminated the first training area. Pits of fire crackled. Steam rose from bubbling water pools. Hot waterfalls and springs streamed together in an interconnected system of pools and streams. Glowing stone walls, painted with scenes of fire and volcanoes, surrounded the training area. It reminded me of my nightmare last night of drowning in lava. The scene of an angel battling hideous beasts was painted on the ceiling. The angel flew high, raining down fire on the beasts. His angelic wings the color of a sunset, he looked like a fire dragon.

I felt everything as though I were standing directly inside the fire area. The soft hiss of rising steam. The pop of bubbling water. The sweet, spicy aroma of cinnamon and orchids.

The platform continued to rotate across the vast fire area. We passed smoky caverns. The smoke swirled together, forming monsters. The smoky tentacle of one of these monsters grabbed a lamp post and dragged it into a cave. Apparently, the smoke could take solid form. Past the smoky caverns, geysers shot up streams of burning water. The tiny droplets sprinkled against my skin like hot mist. I reached out, and my hand bumped against the transparent wall. How had the mist gotten through the wall to touch my skin?

The red glow turned gold. The glass platform had passed into the second training area. A hollow whistle echoed through the tunnels. The raw wind cut like steel ribbons at my skin. There was a flicker of movement from within the tunnels. Someone was in there right now.

"It's a labyrinth in there," Soren whispered to me and Nerissa. "You have to navigate the ever-shifting barriers, battling the wind funnels that try to push you off track."

The platform moved past the wind tunnels to the open field beyond. The air smelled of dry grass and something burning. Lightning flashed across the sky and crashed down to the ground with a thunderous roar that split a tree in two. A second lightning bolt hit a patch of grass, igniting the long blades with purple swirls of magic. The air was electrically charged. It popped against my skin and buzzed in my ears.

"Don't tell me we have to dodge that lightning," Nerissa commented.

"When you're lucky, you get to dodge it," Soren replied. "When you're unlucky, you have to stand there and let it hit you."

"What is the point of that?" she gasped.

"To build up our resistance to elemental magic," I guessed.

Soren nodded. "Yes, only those with an innate talent for elemental magic can cast it before drinking the gods' fourth gift. No matter how long most of you stare at your sword, for example, you won't be able to set it on fire. You can't train it. That's why candidates for level four train their resistance instead. That's the best way to prime your elemental magic—and to maximize your chances of surviving the next ceremony."

We moved into the third training area, and gold gave way to blue. There was nothing but water as far as the eye could see. Either Storm Castle was much bigger than it looked, or they'd made use of some very powerful magic to fit an ocean inside of it. My breath caught when the platform plunged into the water. A few people gasped as a sea monster that resembled a large spiky shark swam past us.

"I take it we have to fight beasts like that?" I asked Soren.

"Yes, you will be training underwater battles. It's harder than it looks. You have to learn to hold your breath for extended periods. Also, the supernatural speed you enjoy on land is seriously impaired underwater. As you build up your water resistance, however, you will regain that speed."

The platform rose, breaking the water's surface like a giant whale. We turned into a frozen tundra, a white wasteland. I inhaled the icy air. It burned like cold fire in my lungs. It nipped at my fingers and nose. My breath froze on my lips. It was even colder in here than it had been during my trek through the Wilds this morning. And I had a feeling the temperatures in this training area could drop even further. This was how they built up our cold resistance.

We moved into the final training area. A warm, green glow dissolved the snowflakes on my face. I looked down at the obstacle course below. Quicksand patches. Tremors. Climbing walls surrounded on all sides by bubbling, gurgling mud pits. A pair of trumpet-shaped ears peeked above the muddy surface.

"What is that?" I asked.

"A mud monster," Soren replied. "Earth elementals use

their magic to create monsters from mud. Using elemental magic, you can do the same with other elements."

"Like the smoke monsters in the fire area."

"Right," he said as we left the obstacle course behind to enter a dense forest. "But summoning these helpers is a master-level skill. Not everyone with elemental magic can do it. It requires a great deal of concentration, magic, and finesse."

"It's beautiful," Nerissa said, looking around.

"It is indeed, but that beauty hides many dangers," Soren warned.

He pointed at a squirrel running down a tree trunk. A nearby cluster of vines stirred. The squirrel froze at the rustle of movement, its nose twitching in the air, trying to sniff out the danger. The vines struck fast and hard. They snapped out like a whip, coiling around the squirrel's body before it could flee, pulling it deep into the underbrush.

"Soul-eater Vines," Nerissa said.

"Lovely name," I replied.

"They are vicious plants. Swords cannot cut them, but they are vulnerable to several potions," she said.

"Potions aren't permitted here," Soren told her.

"So how are we supposed to defeat the vines?"

I turned to hear his answer. My last encounter with sentient vines had been less than pleasant.

"An earth elemental can control them," Soren said. "Someone with moderate elemental resistance can break through them."

"Are there any other vicious plants in that forest?" Nerissa asked.

"Watch out for the moss. It will paralyze whatever part of your body it covers."

The platform clicked. It had returned to its starting point. The glass went opaque, and a runway of lights showed the way out. We followed the four Dragons past the castle's forges and armory. Here was where the Legion's magic weapons and armor were made. Steam hissed. Fire sparked. As I watched the metal magic smiths working, I wondered if the immortal weapons of heaven and hell had been forged within these walls. Creating the Legion's weapons and armor required strong elemental magic, among other things. The more powerful the smith's magic, the better weapons he could make.

Past the armory was a training room. The gym hall was large, but after the training areas we'd just seen, it felt very plain in comparison. A rack of weapons stood against one wall. There was nothing else in the room.

"Candidates," Major Valentine said, drawing our attention to her. "Your training, your first step toward elemental mastery, begins now."

We trained the whole evening and late into the night. We started in the gym hall, but we didn't stay there long. The Dragons divided us into groups for the obstacle course that brought us through the four elemental training areas. Nerissa and I were with Soren. Jace was with Kendra, and Morrows with the pretty petite lieutenant. There were two more pairs here, both from the Los Angeles office. The mentors showed us how to tackle the challenges, and we tried our best not to thoroughly embarrass ourselves.

It was a quadrathlon of elemental magic, one right after the other. We were frozen, drowned, struck by lightning, caught in tornados, set on fire, suffocated in smoke, besieged by carnivorous plants, and thrown into pools of magic quicksand. In other words, day one of elemental training at Storm Castle was nothing short of hell.

Of the six trainees, Jace was the best by far. He was the only one of us who could freeze a fire, if only for a moment. It was only a fragile layer of frost, just enough to slow it down so he could escape, but it was better than anything I could manage. My inability to cast a single spell made me feel horribly inadequate. Compulsion, the power of Siren's Song, had come so easily to me, that I guess I'd thought I was finally getting the hang of things. I'd even dared to think that making it up the Legion's ranks would be easy.

There was nothing like a dose of bitter reality to put my expectations in check. This wouldn't be easy. I was going to have to work my ass off from now to level nine.

"Candidates, gather round," Major Valentine called out just as I thought I couldn't take another step.

In these few hours, I'd come to loathe her voice, the sound of her summoning us to the next course of torture. Getting set on fire and then frozen into a popsicle and electrocuted was not as much fun as it sounded. I hadn't felt this bad since my initial Legion training. I couldn't even twitch without something in my body hurting. And from the looks of my comrades, they weren't faring any better.

"We are finished for today," the Major told us.

I would have sighed in relief—if my chest hadn't hurt so much. It felt like a family of elephants had done the polka across my ribcage.

"Captain Somerset will show you to your rooms," Major Valentine finished. Then she, the Sea Dragon, and the Sky Dragon left the training area.

The candidates and our mentors slept in rooms located in the castle's four enormous towers. Captain Somerset led us to the Fire Tower first, where the four soldiers from Los Angeles were staying. From its fiery peak, you could see the Fire Mountains. The other three lands of the Elemental Expanse—the Sky Plains, the Desert Rose, and the Crystal Forest—were visible from their corresponding elemental towers.

Next, we dropped off Jace, Kendra, Alec, and his mentor in the Sky Tower. Nerissa and Soren each had a room in the Earth Tower. I was alone in the Sea Tower. I walked beside Captain Somerset. She was unusually quiet. The only sound in the spiral stairwell was the hum of the magic lanterns on the walls. The flames blinked against the darkness, casting everything in a pale blue light.

"So, how did I do today?" I asked her with a crooked smile.

"As well as we all did on the first day of elemental training." Her gaze remained forward. Wherever her mind was, it wasn't here.

"That bad, huh?"

"You will improve with time."

With that said, she unlocked the door to my room and walked back down the stairs. A large bedroom with a fairytale canopy bed awaited me. The antique wooden furniture certainly fit with the castle. I swung my door closed, plunked my backpack down on the floor, and explored the rest of the room. I found a private bathroom off to the side. It even had a shower.

I went to the window, brushing aside the thick, velvet curtains to look outside. My room was about halfway up the Sea Tower, and I had a nice view of the Crystal Forest from here. Icicles hung from the branches, glistening and jingling in the moonlight. A waterfall sat at the edge of the woods. It was all so perfect that I almost expected a unicorn to step out of the trees and sip from the sparkling water. I'll admit I was disappointed when that little fantasy didn't come true.

I took a moment to stand there and drink in the beauty of this perfect, magical scene. The moment was over too soon. I didn't have time to daydream. My schedule stated that tomorrow's first session would begin in just under four hours. Today's training had drained me down to my last reserves. I needed rest. I kicked off my boots and fell onto the soft bed. I fell asleep without even changing out of my magic-stained clothes.

CHAPTER TEN
Elemental Trials

MY ELEMENTAL TRAINING continued in much the same way for the next week. I rose early, trained hard all day, then dropped onto my bed, not stirring until the unholy hour of morning when training began anew. Fire, sea, sky, and earth. I'd come to detest the very elements of nature. That which I'd always considered beautiful had turned inside out. I could only see the danger now. Burning, electrocution, frostbite, drowning, mud monsters. Even the snowy forest outside my bedroom window couldn't soothe my frayed nerves.

I felt like my body and magic had been put through an elemental blender. This endurance training was supposed to prime our elemental magic, make it more able to survive the gods' fourth gift, the Nectar that would unlock our elemental magic. There was a certain nuance to it, a process, a procedure. Like everything the Legion did, this process was equivalent to subtly hitting someone over the head with a hammer.

"Face your partner," the Sky Dragon instructed everyone, projecting his voice to every corner of the gym hall.

Jace was my partner. We'd already fought four times this afternoon, and we'd each won twice. Jace was the better fighter, but he wasn't nearly as scrappy as I was. Never underestimate the importance of scrappiness. The Legion of Angels might have been founded on the principles of dignity and honor, but humanity had been founded on dirty fighting.

Jace and I stood facing each other. We held no weapons; we were armed with only our magic and willpower. Our eyes locked, our bodies froze. It was like a good old Frontier standoff—without the guns. Our hands were posed at our sides, our fingers twitching.

Jace struck. He waved his hand up in an arc, igniting the leaves under my boots. I stomped them out.

"You should freeze them," the Sea Dragon told me from the sidelines. There was disapproval in her voice. Like she expected me to be able to do magic just like that.

I couldn't freeze anything. Even after a week, Jace was still the only one in the whole group who could so much as set a matchstick on fire, and his sister knew it. Kendra Fireswift shot me a smug smirk. She was getting on my last nerve. And on Jace's too.

"Make more fires," she demanded.

"I think she wants you to turn me into a bonfire," I whispered to Jace.

He managed to ignite another crinkly dry leaf. It was more smoke than fire, though. The strain on his face was noticeable.

"Indeed," he said.

"Why are you holding your breath?" I asked. "Afraid if you exhale, your breath will put out your fires?" I winked at him.

Jace snorted, and a small laugh escaped his mouth. His tiny fires went out like birthday candles. I chuckled.

"Less laughing, more kicking her ass," Kendra instructed him.

Jace grabbed one of the flaming swords off the rack. I grabbed another. The blades had been pre-spelled for us. The rack charged the magic on them, kind of like how my electric whip worked. As we used them, the magic would slowly wear off.

Fire hissed as Jace swung his sword at me. I parried his strike, then turned and butted him in the face with the hilt of my sword. Soren, who was shooting flaming arrows at target boards with Nerissa, spared us a glance—and a soft laugh. Kendra glared at me like I was a demon, but I was hardly even a footnote to the scorn in her eyes when she looked at her brother.

"You are the son of an angel," she snapped at Jace, whose nose was streaming blood. "You've been training with a sword since you could walk. And you're letting a street urchin best you with her dirty tricks? Our father would be ashamed of you."

"Nothing new there," Jace muttered in a low voice.

"Would it help if I let you kick my ass?" I asked him.

The corner of Jace's mouth quirked up. "Let me? You think I can't kick your ass by myself?" His voice was half humor, half pride. Conflicted, as always for him.

I smirked at him. "Give it your best shot, hotshot."

He rushed forward, so fast I could barely track him. He swung his sword. A tone chimed in the hall, signaling an elemental change. It sounded like ice.

A cold wind cut through the room. The frost froze the

flames on our swords. Tiny ice pieces sprinkled to the floor every time our blades clashed. After a few strikes, there was nothing left of the frozen flames. Jace and I each took a step back, muttering at our swords. We were trying to cast water magic on the naked blades. Unsurprisingly, it didn't work.

From the sidelines, Kendra made a derisive noise. "Pick up the pace, Sniffles."

"Sniffles?" I asked Jace.

"Kendra's nickname for me. She used to beat me up until I cried."

"I thought big sisters were supposed to be nurturing."

"You obviously didn't grow up in a family with an angel patriarch," he said darkly.

We gave up on the swords, tossing them aside. We each grabbed a water wand from the rack, weapons that had been spelled to shoot water. Jace thrust his wand forward, and a stream of water burst out of the tip. It hit me right in the face. I stood my ground, enduring the onslaught. I aimed my wand low and fired. A stream of high-pressure water exploded out of the wand, hitting him in the groin. He doubled over but didn't fall. He turned his back to me, so the stream was only slamming into his back.

The chime sounded again. Rather than a single elemental note, it was a melody of four notes, the signal that it was time for the elemental obstacle course. Oh, goody.

We all waited in front of the door that linked the gym hall with the entrance to the obstacle course. The Dragons could use the castle's magic to reshape the spells and challenges of the course. That meant there was an infinite pool of possible courses, a plethora of elemental combinations they could use to torture us.

"This time, each candidate will enter and complete the course alone," Major Valentine announced. "Mentors will wait here."

"Great," Nerissa said bleakly, stepping into line. She'd been getting a lot of help from Soren in the course.

I moved into line right behind her. "You can do it!" I said brightly.

She frowned at me. "Has anyone ever told you that your unwavering optimism is annoying?"

I grinned back at her until a smile broke out on her face. Every minute a chime sounded, the signal for the next person in line to go. When it was her turn, Nerissa entered the course with rugged determination. Now it was just me and Jace. He didn't say anything. He'd put on his game face.

The bell chimed, and I ran into the obstacle course. An open plain awaited. Lightning crashed down from a purple sky. I danced around the bolts. One snapped against my heels, but I was already jumping into the pool of water at the edge of the plains.

I swam as fast as I could. The lightning hadn't given up. The barrage of charged bolts was closing in on me, and I did *not* want to be hit while in the water. I considered my options. A small island awaited me after a short-but-potentially-electrifying swim. Option number two was the underwater tunnel below me. Taking it meant avoiding the lightning, but I knew from my roughly two million trips through the Dragons' obstacle course that the tunnel was the long way there. I'd have to hold my breath for an indeterminate length of time.

Lightning hit the water's surface just a few feet from me. The resulting jolt of electrical magic made the decision for me. I dove, praying that I didn't met any underwater beasties this time around.

After several minutes in the tunnel, my lungs burned with volcanic fury. This was the longest I'd ever held my breath. The tunnel spilled out into an underwater chamber. A circular platform waited at the center. Hope jumpstarted my muscles. I swam to the platform and stomped my foot down on it. Magic flashed, and then the platform shot out of the water, catapulting me onto the island.

I landed on the cracked ground, rolling to my feet. I sucked air into my lungs in ragged gasps. My body shook. No, wait. That wasn't my body. It was the ground. The ground was shaking. Tremors rumbled deep inside the earth. The ground split beneath my feet. I darted away from the emerging canyon—only to nearly fall into another canyon.

I listened for the tremors, feeling them out. Soren had told me how to predict where the next quake would hit. I had to put myself in tune with the magic creating them. A twinge of magic tugged on my senses. I ran to the right, avoiding a new split in the ground. The edges of the first canyon bumped, sealing together with seamless perfection. It was as though there had never been a canyon there. I dashed over it before it decided to open again.

I crossed the small island, avoiding earthquakes and sidestepping canyons. I reached the far shore, but instead of a sea of water, I met a sea of smoke. It swirled around me, drawing me forward. With every step that I took, the smoke cleared a little. I found hell on the other side.

Not literally, of course. The fire arena was marked by flames. They rolled across the land like a river of fire, consuming everything in their path. A black tree was caught in its wake. The flames pulled it down. Within seconds, it was nothing but ash.

Just past the former tree, a ring of fire burned around Nerissa. She was trapped, and the river of flames was coming. I had to help her. I took a running start up a mound of hardened stone, launching off it to jump over the fire ring and land beside her.

"You ok?" I asked.

She rubbed a smudged hand across her face. "Fantastic." All around us, the fire was raging, burning higher. "I can't believe you just did that."

"Neither can I."

She let out a strained laugh. "You missed the top of the flames by a hair's breadth. If it had touched you, it would have set your whole body on fire. Didn't you think about it?"

"No. At times like these, I find it's best not to think too hard. Overanalyzing things just slows me down."

"That would explain why your hair is on fire."

I squeezed the tip of my braid between my thumb and index finger, putting out the tiny flame. My hair appeared untouched. Hmm.

"I'm going to give you a boost over the flames," I told Nerissa. "Then you run for the exit like your tail is on fire."

"Very funny."

I shot Nerissa a grin, then grabbed her and threw her up high. She shot over the flames, landing safely at the exit. I drew in a deep breath and ran right through the fire. Flames hissed against my skin, but it hardly burned me at all. Maybe my elemental resistance really was improving.

I sprinted for the exit Nerissa had taken, but the opening closed before I got there. It reopened on the other side of the fiery field.

"You have got to be kidding me," I growled under my breath, then headed for the new exit.

Jace burst out of the smoke, speeding past me. I pushed myself to run faster. He'd started a minute after me. He was *not* going to finish before I did.

Flames shot out of the ground all around us. Jace grabbed one of them between his hands and tossed it in my face. I dodged to avoid the fire, but that slowed me down. He burst through the exit. I came out right after him. The first thing I saw was the smirk on Kendra's face. The second thing I saw was my time on the score board.

"Your friend Pandora was the slowest of everyone," Kendra commented to Jace, her full lips turned up into a smile of dark delight.

I longed for elemental magic—if only to set her hair on fire.

"I'm sorry, Leda," Nerissa said. "If not for me, you might have beaten his time."

I knew she was just saying that to make me feel better. In a whole week of training, I hadn't once beaten Jace's time on the obstacle course. I just wasn't fast enough.

"It doesn't matter," I said. "It's not a competition."

Which was why the scores were posted up there in bright shining digits for everyone to see. To see I was a loser. No, I couldn't think like that. The scores meant nothing. What mattered was what happened when I drank the Nectar. I frowned at my pathetic score anyway. It might not be a matter of life-or-death, but it annoyed me anyway.

"You saved my life," said Nerissa.

"You won't die in training. There are too many safety measures in place." I sighed. If I'd been thinking straight in there, I would have just kept going. But, no, I was so busy trying to hold onto my humanity that I'd taken leave of my senses.

"You haven't been paying attention, Leda. This is the Legion of Angels. Of course you can die in training," Nerissa said.

Captain Somerset walked over to me, the skirt of her red Fire Dragon dress swaying like flames in the breeze. "Pandora." Her tone was foreboding.

"Yes?"

"You interfered in another candidate's training. We cannot allow your indiscretion to go unpunished."

Was she serious?

All it took was one look at the hard gleam in her dark eyes for me to realize that she was very, very serious.

"Rules are rules, Pandora. You aren't doing her any favors by helping her. She needs to build up the resistance herself. You can't do that for her. You can't drink the Nectar for her."

Maybe she was right.

"Everyone else is dismissed for the night," Captain Somerset declared. "Pandora, you will train that course, repeating it until you beat Fireswift's time. That is your punishment."

I read Jace's time off the scoreboard. He'd completed the entire course in under four minutes, nearly a half a minute faster than the next best person. I'd never finished the Dragons' obstacle course in under five minutes. This was going to be fun. Since when had Captain Somerset become such a hard ass? She was certainly channeling Nero right now.

The candidates waited until the Dragons had left the

gym. Then they began filing out with their mentors. Alec Morrows walked the other way—right for me.

"That was cool what you did, Leda." He put one arm around me and the other around Nerissa.

I smiled through the bone-crushing creak of his embrace. "Thanks. But Captain Somerset doesn't think so."

He grunted. "Captain Somerset is a killjoy. The woman needs to learn to loosen up. Speaking of loosening up…"

If this was his smooth transition to propositioning me, I was going to punch him.

"The Dragons have a ceremony tonight," he said, grinning. "So we're all planning on taking advantage of the early evening. We're going to the Tranquility Pools for a bit of food and games. You should join us." He glanced at Nerissa. "Both of you."

"I could use a little down time. I'm in," said Nerissa. "Leda?"

I peeled my eyes off the scoreboard. "If I get out of here tonight, I'll try."

"You can do it!" Nerissa said brightly.

"You were right," I told her. "The unwavering optimism is annoying."

"Come on, Leda. Promise you'll join the party."

"I didn't bring a bathing suit."

"You could just come naked," Morrows suggested.

"In your dreams."

"Oh, yes." His eyes lit up. "You have played key roles in my dreams. Especially after our trip across the Black Ruins. The way you handled that cannon." He winked at me.

"Actually, it was Claudia Vance who shot the cannon," I reminded him.

"In my dreams, you all get to shoot the cannon."

My mouth dropped. He did not just say that.

Nerissa pushed him away. "Don't mind him, Leda. And don't let him scare you away from the party. You simply must come. You can buy a bathing suit from one of the castle's shops."

"Wait, what? The castle has *shops*?" I gasped.

"Of course," she replied. "Where do you think the people living here buy things?"

Good point.

"So, you're coming to the party?" she asked.

"I'll try. That's the most I can promise. I have a sinking suspicion I'll be stuck in that obstacle course all night."

Nerissa smiled. "Let me put it a different way: drinks and pizza and scantily-clothed soldiers by the poolside." Her brows lifted. "That should be motivation enough."

Getting out of the repeating elemental hell loop was more motivating than the promise of food and half-naked soldiers at the end. I managed to beat Jace's time after only an hour. I'd figured out his trick. If you stood on the underwater platform at just the right spot, it shot you past the plain of tremors.

I'd like to think I was clever for figuring that out, but I only stumbled upon the answer by mistake when a shark decided to chase me through the water tunnel and I crashed into the platform at an awkward angle.

Technically, skipping a section of the course was cheating, but I wasn't feeling too torn up about it. Firstly, Jace had cheated too. And secondly, Captain Somerset hadn't said anything about cheating being disallowed. No, not cheating. Outsmarting the system. That sounded much better.

I beat Jace's time by under two seconds—a narrow lead, but a lead just the same. I smiled at the scoreboard as I left the gym. It felt good to see my name at the top for once. I guess I was competitive too.

I stopped by the castle shops on the way back to my room in the Sea Tower. There were a surprisingly large number of shops in Storm Castle. Or maybe not so surprising. There were no towns or shopping malls way out here. The castle shops had everything you could ever need —for twice the price you ever wanted to pay. I was stuck at the wrong end of a supply-and-demand problem. The only swimwear I'd brought to Storm Castle was a wetsuit, and I was pretty sure that wasn't suitable for a poolside party. So I forked over the money for a bathing suit, trying not to think about it. It was either overpay or go naked to the party. And I was *not* going naked, no matter how much Morrows would approve.

My only consolation was the outfit I'd found was cute: a bikini under a zipper top and a little hip-hugging skirt. I changed in my room, completing the set with my running shoes. It was not a good idea to walk barefoot in a medieval castle.

On the way to the pool, I passed the armory. The smell of metal, smoke, and fire filled the air, mixing with a strange magical perfume. It wasn't exactly unpleasant, but it was potent. Despite the late hour, the castle's master magic smith was still working. I'd been meaning to speak with him since my arrival at Storm Castle, but I'd finished every day since then too tired to pay him a visit.

A magic smith was like an artist, bending the elements

to his will to create magic weapons. They lived and worked here at Storm Castle, the place on Earth where elemental magic was at its strongest. The master magic smith was the most talented of all the smiths—and he was also the most knowledgeable. He was rumored to know the history of every notable weapon and piece of armor ever made. I hoped that was more than a rumor.

"Master Smith," I said.

He looked up from the whip he was braiding. Lightning sparks danced across his fingers, blending into the black strands of the whip. The master smith looked twenty, but his dark eyes were so much older. They were the eyes of someone who'd seen the end of the world—and lived to tell the tale.

He set down his whip. "You are the one they call Pandora."

So he'd heard of me. This conversation could go one of two very different ways. People tended to either instantly like me or instantly hate me.

"My friends call me Pandora," I replied.

I hoped the master smith had a sense of humor. Too many of the older Legion members did not.

He chuckled. "A fitting name. What can I do for you, Pandora?"

I looked over the weapons around him—swords, daggers, whips. They were all magical, but not one was unique.

"What do you know about immortal weapons?" I asked.

"They are very rare. Few people have ever seen one."

I peeled up the bottom of my top to show him my scar.

"A scar from an immortal weapon." His dark brows

lifted, and he leaned in for a closer look. "A bullet from Shooting Star, one of the weapons of heaven and hell."

Wow, I'd hoped he'd known something about immortal weapons, but I hadn't expected him to be able to identify one by the scar it had left.

"Do you have any immortal weapons?" I asked him.

He didn't appear shocked by my question. He probably thought I was morbidly curious. Truth be told, I wasn't eager for a second encounter with an immortal weapon. I'd barely survived the first.

"We have only two at Storm Castle," he said. "One is Diamond Tear, a dagger used by Colonel Starborn. The Colonel is away at the moment, so I can't show you that one. But I can show you our second immortal weapon. It's too big to be wielded in combat."

He used the key around his neck to unlock an enormous locker that could easily fit two people—stacked on top of each other. But there weren't any people inside the locker; there was only a rod. Except for the runes etched into it, it looked an awful lot like a flagpole. I saw what he meant. A Legion soldier with supernatural strength would probably be able to swing it around on the battlefield, but it was impractical to carry for extended periods of time. It was far too long and heavy.

"This is the Lightning Spear," he told me. "The Dragons sometimes use it in their training rooms. It's indestructible, so it can absorb a lot of magic. I use it to cleanse the castle of excess magic, which I can later put into the weapons I make."

"Do you know how to make an immortal weapon?" I asked.

"No, that magic is far beyond my limited power."

"Who can make them?"

"No one on Earth," he said. "And no one in heaven or hell either."

"I thought the gods and demons used them in their wars." Well, when they weren't warring by proxy anyway.

"There are two classes of weapons used by gods and demons—and, sometimes, by their angels," he told me. "The simple ones are made by gods and demons. Those are their normal weapons. Weapons of the immortal, they're called. And then there are the immortal weapons. Immortal weapons cannot be broken, or so they say. The weapons and armor are powerful, sentient."

"Alive?" I asked.

"In a way. They were forged in the Sea of Souls, where the fallen gods and demons live on. Pieces of their immortal souls were absorbed into the metal of the immortal weapons. Parts of their personalities and their power live inside those weapons. Only an expert magic smith can create a cohesive weapon out of the soul of a god or a demon. Only an expert magic smith can control such powerful, unwieldy magic. There was once someone who could make immortal weapons, an immortal named Sunfire, born long before gods and demons came to be." He lowered his voice to a whisper, as though afraid his next words would be overheard. "Sunfire could manipulate light and dark magic equally. He was the first and only person who has ever been able to forge an immortal weapon. Later in his life, when the wars of gods and demons threatened to tear his world apart, he created the full sets of immortal weapons and armor to fight them."

"There's more than one set?" I asked in surprise. I'd thought the weapons of heaven and hell were the only ones.

"Yes, but they have been lost to the ages. Most of them have not been seen in centuries, if not millennia."

"Where is the immortal blacksmith?"

He shook his head. "No one knows. He disappeared long ago. Some say he is dead. But his legacy lives on in our magic, in our ability to manipulate magic to create enchanted weapons. Every magic smith today owes our power to Sunfire." He sighed. "And yet even the most skilled among us cannot hold a candle to his work."

If Sunfire was alive, I had to find him. I had to speak to him about the weapons of heaven and hell. In my hour of need, I'd been able to control them. What was my connection to them? And what was my connection to the Guardians? I had memories of past Guardians wielding that same armor and those same weapons. Something was going on here—something bigger than all of us—and I intended to find out what it was.

CHAPTER ELEVEN

Tranquility Pools

AFTER LEAVING THE master smith, I continued on to the Tranquility Pools. The magic here was peaceful and calm, very different from the intense, high-density magic of the Dragons' training rooms. Palm trees swayed in the warm, balmy breeze. A velvet-soft bed of sand surrounded the pools of cool water. The sweet scents of coconuts, pineapples, and other tropical fruits flooded my senses.

I was the last one to arrive. Everyone else was already sitting in the lounge chairs on the stone patio, playing cards and sipping tropical drinks out of festive-colored straws. All of the candidates were here. All of the mentors were here too, with the notable exception of Kendra Fireswift. Either she'd refused to come, or she hadn't been invited.

There was food packed onto every side table. Fruit salad and hamburgers and pizza and ice cream. There were a few bowls of chips too. The main table was clear of food to make room for the cards. As I approached, I recognized the deck. They were playing Legion, a popular card game that its makers boasted to be an authentic representation of the Legion of Angels. In truth, it was a watered down version of the real thing. The paranormal soldiers loved to play Legion, something we Legion soldiers constantly teased them about. It was impossible to ignore the irony of a group of Legion soldiers, in the midst of special training, playing the game.

"Leda," Nerissa greeted me, moving over to make space for me on her chair.

"Hey, Pandora," Alec said, casting a long look down my body. "Nice outfit. I like it."

"Thanks."

He wiggled his eyebrows. "I can even see your nipples through your shirt."

"Glad you could make it," Nerissa said quickly, before I could knock Alec upside the head. "So you beat Jace's time."

I shot a triumphant grin across the table at Jace. "By nearly two seconds."

"Until tomorrow." There was a sharp, competitive edge to Jace's voice. I had no doubt that he was going to beat my time tomorrow—and that it wouldn't be by a small margin.

"Pay attention to your cards, Fireswift," Alec told him. "You're already losing badly enough. You could at least try to present a challenge. It's no fun to beat someone so bad at the game."

"I'd rather be good at the real Legion than at a card game."

Alec laughed and gave Jace a hard, friendly slap on the back. Wow, they sure were chummy. I'd always assumed they hated each other. In fact, *everyone* here was acting real friendly. I noticed the sizable pile of empty liquor bottles on the ground. Well, that explained it. Alcohol didn't make us as drunk as it did humans, but it definitely made us more amiable.

Alec dealt me into the next round. I grabbed a handful of popcorn from the bowl balanced on Nerissa's lap. She smiled at me, her eyes sparkling like gemstones. Wait a minute...

I grabbed the liquor bottle out of Jace's hand and took a sip. A sweet, intoxicating flavor danced across my tastebuds. "It's laced with Nectar drops." I put the bottle down before I was tempted to drink it all down.

"Of course it is," Nerissa said, picking up the bottle. "After the week we've had, we need to unwind a little."

A few others raised their bottles in agreement. Nectar drops were a very, very diluted version of the gods' Nectar. Being a soldier in the Legion of Angels was the most stressful job on Earth. Legion soldiers drank Nectar drops to destress. Because we'd already built up some immunity to Nectar through the promotion ceremonies, the drops didn't kill us. Instead it reacted to the magic inside of us. Essentially, it made us drunk.

"You need to unwind too," Nerissa told me, offering me the bottle.

I waved it away. "Not a good idea. I'm too sensitive to Nectar."

"Suit yourself," she said with a shrug, then took another swig.

"Ladies, are you in or not?" Alec asked us.

I dropped a handful of chips into the large pile at the center of the table. "I'm in."

Alec grinned. "Finally, someone who's taking this game seriously." He matched my bet.

I played a weak character. I wasn't surprised when Alec topped my card. I followed up next turn with the Fire

Dragon card. He countered with an angel.

"Giving up, honey?" he asked me when I paused to consider my cards.

"I don't give up."

Alec grinned. "I was hoping you'd say that."

I continued playing. Alec beat my card every round. He beat everyone else's cards too.

"You must be really unlucky in love," Soren grumbled.

"My dance card is always full, my friend."

Soren shot him a skeptical look.

"It's true," Nerissa told him. "The number of women who've come to my office with bizarre injuries after a night with him is simply staggering. I'm not even sure how some of those injuries are anatomically possible."

Alec winked at her. "I'd be happy to stop by your room and demonstrate, Doc. All in the name of science, of course."

"I think I'll pass," she said. "I prefer to keep my knees pointed forward."

He chuckled. "Suit yourself. I'll be right over here if you change your mind."

"I don't believe it. No one that obnoxious can get laid that often." Soren shook his head in disbelief.

"I can't believe *this* either," Jace said as Alec bested his card.

We played a few rounds, Alec winning every one. He certainly had a talent for cards. Around round six, I felt my head going all funny. It was then I realized that I'd been absentmindedly taking sips from the bottle. With all that Nectar in me, it was a wonder I could still think straight.

"Hey, love birds," Alec said. "Are you in or not?"

Sometime during the last few rounds, Nerissa had

relocated to Soren's chair, and they were now making out like there was no tomorrow.

Nerissa slid off Soren's lap with a coy smile and returned to the chair she'd been sharing with me.

"Good move," Alec told Soren with an approving nod. His gaze slid down to the card Soren had played this round. "Unlike that move. That was a very stupid move."

Nerissa leaned in closer to me. "So, rumor has it you've been having clandestine meets with our favorite angel Nero Windstriker," she whispered. "And that Colonel Fireswift marked you. What an idiot."

"How could you possibly know that?"

"I eavesdropped when you and the Colonel were chatting outside my lab."

"You heard that?"

"Sure. I can wallow in self-pity and eavesdrop at the same time."

I shouldn't have been surprised. Nerissa was the gossip queen of New York.

"Colonel Windstriker marked you too, didn't he? That's how you got rid of Colonel Fireswift's mark." She sniffed me. "So why don't I smell him on you?"

"Nero marked me without asking. I made him remove it."

"You convinced an angel to remove his mark?" she gasped in shock.

"I told him I refused to be stuck in the middle of this pissing contest between him and Colonel Fireswift."

"What did he say?"

"He brooded a little, then he removed his mark. But not before giving me a lecture about the ways of angels and how I needed to get used to them because this is my life now. He thinks I can't accept him for what he is."

"Can you?"

I sighed. "I don't know. The ways of angels are so cruel. They think they know what's best for everyone, and they don't hesitate to enforce their will over you. I'm not sure I can accept that."

"Angels are cruel, yes," she said. "But that's not all there is to them. Colonel Windstriker removed his mark. He gave you a choice. He's a good man. But a wicked angel." She licked her lips. "What are you going to do?"

"I don't know."

"He cares about you. If he just wanted to screw you and leave, he wouldn't be doing this."

"That doesn't make this easier," I said. "It makes it harder. He marked me, Nerissa. It's just so… crazy."

"He's an angel. Those are their ways. And, for the rest of us at the Legion, they are to a lesser extent our ways as well. Your ways. A bit of a culture shock, isn't it?"

"You could say that. I didn't expect this to be the hardest thing about the Legion," I admitted.

"No one ever expects that. They think the hard part is the fighting or gaining new magic. But it's the same story for everyone who joins the Legion. We change. Or we die."

"And marking your territory?"

"That one is just the angels. They are very competitive. And territorial. It might seem they are acting impulsively, out of anger, but every move they make is calculated to achieve their desired result. It's a big game of strategy." She waved her hand at the table. "Like this card game, except the stakes are much, much higher."

"It sounds like an exhausting way to live."

Nerissa's brows lifted. "Angels have a lot of stamina."

I groaned at her joke. She was almost as bad as Alec.

"I've heard angels can have sex like twenty times in a row," said Darren, one of the Los Angeles candidates.

Oh, great. My private conversation with Nerissa had an audience.

"Twenty times in a row?" Alec looked at Jace. "Is that true?"

"How would I know?"

"Your father is an angel," Alec pointed out.

Jace looked ill. "We've never discussed his libido. And I would appreciate if you didn't either."

Alec's gaze shifted to me. His expression was one of pure innocence—or his version of it anyway.

"No," I said firmly.

"No what?"

"No, I don't know the answer. So don't bother asking me."

"I've done studies in angel fertility and sexuality," Nerissa said, taking a swig from the bottle. "It's a fascinating subject. The Nectar the soldiers of the Legion drink is a poison, the strongest on Earth. Because we've survived the strongest poison, it's hard to poison us. We hardly ever get sick either. Even when we do fall ill, we typically fight off diseases quite quickly."

Alec swallowed a yawn.

Nerissa wasn't deterred. "But the same poison that made us immune to most illnesses and poisons also has a downside. Legion soldiers are notoriously infertile. The more Nectar you've had, the more magic you have, the less fertile you are. Naturally, that means angels, who have consumed the most Nectar, are the least fertile of us all. But they are also the ones the Legion pushes hardest to procreate. Because the child of an angel has a significantly higher magic potential, a higher chance of becoming an angel."

Her eyes lit up, the scientist shining through. Alec was resting his weight on one of his elbows. He looked like he just wanted her to get to the 'sex' part of this sexuality lecture.

"Female soldiers of the Legion are infertile most of the time, having a fertile cycle only once every few years," Nerissa said. "For female angels, it is even less frequent."

"So they just have to keep going at it. For years." Alec grinned. "Doesn't sound so bad."

"When a female soldier of the Legion has a fertile cycle, she knows it. Her libido jumps," Nerissa said. "And when a female angel has a fertile cycle, *everyone* knows it."

"We had that at my old office last year," said Lieutenant Gardner from LA. "They had to send her off into isolation, far away to another region."

"Why?" I asked him.

"Her presence became disruptive."

"A fertile female angel puts off hormones that drive everyone, male and female, into a sustained state of heightened agitation," Nerissa explained. "They become more violent, more aroused, depressed, excited, reckless. The whole emotional range. It's like everyone is high on Nectar, all at once. Fights break out. There are crying fits, heated arguments, fights."

"Orgies?" Alec asked.

"It's been known to happen."

He grinned.

"It's not pretty," she told him. "Breaking down the control of hundreds to thousands of highly-disciplined

Legion soldiers has disastrous results. People have died."

"I know the guy the Legion mated to the female angel I mentioned," Lieutenant Gardner said. "The Legion sent him off with her for a week. He said it was the best week of his life, so good that he could barely walk without it hurting for the rest of the month."

Gods, what had the angel done to him?

Nerissa must have seen the shock in my eyes. "Sex, Leda. Lots and lots of sex."

The guys at the table let out a collective sigh.

"They are insane," I commented to Nerissa.

"No, they're just men."

"Are we playing or not?" Jace demanded. He was the only guy here who didn't look excited by the prospect of being screwed until he couldn't walk.

"Don't get your panties in a twist, Fireswift. We're playing." Alec set two cards facedown on the table.

We all did the same.

"How long after a woman becomes an angel does this…phenomenon happen for the first time?" I asked Nerissa.

Alec flashed me a grin. "Thinking of becoming an angel, Pandora?"

Lieutenant Gardner cast a long, leisurely look down the length of my body. "She would make a fine angel."

There were some grunts of assent from the male delegation. That's what I got for wearing a bikini to a pool party full of soldiers high on Nectar. I should have worn a robe. Or a suit of armor.

"Is that your own hair?" Darren asked me, reaching across the table.

I batted his hand away before he could touch my hair.

"Yes, mine. My hair. My space. Invade it and I'll break your wrist."

The guys kept on grinning. Apparently, Legion soldiers saw threats of violence as foreplay. They really were just like angels. But that meant…so was I. Before joining the Legion, I'd never threatened anyone with violence. I'd instead plotted what pranks I could use to get back at them. Whether I liked to admit it or not, I was changing. And I didn't like it.

"Each level of the Legion we gain, we get a progressively larger dose of Nectar," Nerissa told me. "The jump to becoming an angel requires Nectar twice as potent as the previous level. It spikes the poison in your system so high that you're not fertile for years, maybe even decades."

Thank goodness. Maybe it was a stupid thing to worry about this far out, but I was determined to become an angel and acquire the power to find my brother Zane. I didn't have time for games and wonky hormones. I wanted the powers, but not any of the nasty side effects. Nero would have called me a hypocrite for thinking that, and maybe he was right. But I wasn't just going to wait around and pray for someone else to save my brother. I was taking matters into my own hands. I'd save him and worry about the angel side effects later, when I had time.

Everyone else at the table had already flipped over their two cards—and lost to Alec's twin captains.

"Ok, let's see what you've got, angel." Alec blew me a kiss.

I flipped my cards. His smile melted when he saw my angel and Sea Dragon.

"It can't be."

"And yet it is," I said cheerfully, claiming the pile of

chips that I'd just won.

"You lost every round before this. How can you win?" Alec demanded as I dealt out our new cards.

"It's not about the battles," I told him. "It's about winning the war."

Darren laughed. "She is as cunning as an angel."

Alec blinked. He still couldn't believe it.

"I wasn't playing those rounds to win. I was playing them to see how everyone else played, how you ticked, how you responded to different cards. I've got you figured out, Alec Morrows."

"I'm not that predictable," he stated, setting a card face down on the table.

"You just played a strong mid-level card, either a captain or major." I watched the flicker of his eyes. "No, a Dragon."

"Flip the card, Morrows," Darren said. "Let's see if she's right."

Alec's lips pressed together into a hard line, and he flipped his card. The Earth Dragon stared back at me.

Jace laughed out loud. I'd never seen him do that. He must have had way too much to drink.

"Your strategy is to be unpredictable," I told Alec. "But that strategy falls apart as soon as someone finds the pattern in your unpredictability." I tapped the card he'd just set facedown on the table. "Your card is something really low, like an initiate. You want to force the rest of us to waste our strong cards."

When Alec didn't turn his card, Jace turned it for him. The picture showed a scrawny initiate, one of the weakest cards in the whole deck. This time, Jace wasn't the only one who laughed.

"This is getting really annoying," Alec grumbled.

"On the contrary, it's just starting to get interesting," I declared, claiming the pile of chips.

"What's he going to play next?" Jace asked me.

"I'll tell you after everyone has played."

Jace frowned at his hand of cards. "That's not helpful."

I shrugged. "I have to beat you at something."

We all played our cards facedown. I declared that Alec had played an angel card.

"That's uncanny," Nerissa gasped when I turned out to be right.

"Pure logic," I said.

"This isn't logic," Alec griped. "It's sorcery."

"Your facial expressions give it all away," I told him. "Your gaze lifts slightly to the left when you're about to play an angel card."

"Remind me to bring sunglasses along the next time I play cards with you, Pandora."

"Sure thing. If you think that will help." I flipped over my own angel card, winning the round.

"I never get tired of looking at that face," said Lieutenant Jenson, Alec's mentor.

"More than just the face," sighed Liana, a candidate from LA. She slid her finger across the painted chest of Nero Windstriker. The artist had exaggerated every muscle on Nero's body—and given him a sword too long for even an angel to wield.

"Colonel Windstriker is definitely the hottest angel," said Lieutenant Greer, Liana's mentor.

"Definitely," Nerissa said, giving me a wicked look. "Don't you think, Leda?"

"He's all right," I said casually. "If you can get past the

insufferable know-it-all angel demeanor."

"But you got past it, right? What is it like to kiss Colonel Windstriker?" Liana asked me.

Like kissing lightning—and not in a bad way.

"What does his blood taste like?" Lieutenant Greer asked.

Like the sweetest Nectar I've ever known. And how the hell did she know I'd tasted Nero? It's not something I'd advertised. The Legion didn't forbid blood exchanges between their soldiers, but it did frown upon the practice.

"Well, ladies and gentlemen, it would appear most of you are nearly out of chips," I declared, trying to change the subject.

"I knew I played my angel card too soon," Lieutenant Greer said.

"I waited too long to play mine," said Darren.

"Which one did you have?"

Darren looked at Jace. "Colonel Fireswift."

"Colonel Windstriker is much better. He has the better stats," Lieutenant Jenson said.

Nerissa nodded in agreement. "And word is he's going to be promoted soon. They'll have to update his card."

"If he survives," said Lieutenant Gardner. "The jump to level ten is supposed to be unlike any other promotion. It's not just drinking Nectar. There are a whole bunch of trials leading up to it."

Liana sighed. "Kind of like these trials."

"No, harder," Lieutenant Gardner told her. "Much harder. But no one knows anything about them. They are shrouded in secrecy."

That wasn't entirely true. Someone knew about the level ten trials, and he was willing to help Nero pass them too.

Damiel. Nero needed his father's help, whether he was willing to accept that or not. Nero would never ask for Damiel's help. He was far too proud. So I'd just have to ask Damiel to tell me everything he knew about the trials, and then I'd use the knowledge to help Nero survive.

"Hey, daydreamer, time to deal the cards. You can fantasize about Windstriker naked later."

Alec's voice brought me out of my mind. Cards, right. I began dealing them out.

"Just for the record, I was not fantasizing about him naked," I told Alec.

He braided his fingers together and hit me with an innocent smile. "Your gaze lifts slightly to the left when you're thinking about Colonel Windstriker naked."

"Actually, it's to the right."

I snapped my head around, nearly falling off my chair. Nero stood in front of the open door. He wore a black leather suit that fitted his broad chest perfectly. His thick arms, built by centuries of continuous physical exercise, were folded across that chest. His blond hair was slightly windswept, a few strands out of place, as though he'd flown all the way here. His eyes shone out like a laser, sharp and deadly. Being here, in Nero's shadow, I felt so small, so mortal. I'd been so wrong. The artist of Nero's card had captured the angel's essence perfectly.

No one said a word. It was like all the air had gone out of the room. I had to remind myself to breathe. I rose slowly and walked over to him.

"What are you doing here?" I asked him quietly.

"Basanti told me of your performance," he replied coolly. "I've come to put your ass into gear." He looked over my shoulder to address the others. "Leave."

His voice was cold, loaded with command. Like a weight pressing down, crushing all freewill out of the room. Everyone scrambled to their feet and hurried away. A telekinetic tug from Nero slid the door shut behind them.

I gaped at him in shock. He'd just compelled nine hardened soldiers into a state of cold panic.

"Put my ass in gear, you say? Did you come all the way here to give me that little pep talk?"

"No," he replied patiently. "I came all this way to train you so that you'll survive the next promotion ceremony."

Despite the fact that I was still upset with him over the whole territory-marking thing, I was also glad to see him. If he was glad too, he didn't show it. His face was perfectly neutral, completely professional.

I dared to take another step toward him. "You came all the way here, taking time out of your busy schedule preparing for level ten, just to help me?"

"Not entirely. Nyx asked me to come here."

"Why?"

"It's one of the tasks I must complete before the trials."

"What task?" I didn't think he was talking about helping me.

"Colonel Leila Starborn, the Fire Dragon, was not called away on Legion business. That's just the cover story Nyx told the other Dragons, the one they tell anyone who comes here."

"If Colonel Starborn is not on a mission, then where is she?"

"That's the thing," Nero said. "No one knows. She has vanished without a trace."

CHAPTER TWELVE
A Storm Is Raging

"NYX HAS SENT trackers to find Colonel Starborn," Nero told me. "They've all come back empty-handed. They can't track her."

"Why not?" I asked.

When the Legion's regular teams could not find someone, Nyx sent in the trackers. They could find anyone, anywhere on Earth.

"The Legion suspects that Colonel Starborn has gone dark," Nero said.

It suddenly all made sense. The Legion's trackers tracked light magic. If Colonel Starborn had switched sides, her magic had switched too.

"The trackers can't follow her dark magic," I said. "But you can." The darkness inside of Nero gave him that power. "That's why Nyx sent you here."

"Nyx sent me here to find Colonel Starborn, but I came to find you. I need your help. You can track dark magic even better than I can."

I possessed what Nero called a 'perfect balance' of light and dark magic. *Perfect* certainly wasn't the word the gods, champions of light, or the demons, champions of darkness, would use. Both of them believed in the purity of magic; they just disagreed as to which kind of magic should reign supreme.

"I don't know, Nero. I've never tried to track anyone before."

"You were a bounty hunter before you joined the Legion. You have tracked down many people," he pointed out.

"That was different. I tracked down humans—or an occasional supernatural when I was desperate for money. I used mundane means to find them, not magic. I'm not even sure how to use magic to track people."

"You will figure it out."

Figure it out or die trying. That was the way of the Legion. Of the angels. Even though I had Nero with me, tracking down a rogue angel was at best a recipe for a whole lot of pain. At worst, it was a suicide mission. I'd learned that very well in the Lost City. And I wasn't eager to repeat the experience. Somehow, I didn't think the Legion was giving me a choice. Holding onto every angel they had was important to them—and I just wasn't. I was expendable.

"I hope you're stronger than Colonel Starborn," I sighed. "Because I really don't want to die."

"She's been an angel longer than I have. And she was trained by a legendary angel warrior. If it comes to a fight, defeating her will be difficult."

You had to love Nero's brutal honesty.

"Then let's hope it doesn't come to a fight," I replied. "Maybe we can catch her off guard."

"Angels aren't caught off guard."

I laughed in his face. "You just said that because it

139

sounded good, didn't you?"

"Of course." His poker face didn't even crack.

"So, how do we begin this foolhardy mission to capture a formidable angel warrior? Do we get a team, or is it just the two of us?"

He said nothing.

My heart sank. "Don't tell me I have to do it alone. Nero, I can't go after an angel alone. She'll kill me. You know that. The Legion knows that. And if I'm dead, I won't be able to bring her back."

"Relax, I'm going with you," he said. "But no one else. We need to keep this quiet. No one can know Colonel Starborn is missing."

The Legion had already lost an angel recently: Osiris Wardbreaker, who'd decided he'd rather torture people than protect them. General Wardbreaker was dead now, but the Legion's image had taken a heavy blow. This wasn't just about having powerful soldiers. It was about maintaining an image of absolute power and competency. That's how the Legion kept order.

"Don't tell anyone, not even other Legion soldiers," Nero said.

We couldn't even trust our own? That was taking paranoia to a whole new level. Nyx must really be on edge right now.

"Who knows Colonel Starborn is missing?" I asked.

"Nyx and myself. And now you."

He trusted me. I tried not to let that go to my head. Just as I was trying to not think about the last time we'd seen each other—and our blood exchange. Even knowing he'd marked me in that exchange, I couldn't help but remember how good it had felt. I'd been remembering it for a whole week. I couldn't shake the memory. His fangs popping my skin. My blood flooding into him. A rush of heat bathing my body, starting at his mouth and spreading like wildfire, consuming me. His pulse throbbing beneath my lips. His blood spilling into my mouth, as sweet as Nectar. Drowning in a river of liquid ecstasy.

"Leda."

I met his eyes and saw that familiar spark of desire. Either he'd read my thoughts, or he was responding to my body. I dropped my hand from my neck.

His eyes went hard again. He looked so serious. I had to get serious too. And, seriously, I didn't want him to bite me, to mark me. He'd made his point, and I was making mine. I wouldn't let him mark me—and I certainly wouldn't ask him to do it.

"Leda," he said again.

Was it crazy that the sound of my name on his tongue sent shivers down my spine. Yes, it was very wrong, I decided. I should never have drunk all that Nectar tonight. It was making my head all funny.

"So the other Dragons don't know about Colonel Starborn?" I asked, keeping my tone professional. Professional was the way to go.

"No, and we need to keep it that way. News of her disappearance—and possible defection—would unsettle them. The Dragons need to be calm. They need to be balanced. They are the keepers of the Earth's elemental magic. The ones who keep everything in balance. This castle is a conduit of power, drawing on the elements. It links the elemental magic of heaven to Earth. If the Dragons fall out of balance, it could affect the weather everywhere on Earth, overriding nature with magic. The results would be devastating. We cannot allow that to happen. We must keep the Dragons in the dark. All but one of them."

"Which one?"

"Basanti is holding Colonel Starborn's place. The other Dragons should have petitioned the Legion for a replacement in Colonel Starborn's absence, but they were clearly too impatient. And desperate."

"Desperate about what?"

"The four Dragons link with the castle, keeping its magic in check. If any one of the Dragons is gone for too long, the castle's magic becomes unbalanced."

Which could lead to the weather everywhere on Earth going crazy.

"So, we're telling Captain Somerset?" I asked.

"Nero has already told me," she said as she closed the door behind her. She turned toward him. "I spoke to the Dragons about Leila."

"I trust you were discreet."

"Of course. Before the Elemental Rites tonight, I asked them what Leila had been working on prior to her departure. I tried to make it seem like I just wanted to be thorough in taking care of her responsibilities until her return."

Nero dipped his chin. "What did they say?"

"For the past few months, Leila has been experimenting with new magic. She was sure she could make the castle better, more powerful, more in control. That she could maybe even control the weather in the monsters' lands. She wanted to change the elemental magic in the wild areas to make the weather hostile to the resident monsters, clearing the lands for humanity."

"That is a bold endeavor," commented Nero.

"Leila was trying new spells."

"It sounds like she dug too deep into the magic wells," I said.

"Yes," Nero agreed. "She could have hit dark magic. It has the power to seduce, to lead astray."

"Leila is almost entirely light magic," Captain Somerset said. "That's how she is and how she was trained. She wouldn't dip her toes in dark magic."

"Perhaps not intentionally, but darkness is very seductive. Especially to those with no experience fighting it."

Captain Somerset planted her hands stubbornly on her hips. "She hasn't fallen, Nero. I know her. She lives and breathes the Legion—duty, honor, and propaganda in all."

He set his hand on her shoulder. "That was long ago, Basanti. People change."

"Not angels." The pained look on her face was undeniable. That was the look of someone whose heart had been broken. Of someone who had loved and lost.

"Colonel Starborn is the angel you were involved with," I said.

She gave her hand a dismissive wave. "As Nero said, that was long ago."

"We'll try to bring her back," Nero promised her. "If you sense anything from her, it would greatly help with our search."

"Our connection is not as strong as it once was," Captain Somerset replied. "I feel…something. It's so weak. I'm not even sure if it's her."

"I trust your feeling," said Nero. "You point us in the general direction, and we'll track her from there."

"The Fire Mountains. I think she's there. Or at least she was there."

"We'll check it out," Nero told her.

"Now?" I asked.

"No. A storm is raging tonight on the Elemental Expanse. I barely made it here. I couldn't see three feet in front of me."

That explained his disheveled hair.

"We'll set out tomorrow morning. The cleansing storm will have run its course by then."

Every month, the Dragons got together for the Elemental Rites. They combined their magic with the castle's to cast a great storm over the Elemental Expanse, a storm that cleansed the whole area. It kept the magic here in balance.

"Are you really taking her along?" Captain Somerset asked Nero, but she was looking at me. "She is in the middle of a very important training."

"I am personally taking over Leda's training for the duration of this mission. I'll make sure she's ready. There will be plenty of opportunities for training during the mission. She needs an extra push anyway."

I knew Nero's training would be rougher than the Dragons' obstacle courses. He'd never taken it easy on me. I couldn't really complain. He was exactly what I needed—someone who pushed me to be better, to become stronger.

"We'll leave at first light," Nero told me. Then he patted Captain Somerset on the back and left the room.

I wondered which tower he was staying in.

The Sea Tower, just like you, he spoke in my head. *But if you try to prank my hot water, Pandora, I will retaliate.*

The delightfully vicious way that his words hissed

through my mind shot shivers up my spine. Nero would have made an excellent ghost story teller.

"Are you all right?" Captain Somerset asked me.

"Are you?"

"It's all water under the bridge," she said unconvincingly. "You need to worry about your mission and your training."

"Actually, I'm more worried about the angel who will be taking me on the mission—and training me."

"Nero will be good for you. Maybe he can get some of that nonsense out of your head. What were you thinking, swooping in and saving Nerissa like that? This isn't a storybook, Leda, and you aren't a knight."

"I was just trying to help."

"You can't save everyone."

"Nerissa is your friend too," I reminded her.

"This isn't about today. It isn't even about her. It's about you. The mortality rate in the Legion isn't all that great. You have to learn that you can't save everyone. There's a time to be a hero—and a time when trying to be a hero will just get everyone killed. Do you know the difference?"

"Yes."

"Do you? Because I'm pretty sure that you're telling yourself right now that there is no such thing as a no-win situation."

"I don't give up on friends."

"You have to learn to let go. If you can't, you'll lose more people than you'll save."

I had a feeling this wasn't about me and my training. "What happened between you and Colonel Starborn?" I asked her. "Was it the reason you pushed back and reclaimed your humanity?"

"You ask too many questions."

I smiled at her. She did not return the gesture. For a moment, I was sure she was going to tell me where I could shove my questions. But then her expression softened, and she let out a heavy sigh.

"I couldn't take the angels' power games," she said. "The blind faith in everything the Legion said. The need to mark your lovers and family as property."

"I'm with you on that one."

"And the jealousy over every single person who looked at your lover," she added.

"So she didn't approve of your admirers."

"Of course not, but that wasn't the problem. I could handle her jealousy. It was my own that I couldn't take. She made me mad with jealousy. That's what being with an angel means. You become like them. You lose your mind. You want to attack anyone who might take her from you, even your own friends." Her eyes burned with regret. "I had to let her go. It was the only way to save myself."

"How long ago was this?"

"It's been nearly a hundred years."

If letting go had really been the right thing to do, then why did her heart still ache a century later? Why did regret mar her face when she spoke of her former angel lover? If I let Nero go, would I end up like Captain Somerset, regretting that decision for the rest of my immortal life? I cared about Nero. His angel ways were a lot to take, but then again, so was I.

"You should get to bed," Captain Somerset said, interrupting my thoughts. "You have an early morning tomorrow, and you'll need your strength. Who knows how many things will try to kill you along your journey."

"You have got to work on your pep talks," I told her.

A wicked smile spread across her lips, pushing out the melancholy. "I'm just trying to prepare you for your date with Nero."

"Date? I'd hardly call tracking down an angel who might have gone dark a date."

"Then you haven't been paying attention, Pandora. This is the Legion of Angels. Grab life by the horns and pray you never fall off this wild, wild ride."

CHAPTER THIRTEEN
Charging into Oblivion

THAT NIGHT, I dreamt I was once again drowning in lava. The lava hardened and froze around me like a shell, lodging me in solid rock from the waist down. I looked up to find Nero standing over me. He reached his hand toward me.

I woke up before I'd decided if I was going to take it.

Yeah, I knew what that all meant. It meant I still didn't know what to do about Nero. I could have at least dreamt a little longer to learn what my mind wanted. But I'd woken up instead.

Better yet, it was Nero who'd awakened me. He stood over my bed just as he'd stood over me in that volcano. Maybe the universe was trying to send me a sign. But if so, what kind of sign? I sure as hell didn't know.

I sat up, pushing the hair out of my face. "How did you get in here?"

"Put on some clothes, Pandora," he said, then opened the door and left my room. I thought I caught a hint of humor in his eyes.

He'd probably gotten in here by overriding the magic

lock on my door, I decided as I pulled my clothes out of the closet. We were headed for the Fire Mountains today, so I opted for my hot weather set: the tank top, shorts, and trekking boots. I splashed my face with cold water, braided my hair, then headed out.

The castle was still asleep—and so was the sun. I moved quickly and quietly through the halls. Nero was waiting for me just outside the castle gate.

"Did anyone see you?" he asked.

"A few of the castle guards tried to get the jump on me, but I was too fast for them. I left them tied up in the linen closet," I drawled.

"Very funny."

"They didn't think so." I dropped my voice to a whisper. "Are we doing something we shouldn't?"

"No, but due to the sensitive nature of this mission, it's best to be discreet."

"I can do that."

"Basanti will tell anyone who asks that I took you out onto the Elemental Expanse for extra training," Nero said.

Everyone would believe that too, especially after my epic failure on the obstacle course yesterday.

"Let's go." He walked to the edge of the mountain. "The sun will soon rise."

"You aren't flying?" I asked as he began to climb down the cliff alongside me.

"You can't fly."

"I know. I just figured you would fly down and stand there, watching me in judgmental silence."

"Do you want me to do that?" he asked.

"No." I had a thought. "Is this all part of your new training?"

I could tell he'd been doing a lot more physical training lately. The question was why. Level ten was a test of magic, not physical strength.

"Worry about your own training," he said when my foot almost slipped.

I concentrated my efforts on climbing—and not falling. "This would have been easier with climbing gear," I muttered to myself.

Of course he heard me. "That would be cheating," he said.

"I knew you were going to say that."

He merely grunted in response, and we passed the remainder of the descent in silence. At the bottom of the mountain, we took the same car Captain Somerset and I had brought here. Nero drove us toward the Fire Mountains, the lands of fire magic. A warm wind blew across the burning field of grass, carrying along the scent of frying bananas. The smell was pleasant, if not unexpected. I didn't see any bananas anywhere.

"The new look is good," I told Nero.

"What new look?"

"This windswept look." I waved my hand to indicated his hair. "Tousled hair and all."

"It wasn't intentional."

Ok, then.

"So, how was your flight to the castle yesterday?" I asked him.

"Next thing you'll be commenting on the weather."

"I will not."

"You are making smalltalk to fill the awkward silence."

"There is no awkward silence," I told him.

"Not on my end."

"Have you ever considered the possibility that I genuinely can't shut up?"

He snorted. "Now *that* I believe."

Nero appreciated silence, moments of reflection. I liked to talk. He'd chastised me on more than one occasion about chatting when I should have been training. Or about my battle banter when fighting. He thought I was splitting my attention. He didn't realize that talking helped to calm me. It helped me keep my wits about me. Silence calmed him. Talking calmed me. In so many ways, we were total opposites.

"So how was your flight?" I repeated.

"Rigorous. It was good training."

Of course it was.

"Tornados, lightning storms, rain," he listed off.

"The storm last night was perfectly dreadful."

The corner of his mouth drew up. "I knew you'd comment on the weather."

"I didn't..." I stopped and took a deep breath. "You tricked me."

"I have no idea what you're talking about." The look on his face was so deliciously evil.

I changed tactics. "Why have you been doing so much extra physical training lately?"

"I am simply preparing myself for the trials."

I allowed my gaze to trace the contours of his body. "What kind of trials?"

His brows swept his hairline. "Are you checking me out?"

"No, I..." I caught a spark of mischief in his eyes. "Maybe a little." I grinned at him. It was either that or blushing as red as a cherry.

"Good," he replied, to my surprise.

"Good?"

"Yes."

"Why do you want me to check you out?" I asked, almost afraid of the answer.

What he said surprised me. "Because if you're checking me out, it means a part of you doesn't think I'm a monster."

"I don't think you're a monster," I told him. "We're just different. Our cultures are…different."

"So you said."

"Because it's the truth."

"Your life is changing, Leda. You are changing with every sip of Nectar you drink, with every magic level you gain. You are slowly becoming more like an angel. Sooner or later, you will have to deal with that. Much sooner, given your progress."

It wasn't a judgment. He wasn't telling me what to do. He was just telling me how it was. And he was probably right. Captain Somerset had held onto her humanity, but she didn't have any aspirations to become an angel. I did.

"I know," I said. "And I'm trying to deal with it. Some things are just a lot to take."

"I am a lot to take." He didn't look offended or upset. It was just another statement of fact.

I smiled. "Yeah, you are. You're just…an angel."

"I don't blame you for feeling like that. We can't stand one another either."

"I have witnessed your interactions with Colonel Fireswift, you know."

"He is just…an angel." Nero shot me a wicked look.

I laughed. "He is indeed."

It felt so nice to be with him, laughing like this. The

stress had lifted from my shoulders, if only for the moment. I preferred this Nero to the cold, distant one who had come to Storm Castle last night.

But my mind kept returning to my conversation with Captain Somerset—and her comments on what being with an angel did to you. Nero's hand was so close I could feel his pulse. And I could feel my own pulse syncing with his. I wanted so much to reach out and take his hand, but what then? What would happen to me if Nero and I got together? Would I go crazy with jealousy like Captain Somerset had once felt with Colonel Starborn? Would I become more like an angel? And why did that suddenly not sound so bad?

It was already starting. I was falling too fast and hard for him. Soon, I wouldn't be able to come back from this. I wasn't sure I was ready to give up my humanity. No, I couldn't think about this right now. I had to keep my head in the game. We had to find Colonel Starborn. If she'd truly gone dark, a lot of people could be in danger.

"Do you know Colonel Starborn well?" I asked Nero.

"Fairly well. She was my mother's protege." He looked at me to gauge my reaction.

I didn't have time to react. A deep howl thundered across the expanse. My skin went cold, my body stiff. I looked toward the Fire Mountains. A pack of wolves stood in front of the burning rocks. There were dozens of them, each one as large as a pony. Their eyes burned as red as the mountains' five fiery peaks.

A streak of orange lightning flashed across the expanse, then slowed to match the truck's speed. A dragon-like lizard was running alongside us. Seven more giant lightning-fast lizards surrounded us. One of them slammed its spiked tail against the truck, and the vehicle jumped like it had hit a massive pothole. The wheels slammed down on the road again, the impact nearly throwing me from my seat. Another lizard readied its tail to hit us, but Nero spun the truck away from the beasts.

"Monsters?" I gasped. "The wall is supposed to keep them out. They shouldn't be here."

"No, they shouldn't," he agreed, turning the truck to dodge another lizard. They were much smaller than the wolves, but still too big to run over.

Speaking of the wolves, they were charging at us. They ran so fast, their paws were on fire. Or maybe that was just their magic. I drew my guns and fired. But for every wolf I hit, two more joined the fray. They spilled out of the Fire Mountains like a river of fire. I was going to run out of bullets long before the mountains ran out of monsters.

"It's like trying to sow a field of corn using only a hairbrush," I commented. I pulled out my lightning whip and snapped a lizard off the hood of the truck.

The monsters' numbers were swelling too fast. Enormous rats had joined the wolves and lizards. This was quickly becoming a horde.

"I wonder," Nero said.

"About what?"

Without bothering to answer, Nero turned the truck down the road that led into Desert Rose, the earth elemental lands. The grass, bushes, and sand—everything really—were in constant motion, always shifting, never resting. As we sped away from the Fire Mountains, the monsters slowed.

"They aren't following us," I said. "They were just trying to drive us away from the Fire Mountains."

"Which is precisely why we should go there."

I looked back at the tidal wave of monsters between us and the mountains. "How?"

"First things first. We need to take out the monsters." He said it casually, as though it were a small matter for two people to take out several hundred monsters. "We have to kill every single one. We cannot allow monsters to live here, on this side of the wall. They will breed and overwhelm the lands. If their numbers grow, we won't be able to contain them."

"Their numbers are pretty significant already. How do we stop them?"

"You need to control the beasts like you did back on the Black Plains," he told me.

"I thought I wasn't supposed to show I had that power."

"No one will ever know. Not out here."

I looked around, but all I saw was nature—and monsters. "There sure are a lot of them, Nero. I'm not sure I can control them."

"We'll do it together."

"Do it," I said without hesitation.

He took my hand, flipping over my wrist. His eyes traced my arm, his gaze sensual, penetrating. Before I could blink, his fangs pierced my skin like two hot irons. A flash of pain shot through me. One hand was on the steering wheel; the other held mine in a hard, almost ruthless grip. With every draw of his mouth, heat flashed through my veins, consuming me in a firestorm of sensations.

His mouth lifted too soon. He flipped over his wrist and offered it to me. My pulse racing against my skin like popping popcorn, I grabbed his hand in mine. My fangs descended. The icy hot sweetness of his blood ignited in my mouth. I gripped his hand with desperate thirst, like I hadn't drunk anything in days. It poured down my throat like liquid lightning—hot, smooth, deadly. I was drowning, a feverish madness taking hold over me.

"That should be enough," Nero said, pulling his hand away.

No, it wasn't. I didn't want to stop, but if I held on, my fangs would tear open his wrist. That would make it harder for him to fight the monsters. He was right. It was enough. We'd exchanged enough blood to link magic. I licked the last drop of his blood from my lips.

"Are you ready?" His voice was steady, but his eyes were burning silver.

I reached out, allowing his magic to help me find the beasts' minds. I could feel them all, their primitive minds flicking like hundreds of angry stars.

"Yes. I can feel them," I said.

"Take the wheel. I need you to drive. Use your power to get the monsters to follow you. Drive toward the Legion base at the center of Desert Rose," he instructed me. "I am going to fly ahead to the base and have them put up the Magitech barrier."

Gods, he wanted me to slam the beasts against the base's barrier. All Legion bases and buildings had a Magitech barrier in case of an emergency. They just never thought they'd need them. And throwing beasts against the barrier was definitely not in the Legion's handbook. It was the sort of plan I'd have come up with, not by-the-books Colonel Windstriker. My maverick behavior must have been wearing off on him.

"Will the barrier hold?" I asked him as we switched places in the truck.

"I don't know. It should. And it's the best shot we have. We don't have any other weapon with so much magic at our disposal. The barrier is all we've got."

He brushed his hand across mine, then rose to his feet. His wings spread out from his back, and he shot up into the air.

The monsters aren't heading for the base, I told him in frustration. I'd been trying to get them to change direction without success.

Keep trying, he said in my head. *I'm going to put up magic barriers to encourage them to change direction. That will help us direct the beasts where they need to go, but you have to send them at that barrier. It's the only way we can kill them all. If we allow any of them to live, they will breed so fast that the lands on this side of the wall will be overrun.*

Yeah, no pressure then. *I'll try,* I promised.

I could feel the beasts' consciousnesses. The weight of their minds inside of mine was overwhelming, crushing. Controlling them was like trying to move a mountain. Nero set off a few magical explosions, and I felt the monsters change direction to avoid the blasts. I went with that, nudging the herd toward the base. Surprisingly, they responded. Wow. It really *was* like moving a mountain— hard to start, but once you got it started, it flowed like an avalanche.

I drove the truck full-speed across the desert. In the distance, I saw Nero setting down inside the base. A few moments later, he flew up again. Magic flared up on the wall built around the base, surrounding it in a golden glowing bubble. Psychic blasts pounded at the horde's flanks, speeding up the avalanche. I herded the river of monsters toward the base. I could feel the sparks of other monsters' minds in the distance. I reached out with my magic, pulling them into the horde.

The monsters' minds smashed against the walls of my control, trying to get free. Blood dripped out of my nose, splashing against the dashboard. My head pounded like a mountain of rock was slowly burying me alive, but I didn't let go. I gritted my teeth and clutched the steering wheel with my shaking hands.

The truck wasn't faring much better. It thumped across the cracked, bumpy earth. My seatbelt was cutting into my skin like a hot knife, but I didn't have time to adjust it. I held onto the steering wheel—and the monsters' minds. I couldn't allow a single beast to escape. I had to push them at that barrier or they'd survive—and a lot of people would die as a result.

A quake rippled across the desert. Broken chunks of earth shot out of the ground, shooting toward the truck. I tried to swerve out of the way, but there were too many of them. A rock as big as a boulder slammed against the truck, shooting it into the air. I clicked out of my seatbelt and jumped out of the turning vehicle as a second boulder crushed it into the ground.

Hands snatched me out of the air before I could fall to a similar fate. Nero held me against him as he flew over the monster horde.

"Did you really have to set off all those earthquakes?" I demanded.

"I didn't. The quakes came from the magic in these lands. Desert Rose has never seen monsters before."

"So, you're saying the land panicked?" I asked.

"Not exactly. It's not sentient. It was simply reacting to the monsters' magic."

"Well, its timing was miserable."

The desert groaned, almost as though it had heard me. But it couldn't have. Nero said the land wasn't sentient. It certainly was beautiful, though. The sand shimmered like gold powder, and the prickly plants sparkled like precious gemstones. A melancholy melody hummed across the desert, singing to my soul. I drew in a deep breath.

And then I snapped out of it. The sight of the monster horde woke me right up. They were veering in the wrong direction. I nudged them back toward the base. It felt so weird—so wrong—to be sending monsters toward all those people. I hoped Nero was right and the barrier could take the impact of so many beasts.

A shriek pierced the sky. I looked up to find a beastly bird diving toward us. It was as large as a car—and it had two friends. I tried to grab hold of the birds' minds, but they eluded my control. Two of them rammed Nero from both sides. The impact knocked me down.

I fell to the ground, landing in a rolling crash. I pushed off with my hands, trying to peel myself off the scorching earth. I looked up and searched for Nero. The air was thick with flying beasts, a dozen of them now. Feathers and smoke rustled in the wind. I didn't see Nero anywhere. Where was he?

Fear surging inside of me, I grabbed control over the flying beasts and sent them at the golden glowing barrier. They exploded into puffs of dark smoke when they hit the wall of magic. The land beasts followed them into oblivion. The glowing barrier shook and hissed as hundreds of monsters slammed into it.

A few dozen beasts broke away from my control. They turned and charged at me, anger burning in their eyes, as though they knew it was I who had tried to send them to their deaths. I fired into the storm of their fury. When I ran out of bullets, I threw down my guns and drew my sword. I darted between the monsters, slashing and cutting. Adrenaline pushed me forward, powering my sore, tired muscles. I kept fighting, never stopping.

It wasn't enough. The barrier had eaten most of the monsters, but too many remained. I was horribly outnumbered. A giant wolf pounced over the others, tackling me hard to the ground. I pushed up, trying to free myself from its enormous weight, but it didn't budge. Two rows of dagger-like teeth glistened under a layer of thick saliva inside a thick, bone-crushing jaw. The beast snapped its teeth at me—and then it exploded.

I brushed off the burning embers and looked up into Nero's enraged eyes. There was nothing left of the monster but ash. I'd seen a Magitech barrier do that to a beast—but I'd never seen a person do it.

Wait, that wasn't quite right. I'd seen Damiel do the same last week. He and Nero shared some terrifying powers.

"Are you all right?" Nero asked, helping me to my feet.

I blinked, too shocked to say anything. Nero nodded, then spun around and ran at the wolf trying to sneak up on him. He jumped onto it and plunged his sword through its back. He pushed off the dead beast and quickly dispatched what remained of the horde.

"That was the last of them," Nero said as he pulled his sword out of the last lizard.

He was right. I didn't feel any more monsters.

"You look awful," I told him, taking in his battered appearance. One of the arms had been torn clear off his uniform. The rest of the leather armor didn't look much better.

He snorted. "So do you."

We limped to the gate, passing fallen monsters and what remained of our truck. The collision of several hundred monsters had been too much for the base's Magitech barrier. It had overloaded. Magic sizzled in waves across the stone wall, weak and erratic. Black smoke rose from the base, carrying with it the stench of burning metal. From the looks of it, the barrier was done for.

I really hoped there weren't any more monsters hiding on the Elemental Expanse because we'd just blown up our best weapon against them.

CHAPTER FOURTEEN
The Fire Mountains

WE ENTERED THE base, which looked more like an old Frontier town than a Legion stronghold. Buildings stood several stories tall on either side of the single dirt road that cut through the base. A hot, dry wind blew sand across our path as we walked toward the big building at the end of the road.

Barbed wire was tangled like thorny vines across the stone wall that surrounded the base. The last remnants of magic had sizzled out. The Magitech generators we passed were completely silent. It was a testament to the professionalism of the Legion's soldiers that everyone here was on high alert, guarding the wall, not standing around dumbstruck. It wasn't every day that even a single Magitech generator blew out. They were pretty much indestructible. Yet Nero and I had blown out all six at once by throwing a horde of monsters at the wall.

How many monsters had there been? Three hundred. Four? Five? The cameras had probably captured it all. That was some new data for the Legion's scientists. I only hoped Nero was right, and no one would realize I'd been the one controlling the monsters. My power over beasts was not something I should be advertising.

Centuries ago, when the beasts began to interbreed, mixing light and dark magic together, the gods and demons had lost control of their creations. As it turned out, gods could only control beings made from pure light magic, and demons could only control dark magic beings.

If the gods and demons found out there was someone who could control mixed magic monsters, they wouldn't just ignore it. There was already a god interested in using me to find my brother, a uniquely powerful telepath. I didn't also need deities after me for my weird monster-herding powers. The power to control monsters wasn't a very glamorous superpower. And was it supposed to hurt so much?

I kept walking down that road, trying not to move like every bone in my body was screaming in protest. The scar from the immortal weapon on my abdomen was screaming with renewed pain. It tended to do that whenever I pushed myself too hard. The damn thing really needed to heal already.

"Get that barrier up and running again," Nero told the grim-faced major in charge of the base we'd just left defenseless. "There might be more monsters in the area."

"I have my best people working on it, Colonel," Major Horn assured him.

His tone was perfectly professional. If I'd been in his place, I would have screamed at the people who'd broken my barrier and then demanded I fix it. But Major Horn was too much the perfect soldier to lose his temper. Nero surely approved.

Then why was he being so curt with him? "That won't

be good enough," Nero said. "I have called in extra support from the Legion to get that barrier up. There's no time to lose. We need to get it back up right away."

Major Horn did a good job trying not to look offended by Nero's lack of confidence in his best people.

When in all of that chaos did you have time to call in extra support? I asked Nero.

Controlling a few hundred monsters had nearly drained the magic from our blood connection. I didn't have that many more silent questions left. Sure, I could think them, and he might pick them up if he happened to be eavesdropping on my thoughts. But once the power of our last blood exchange was spent, I wouldn't be able to project my thoughts into his mind.

I can multitask, was all he said as we left poor Major Horn behind to pick up the pieces of our operation.

"Where did all those monsters come from?" I asked. "It's like they popped out of nowhere."

"That's exactly what happened. They popped out of nowhere."

"They appeared when we tried to go toward the Fire Mountains, where Captain Somerset felt Colonel Starborn might be," I said. "I think she's right and Colonel Starborn is there. The monsters tried to keep us away for a reason."

"It appears so."

"Captain Somerset and Colonel Starborn still have a connection, even after all these years."

"Yes." He looked thoughtful.

"I thought the wall kept out monsters," I continued. "But somehow they just popped up here. They shouldn't be able to do that. Not by themselves. Someone is controlling them."

I didn't feel anyone else's mind inside the beasts, he spoke into my mind.

I don't mean controlling them like we did. It's more subtle. Like they were conditioned for this purpose, to keep people away from the mountains.

Like guard dogs.

Exactly, I replied. *Except they're guard wolves. And guard lizards. If someone is training monsters to be guard animals, then a missing angel might be the least of our worries.*

Her recovery is still our top priority. I'll let Nyx decide what to do about the monsters.

There's still something I don't get. Even if someone has those monsters under their control, how did they get here? I thought the wall blocked the monsters' magic.

Apparently, our defenses aren't as good as we'd thought. He paused. *You did well out there. You kept those beasts under control. It took a lot of willpower to override their survival instincts and make them throw themselves against the wall.*

When he said it like that, it made me sound like a mass murderer. I reminded myself that they were monsters. And that the last time monsters had overrun the Earth, millions of humans had died.

I didn't do it alone. You helped me. During the battle, I'd felt him in my mind, directing my magic.

You did most of it yourself. I just gave you a little nudge.

Not so little. I'd felt him there, as though he were fighting beside me. It had felt...nice.

So he'd fought monsters in the air and on land, warned the base to put up the barrier, helped me control the beasts, and made a call to the Legion. Multitasking? That was a severe understatement. He must be amazing in bed. And why did I just think that? I stole a quick look at him, but his expression hadn't changed. He must not be tuning into my thoughts at the moment.

Did you feel something interesting from the monsters? he asked me.

I knew what he was getting at. The beasts just happened to be guarding the area where Captain Somerset believed Colonel Starborn to be? No, there were no coincidences. The beasts and the angel were connected. Somehow.

The Legion thought Colonel Starborn was experimenting with dark powers, pulling them into her to boost her magic. And everyone knew the darkness, the magic of hell's demons, always pulled back.

They weren't dark beasts, I said. *They were a mixture of both light and dark magic, just like the other monsters on Earth. If they'd come straight from hell, shouldn't they be purely dark?*

Yes, they should be, he replied.

It's more than that, I said as we entered the base's garage. *The monsters weren't just a mixture of light and dark magic. They were an even split, a perfect balance of the two.*

I felt that too, he said. *It's likely why it was easy for you to control them.*

I was an even split of light and dark magic too. That had to mean something, hopefully not that those monsters and I were blood relatives.

Nero moved toward a big, beige truck suited for mountainous terrain. He got into the driver's seat.

"We're heading for the Fire Mountains?" I asked as I took the seat next to him.

"Someone is trying to keep us away. That is reason enough to go there."

We passed the drive in silence. As we crossed the border into the fire lands, the desert sands gave way to cracked earth. Hot steam rose from crooked fissures in the ground. The sky was black, smoky. Sulfur puffed out in ragged gasps from the tops of burning volcanoes. Despite the foreboding atmosphere, not so much as a mosquito attacked us. I didn't feel monsters anywhere. I hoped that meant we'd gotten them all.

We parked at the entrance to the Fire Caverns, a system of caves and fire pools within the volcanoes. Inside, steam baked the air. It was like stepping into an oven. The heat was so intense, I could barely stand it. My movements were staggered, my head dizzy. Sweat sizzled against my skin.

"I wish Captain Somerset had been more specific than just the Fire Mountains," I said groggily.

"That's all she felt. Now it's up to us to follow the trail of Colonel Starborn's dark magic."

"I feel a lot of dark magic in here, but I'm not sure it's Colonel Starborn's. There's light magic too." I coughed. "There's something familiar about the magic." I blinked, trying to clear my blurry vision—and my foggy head. Gods, I hated this place. "A perfect blend of light and dark. Mixed magic."

Nero caught my arm as I stumbled. "Just like the monsters we just fought."

"Right. That's it." I snapped my fingers, looking at him. "The monsters were born from these mountains."

Nero's expression was hard.

"Sorry, that sounded stupid."

"No, you're right. The monsters were made here." He brushed a strand of hair from my face.

I leaned my cheek against his lingering hand. "Nero…"

"We should keep going," he said, turning away.

We moved deeper into the caverns. Either it was getting cooler, or I was getting used to the heat. I was going for the latter. It meant my elemental resistance was growing stronger, which gave me a needed ego boost.

It wasn't just the heat. Something else felt different. There was another magical trail now. Unlike the monsters' magic, this one was not a natural, harmonious blend of light and dark powers. It felt wrong, discordant, like the revolting screech of nails on a chalkboard. Like one magic had been grafted onto another. Like the two kinds of magic were fighting each other every step of the way.

"I feel it too," Nero replied when I voiced my thoughts.

We followed the trail of foreign mixed magic, buried within a sea of tranquility. It was like listening to a symphony with a few notes out of place, a few notes that did not belong. We had to follow those stray notes.

The caverns were dark, lit only by the harsh red glow of the fires sprouting out of the rocky walls like fiery flowers. If this were a movie, ominous music would be playing right now. I had a sinking feeling that we wouldn't like whatever was waiting for us at the end of this path. My nerves were shot already, and the hazy smoke shapes floating around like phantoms weren't doing wonders for my state of mind. I needed a distraction.

I looked at Nero. "Your father…"

I stopped when I saw the dark expression in his eyes. Like blackout curtains: this way barred, not safe for entry. I changed directions.

"My sister Tessa has a thing for him," I said. Tessa certainly had been sending me a lot more mail lately, ever since Damiel had visited our house.

Nero responded with a noncommittal grunt. Call me an optimist, but I took that as a sign to continue. It was probably more like 'continue at your own risk'.

"Tessa has decided she's going to marry Damiel," I said. "His lack of love letters are just him being a gentleman and not wanting everyone to know about them, or judge their forbidden love. That or him playing hard-to-get. Apparently, Paranormal Teen says angels like to play hard-to-get."

"No, we're just good at evasive maneuvers."

I snorted at the corny joke. "Tessa has their whole love story worked out. It involves me passing secret messages to him."

Nero moved around a fire geyser. "And did you?"

I smirked at him. "Nah, I didn't want to encourage Tessa's silliness. Besides, Damiel is obviously still in love with your mother."

"I'm sure he thinks so," he said coolly.

"He didn't kill her. We know that now. Raven, that vampire, saw her."

Nero said nothing.

"In fact, he has been searching for her for two hundred years," I continued. "He's never given up on her. He knew in his heart that she's alive. We can find her. She's with the Guardians. If I could get the weapons of heaven and hell working—"

"You are naive. You shouldn't trust Damiel." Nero's voice snapped like a whip. "Perhaps he wants to find my mother, but that's not all there is to it. There's something else going on too. I know it. Finding my mother is not the only reason he wants you to get the weapons of heaven and hell working. An angel always has many motives to whatever he does. It's efficient. And my father is nothing if not the epitome of efficiency."

"Are you speaking from personal experience?"

"Yes. He never did anything that wasn't calculated to accomplish at least four things he wanted."

"That wasn't what I meant," I said.

"I know what you meant. You meant me. If what I do has many reasons. The answer is yes. I can't seem to help myself. Whether I like it or not, there is a lot of my father in me." He frowned.

"He's not all bad."

"It's always been the same with him. He always manipulated everyone and everything perfectly to make us think we were actually deciding things, but in the end, we just did what he wanted. He never put trust in others."

"Is that a touch of regret I sense in your voice?" I asked.

"No. I can't bring myself to regret or feel sorry."

"I'm the same."

A hint of a smile graced his lips. "I know." He seemed to like that about me.

"You should have trusted me," I said quietly. "You should have told me what Colonel Fireswift had done. And let me decide what to do about it."

"And what would you have done?"

"I don't know. He's too powerful for me to beat in a fight. But I'm not above spitting in his coffee."

"Since when does he drink coffee?"

Nero had once told me that caffeine was a clutch, a weakness. And to drive the habit out of me, he'd coupled depriving me of my morning coffee with waking me up at four in the morning for weeks on end.

"Since after the incident on the Black Plains," I told

him. "I think I stress out Colonel Fireswift. I'm that little annoying thing he cannot control. Like a paperclip that keeps hopping out of the jar on his desk. He drinks a lot of coffee now. I bet it's laced with Nectar too. I'm hoping to give him an ulcer."

"Angels don't get ulcers."

"Shush. You're ruining my plan."

"What else is part of this plan of yours?" he asked.

"The usual. World domination. Getting Colonel Fireswift demoted to the mail room. Getting you back at the New York office. I have charts and diagrams and checklists and everything."

He was grinning.

"What? I can be organized when I want to be," I told him.

"Oh?"

"Of course. I just have to be properly motivated."

"And getting me back to New York is motivating?"

"Don't let it get to your head. Your stern scowl of quiet disapproval is much easier on the eyes than that look Colonel Fireswift has, like something nasty died under his nose." I crinkled up my nose.

"Alas, I don't think that's reason enough for Nyx."

"She thinks I'm a bad influence on you."

"Can you blame her?"

"No," I admitted. "Not really. Apparently my complete disregard for rules and regulations is contagious."

"Yes."

The way he was looking at me made me uncomfortable. He wasn't even touching me, not even kissing me, but I felt a flush of heat that had nothing to do with the Fire Mountains.

I kept walking. My foot hit a loose rock, and the ledge collapsed. Nero caught my arm before I tumbled into a nasty fire pit. His other hand rested on my back, holding me steady, safe. My heart sped up. I had to kiss him.

Wait, that was a really bad idea. Kissing him would be forgiving him for marking me. No, worse. It would be an acceptance of that act. He didn't even want to be forgiven. He thought he was right—and any other angel would agree with him. I'd read all about angels marking people in the angel book I'd brought to Storm Castle. Inside that book lay a whole new world—a world of dangerous delights and brutal sensuality. It was so easy to get sucked in, and once you did, you might never find the way back to your humanity.

"Can I ask you something?" I asked.

He let go of me. "You can ask me anything, Leda." His voice dipped deeper, as smooth as silk over naked skin.

Why did he have to be so sexy?

"Was that your question?" he asked.

I blushed.

"I wasn't sure because you didn't say it aloud." His face was perfectly serious. Too serious to be real, even for him.

"This isn't funny."

"I have no idea what you're talking about," he said. "Now, what did you want to ask me?"

I buried my face in my hands. "I don't remember."

"Ask me." The hint of a plea hid beneath his facade of pure arrogance.

"Do you promise to behave?"

"No."

Ask a stupid question…

He was smiling, waiting patiently.

"Have you ever marked anyone else before?" I asked.

"No." His answer was immediate.

Oh.

"Never before have I known someone I wanted to declare mine."

He knew just what to say. But the thing was, I had no doubt he was completely serious. Nero never lied. He was honest. Too honest sometimes. He didn't lie to spare anyone's feelings, and he didn't lie to his advantage.

"You were expecting a different answer?" he asked.

"I was hoping for that one." He'd always been honest with me; I owed it to him to be the same. "I'm sorry. I know it's really hypocritical of me." I didn't want to be marked, but at the same time, I wanted to be the only one he'd marked.

"It's all right. It's not so simple. Nothing with angels ever is. We are painfully difficult to tolerate, let alone get along with."

He wasn't pushing me. He was letting me work it out on my own. He wouldn't be with me until I got myself ok with this, until I reconciled myself with his angel ways. That was the right thing to do, the proper one. Either I was ok with how he was, or I wasn't. It was my choice.

He sure was being awfully mature about this. It was annoying. It would have been so much easier to hate him if he'd tried to force me to accept his ways. But, no, he was understanding of the fact that not everyone wanted the drama that came with angels.

"Damn you for being so reasonable," I muttered.

"Would you rather I be unreasonable?"

"Yes."

He chuckled. "I'll remind you of your words the next

time you train with me."

The cavern rumbled. Fire sprayed up. Nero jumped at the fiery geyser, freezing it solid. A dozen more fire pillars exploded into the air, merging together, trapping him behind a solid wall of fire. A second quake shook the mountains, throwing me into a deep chasm.

CHAPTER FIFTEEN
Darkness Descending

THE FIRE PIT swallowed me whole. Only this week's extensive elemental training at Storm Castle—which had involved being set on fire, continuously—kept me from burning up. As soon as my boots hit the ground, I ran straight out of the fire pit into the adjoining cavern. My elemental resistance had very real limits. I could only withstand the heat for so long, and I had no intention of being burned alive.

I followed the rocky tunnel. It felt as hot as hell down here, so close to the raging lava pools. The hiss of steam echoed like screams in my ears. The solid walls blurred and shifted. I blinked, but my vision didn't clear. I stumbled down the wide tunnel, avoiding puddles of burning lava. Suddenly, my nightmare of drowning inside a volcano felt very real. I had to get out of here before it came true.

"Leda," a voice whispered over the hissing steam.

I paused at a fork in the path, looking around in every direction. A blurry figure streaked down the left tunnel, its wings trailing smoke. I ran after the angel.

"Colonel Starborn!" I called out.

The angel kept running.

"Leila!"

She didn't stop running until the tunnel ended. Then she turned around slowly. I gasped when I saw her. Her feet were bare and dirty. Her wings, a beautiful blend of white and pale gold feathers with sunset accents, hung limply. Their tips dragged on the ground. She wore only a black tank top and boy shorts. Slashes cut across the front of her top. Soot smudged her face. Her pale orange hair, stained with blood, brushed the tops of her dirty shoulders.

"Help me," she said through cracked lips.

I looked into her trembling pale blue eyes. "What happened to you?"

She choked out a terrified gasp, then pushed past me and ran back down the path. I followed her to the fork. She took the other tunnel this time. I felt a rush of wind and looked up. Two dark angels, dressed in the shining armor of hell, flew high above us. In a flash of movement, they swept down like a flock of attacking crows. I never saw their faces. When the smoke cleared, Colonel Starborn and the dark angels were gone.

I'd reached a dead end. Sheer rocks towered in front of me. They were as smooth as satin. I couldn't climb them. Dozens of lava pools bubbled and popped all around me. They were spreading, rising like the ocean's tide. Soon, this entire cavern would be covered in burning lava. I blinked, and the lava disappeared. I blinked again, and it was back. What the hell was going on?

The two dark angels appeared once more overhead, their faces masked in smoke and haze. They swept down to the ground and snatched Colonel Starborn. The scene played out again and again, every time just the same.

"She's not really here," I realized. "At least not anymore." I looked at the blurry lava that wasn't really here. "This happened days ago."

"You are seeing what I saw," a voice echoed.

It sounded distorted, like words spoken underwater. Or words caught on the wind, carried to me from far away. I didn't recognize the voice. I couldn't even tell whether it was a man or a woman.

"What happened to her?" I asked, looking around. I didn't see anyone. I was alone down here.

"It happened just as you saw," the voice replied. "Dark angels took her."

"But how? What was she doing all the way out here?"

"She has not gone rogue."

The voice had guessed my thoughts. Or read them.

"She's been working too hard, straining her magic too much," the voice said. "It weakened her mind, her defenses. The dark angels invaded her dreams, taking control of them over the course of many weeks. Dream by dream, step by step. Caught in a trance, she came here. She thought it was just a dream."

"Where did the dark angels take her?"

"They drew her into a dimension between Earth and hell. A dream dimension. Let me show you."

Visions flashed through my head. A dark room. Colonel Starborn being chained to a wall. Shadowed figures swimming around her. Her tortured screams.

"Where is she?" I asked, my voice shaking. The voice hadn't just shown me the angel. It had bombarded me with everything Colonel Starborn was feeling right now. Pain. Anger. Despair.

"I don't know," the voice replied. "My powers cannot

find her. The dark angels are blocking me."

"Then how am *I* supposed to find her?"

"Someone with a connection to her can lead you to her location."

"Captain Somerset?" I asked.

"No, that connection is broken. But there is another."

"Who?"

The voice didn't answer in words. It showed me, hitting me with a thousand different images at once. Flashes of Colonel Starborn training someone, her protege. Flashes I couldn't process, couldn't believe.

"You must go," the voice told me. "*Now*."

I blinked back the visions and looked around. The lava was rising again—and this time it was real. I had to get out of here before it reached me.

"There's a way up that wall," the voice told me.

I looked up. The wall was tall, but it wasn't completely smooth. I began climbing, trying not to panic as the temperature rose. As long as I stayed ahead of the lava, my elemental resistance would protect me. I was *not* going to die. With that settled, I wiped my sweaty hand on my shorts and kept climbing.

I found Nero at the top, a shattered wall of rock behind him. "You're late," I told him with a smirk. It was easy to smile now that I was on solid ground again.

"The mountain gave me trouble," he said.

I looked through the shattered wall to find many more shattered walls behind it. "I see you showed it who's boss."

"Yes." He looked down into the pool of rising lava. "Did you find anything interesting down there?"

"More like something interesting found me. Colonel Starborn was here, but she's not anymore. She's been abducted by dark angels."

I told him everything the mysterious voice had shown me.

"And you believe it?" he asked.

"Yes. I can just feel it's telling the truth." I looked at him, expecting a lecture about not being so trusting.

He merely nodded. "Ok."

"Ok? That's it? No lecture?"

His brows arched. "Do you want a lecture?"

"Not particularly."

"I trust you, Leda. If you feel the voice was telling the truth, then that's good enough for me."

My mouth dropped in shock. "I..." I covered my surprise with a big smile. "Careful, Colonel, some people might think you're going soft," I teased him.

You could have cut diamonds off his face. "If you'd like to test that theory, Pandora, then by all means, continue."

"Oh, no. I'm fine." I swallowed a chuckle. "We all know you're a badass."

"And don't forget it." He waved me toward the substantial hole he'd made in the wall of solid rock. "Let's get out of here before you get heatstroke."

I didn't argue with him. Even my pride knew he was right. Sure, I'd been training my elemental resistance, but we were inside a volcano. It was still too much for my feeble magic. I was getting dizzy, and if we didn't leave now, Nero would have to carry me out. That was considerably less badass than walking out on my own two feet.

The truck was waiting for us right where we'd left it. Lava hadn't eaten it for lunch, and neither had any monsters. As we drove back to the base, I thought about doing the right thing. What did that even mean?

Sometimes it was the hard choice, the one that was best—but not necessarily what I wanted. A sacrifice. Is that what Captain Somerset had done with Colonel Starborn by letting her go? Had she made the choice that was right for everyone even though it hurt her?

The base was bustling with activity when we got back. Nero hurried off to hear Major Horn's report, while I went up to the top of the tallest tower. It was the perfect place to think. No one else was up here. I looked across the vast desert. The sun was setting, its red-orange rays lighting up the sea of sand, making it sparkle like millions of diamonds. The air was clear and still tonight. I couldn't believe how late it was already. How long had we been in those caves?

I'd watched the sun set at Storm Castle too. It was so different from here. From the top of the castle, I could see all four elemental zones. At sunset, when the sun's rays ignited their magic, it was like watching four distinct light shows. Lightning cut across the sky of the Sky Plains, and below wind funnels danced on the ground. Down in the Crystal Forest, the sunlight caught the tiny raindrops beaded on the trees' needles. Snowflakes turned and twirled, changing color as they fell softly down. The smoke that rose from the Fire Mountains glowed with the colors of the sunset. And these earth lands shone just as brightly from the castle.

The Dragons' castle sat at the cornerstone of the four elements. It lay at the crossroads. This base, on the other hand, was firmly in one zone. One choice. One way.

After I watched the sunset, I went downstairs to the base's underground training rooms. They even had a few rooms to train elemental magic. They weren't as extensive as the castle's offerings, but they were more than sufficient for me. I really should be practicing.

I found a closet of sports suits designed to withstand cold, heat, wind, and fire. They also dried instantly. It was the perfect clothing for elemental training. After changing into one of the suits, I entered the wind tunnels. The great thing about navigating an obstacle course on a timer with the wind trying to blow me away was I really couldn't think about anything else. I had to concentrate on what I was doing.

The wind tunnel spilled out into an open room. Lightning crashed down from rotating balls on the ceiling. I sprinted across the room, dodging them. But the room wasn't done with me yet. Beasts made of air magic spawned all around me. I lashed out with my lightning whip. Whenever it hit its mark, the beast exploded into tiny magic particles. The particles stung when they hit me, but I kept going. Pushing through the pain was what this was all about. The room provided an endless supply of monsters, and I provided the single-minded will to destroy them.

There was something soothing about losing myself in this single purpose, in having no other choices. I wouldn't call it therapeutic because I was avoiding reality. The world rarely gave you only one option. It was full of choices—and the consequences of those choices.

I swung my whip around to blast apart the monster sneaking up on me. I found Nero there instead. He'd caught the coil of my whip around his wrist.

"Didn't anyone ever tell you not to sneak up on people?" I demanded.

"Didn't anyone ever tell you to look before you leap?" He didn't seem bothered by the lightning storm raging across the length of my whip.

"I think a wise angel once said something to that effect."

He flicked his hand, and my whip wilted from his wrist. I shook it out, reigniting the spark. He moved in to attack.

"Are you serious?" I said, lashing out with my whip to block his path. "You want to fight me? I have a weapon, and you don't."

"It's cute that you still think that matters."

He cut around me faster than I could track him. A fist hammered down on my hand, breaking my hold on the whip. Nero grabbed the weapon out of the air and snapped it at me. It collided with my body, its lightning bite zapping through me so hard that I hit the ground. A week ago, a hit like that would have knocked me unconscious. Thanks to the Dragons' training, it only knocked me on my ass.

"On your feet, Pandora," Nero chided me.

I jumped up and followed him into the next room. A light drizzle sprinkled down from the high ceiling. The water drops hissed against the lightning whip in Nero's hand. The Dragons had lectured us on the dangers of crossing elements, like holding a lightning whip in a rainstorm. That was a sure way to get electrocuted. Well, unless you were an angel with absolute control over all the magic in the room.

Nero tossed the whip aside. "Try to attack me."

I moved forward cautiously. This had to be a trap.

"Today, Pandora."

I sprinted toward him. A stream of water shot at me. I dodged it and angled toward him again. A second water stream shot out of the wall—and I was too slow this time. It hit me with the force of a train, throwing me across the room.

"Your resistance is too low."

I spat out water, looking up at Nero. He was standing right over me. I couldn't even fathom how fast he'd moved to get here.

"What's the trouble with your elemental magic?" he asked as I rose to my feet.

"Something is blocking me. I can't even make a spark of magic when I snap my fingers. The brats can do that."

"There's a lot holding you back, not just your magic," he told me, his words caressing my face.

He didn't seem bothered by our closeness, but I was. His heart beat in a slow, steady rhythm. How could he be so calm? Every part of me was screaming out exactly how I felt about him.

"What is that supposed to mean?" I demanded. "What is holding me back?"

"You still see yourself as human. You need to let go of these boundaries and sensibilities, this insistence on labeling things as impossible. The Legion has opened up a whole new world to you."

A whole new world that was nothing like the one I'd left. Yes, left. When I'd joined the Legion, I'd chosen this world and everything in it. I wanted to be an angel, to gain the power to save Zane. But how could I ever be an angel? Their ways were so strange, so alien. I didn't belong here. But I didn't belong in the human world either. I'd come too far already. I was caught, trapped, drifting.

The door to the training room opened, and Major Horn stepped inside. Another Legion soldier was with him, someone I'd sincerely hoped to never see again: Major Selena Singh, the brutally intelligent Interrogator I'd seen at work last week. I hoped she wasn't here to interrogate anyone, but I feared that was a futile hope. A Legion Interrogator didn't visit the Elemental Expanse for fun.

The last time I'd seen her, she'd worn the white uniform of an Interrogator. Today, she was dressed in a tank top and shorts outfit that looked a lot like the one I'd been wearing just an hour ago. She carried a lot more weapons than I ever did, though. She wore a long sword on her back, straps of throwing knives on her arms and thighs, and a gun at each hip. Her long, dark hair was pulled back into an elaborate braid that extended down to her bottom. Tall, strong, and toned, she'd managed to keep her feminine curves—and her agility. She moved with liquid grace— strong, powerful, yet soft. Like a ballet dancer.

"Colonel Windstriker," Major Horn said, his voice strained.

Nero turned away from me to look at the new arrivals. "How are you getting along with Major Singh?"

Major Horn's lips drew together into a thin line. Apparently, the answer was not at all. "She has been an asset. She placed a call, and an hour later, six new Magitech generators arrived here via airship. And thanks to her magical expertise, the barrier is up and running well ahead of schedule." He was pointedly avoiding eye contact with her.

So the soul-crusher could fix things as well as she broke people. Who would have guessed?

"Glad I could help," Major Singh replied with a smile. If I hadn't seen her in action in the interrogation room, I'd never have believed she could be anything but pleasant.

Nero went to speak with her about the repairs, and Major Horn pulled back until he was standing beside me. It was as far from her as he could reasonably go in this room.

"Not a fan?" I whispered to him.

Major Horn turned his head toward me. "I've heard you don't know when to keep your mouth shut."

I grinned at him. "Nero tell you that?"

"Colonel Windstriker does not speak to me of personal matters." He said Nero's name with reverence, like he'd swim through a pit of burning lava just for the chance to kiss his ass. "Basanti has told me of your unique...quirks."

So he and Captain Somerset were friends. I wasn't surprised. People respected her, especially other Legion officers. It was hard not to. She was a competent soldier, *and* she had a wicked sense of humor. The nature of the Legion—what they put us through—made that a rare combination.

"Yes, I can't shut up. Some people think it's endearing," I said.

"Like Colonel Windstriker?"

"Why don't you ask him yourself?" I said wickedly.

"You and Basanti are a lot alike."

"Is that your coy way of saying you want to be friends?"

"I'm not sure my career would survive that friendship. You have a talent for trouble." A calculating gleam shone in his eyes. "Perhaps you could befriend Major Singh instead."

"Somehow, I doubt she would appreciate my wanton wit."

"You're undoubtedly right." He sighed with genuine disappointment. He must really hate her.

"Maybe you should ask her to be *your* friend," I

ELLA SUMMERS

suggested.

"I tried that long ago, back when we were initiates. She deemed me unworthy to be in her company."

"Why?"

"Because I don't have an angel parent."

Ah, so Major Singh was another Legion brat.

"She and Colonel Windstriker were lovers once, you know," Major Horn told me.

"Oh?" I replied casually, even as jealousy flared up inside of me.

Major Singh was beautiful and intelligent. It didn't matter that she wasn't flirting with Nero. Whatever had once existed between them, it was clearly over. In fact, they were both being perfectly professional. So then why did I want to punch her in her pretty face?

I counted down from ten, trying to calm myself. This was what Captain Somerset had warned me about, this jealous, murderous streak that the angels brought out in us. This wasn't me. This wasn't who I was.

"Rumor has it she is close to becoming an angel," Major Horn told me, oblivious to my inner turmoil. "Her chances are good. She's stationed in Los Angeles, working directly under the First Angel."

I tried not to dwell on the fact that Nero had spent the past few weeks in Los Angeles, also working under Nyx. Maybe working with Major Singh. Maybe even working with her very closely.

So much for not dwelling. It was a good thing I didn't have any telekinetic powers because my fury would have brought the roof down on her head. I was pretty close to getting elemental magic, though. A good earthquake would collapse the roof nicely.

186

"Are you all right?" Major Horn asked me.

I glanced down at my clenched fists, then smiled at him. "Just tired."

I wasn't tired. In fact, I'd never been so awake in all my life. There was nothing like seeing red that shot your body into overdrive.

Her discussion with Nero finished, Major Singh left the room. With her out of sight, my mood slowly began to cool, and reason returned to my mind. I couldn't bring the roof down on someone just because she and Nero had once been lovers. It wasn't nice to be a psychopath.

Major Horn's wrist beeped, and he looked down at his watch. "Colonel, your next guest has just arrived."

"What guest?"

"The one you asked the First Angel to send here to assist you in your mission."

Nero gave him a hard look. "I never asked Nyx to send me anyone."

The doors to the gym parted. Artificial light streamed inside, lighting up the silhouette of a man in a Legion uniform. My eyes adjusted, and I looked into the face of Major Harker Locke, the man who'd tried to poison me just half a year ago.

CHAPTER SIXTEEN
The Sea of Ice

NERO DREW HIS sword, flames erupting across the blade. He pointed it at his former best friend.

"Nice to see you too, Nero." Harker dipped his chin to me. "And you, Pandora," he added with a smile on his lips.

"How did you get out?" Nero demanded. The flames were burning so hot that the room's drizzling rain was turning to steam.

Harker's gaze shifted from me to Nero. "Leda didn't tell you? She called the First Angel and asked for me."

The look of betrayal on Nero's face nearly broke my heart. Nero quickly recovered his hard shell, but I knew it was still there, buried beneath centuries of training. That was the thing about the hard choices we made for the greater good. They were often horribly dissatisfying.

"We don't know where Colonel Starborn is," I told Nero. "She is beyond our reach. We have no connection to her, no way to find her." I looked at Harker. "But he does."

"The connection between mentor and student," said Nero.

That's what the voice had shown me in the Fire

Mountains—that Harker was Colonel Starborn's protege, the person she'd trained to know everything she did.

"Harker is the person on Earth she has the strongest connection to," I said. "I hoped he could help us find her."

"I can," Harker assured me. "Odd that Nero didn't think of it."

"I thought of it. And decided it wasn't worth the risk of letting you out," Nero said, his voice dangerously low.

Harker met his cold stare without a hint of fear in his eyes. "It seems Nyx doesn't share your feelings. And neither does Leda."

Nero's face was impassive. Oh, no. Harker was not going to put me into the middle of their quarrel.

"We need Harker. Trust me when I say he's a last resort," I told them both.

Harker's smile never faded. "Of course I am."

The look in Nero's eyes put the lava pools of the Fire Mountains to shame.

"An angel is being tortured by dark angels. One of our own, Nero. Despite everything that has passed between us recently, we must work together for Leila's sake." Harker held out his hand to Nero.

"Very well. For her sake," Nero agreed, but he didn't shake his hand.

"We were friends once, Nero. Like brothers."

"No longer. Not after what you did."

"You are so unforgiving."

"Some things cannot be forgiven," Nero declared.

"Guys, we need to work together," I said. "Colonel Starborn is in pain, probably being tortured for secrets. Or they're trying to turn her. Nero, we have to get her out. If they turn her, if they make her dark, there's no going back.

And if they don't turn her, she'll be broken, worse than dead. That's why I asked Nyx to call in Harker."

Gold flashed in his eyes. "You went behind my back."

"I knew you wouldn't agree to this, but it had to be done."

A low grunt buzzed deep inside his throat. "Not long ago, you shouted at me for doing exactly the same thing. You might not be an angel, Leda, but you think just like one."

My mouth dropped in outrage. I was completely ready to argue with him—but then I stopped. He was right. I was acting just like an angel.

No, this was different. This was about saving a life. Saving Colonel Starborn from death and suffering. It wasn't the same as what Nero had done.

Or was it? Under the angels' rules, if I was considered Colonel Fireswift's property, Nero couldn't even protect me anymore. He wouldn't have the right. I would be Colonel Fireswift's to protect. Or to harm. And he *would* harm me. I knew Colonel Fireswift, knew his cruelty, how he treated his children. He'd kill me to be rid of me if he could. Knowing that, could I really say that what Nero had done was any different than what I'd done?

These thoughts made me dizzy. There was no time for that now. I had to worry about saving Colonel Starborn. These moral conundrums, these philosophical debates, would have to wait for later.

"You did the right thing," Harker told me. "The Legion cannot afford to lose another angel to the demons. We've lost too many already. Nyx has ordered us to set out immediately. I can sense Leila, but our connection is growing weaker. They're breaking her."

Nero's face went cold. He was bottling his emotions to deal with the matter at hand.

"What happened? How did they get her?" Harker asked us.

I shared my visions of Colonel Starborn's capture.

"She connected to you?" He looked surprised.

"Yes." I didn't tell him about the voice who'd spoken to me. "But I can't hear her anymore. She's gone."

"She is on the wrong side of the wall. The barrier blocks most magic from passing. Our connection runs deeper than that, but it won't last long."

"Where is she?"

"The Sea of Ice," Harker replied. "You said the dark angels invaded her sleep, controlling her dreams?"

"Yes."

"They brought her through a dream dimension to move her beyond the wall's protection," he realized. "A loophole. I never thought of that."

"We can discuss magic deviations later. It's time to bring Leila home," Nero declared.

Harker nodded. On that, they were obviously in clear agreement.

The road to the Sea of Ice brought us through the Wetlands. The Elemental Expanse's water magic lands were pretty much what you'd expect: warm, wet, and marshy. A small rainforest hugged the banks of the great river that bordered the road.

But with every passing minute, the air grew colder. Warm marshes gave way to snowy fields. Snowflakes fluttered down like crystals falling from the heavens, light and delicate. They jingled like sleigh bells as they twirled in the breeze. Far down the road, a bright blue sky shone behind snowy mountain peaks.

"So are you two a couple now?" Harker asked, breaking the silence that had reigned in the truck since we'd left the base an hour ago.

When Nero didn't answer, Harker looked at me. I didn't answer either. What was I supposed to say? It was complicated.

"I see," Harker said. "Well, my offer still stands, Leda."

He was hitting on me? Now? Sure, he was a nice guy. And loads of fun. Well, up until the part where he'd betrayed me. Harker's first priority would always be to his career—and to the god he served. He was a champion of light, a pious warrior. Collateral damage was fine with him, expected even. But none of that even mattered because Nero was the only one I wanted.

"I'm sorry, Harker," I said. "I don't date people who try to kill me."

He frowned. "You would have survived the Nectar."

He was still saying that? Surely, he did not believe I could have survived a dose of pure Nectar? He was lying to himself. Maybe that helped him live with what he'd done.

"You survived the Venom," he said.

I blinked at him in surprise.

He shrugged. "I hear things."

"You hear a lot of things for a man in prison."

He looked fit, good. He didn't have that haggard look of suffering, torture, or being in a Legion prison for months. I had to wonder if he'd even had a visit from the Interrogators. Nyx had admitted to me that she didn't have anything substantial against him. All she had was Harker's act of killing someone the Legion wanted to interrogate—and her suspicion that he was up to something.

Nero and I couldn't tell the First Angel the truth about what had happened, that Harker had tried to get me to drink pure Nectar. If we did, then the Legion would find out about my brother—and that we were trying to keep Zane away from them. What we were doing, keeping a powerful telepath hidden from the Legion, would be considered treason.

I suspected Harker's prison stay was more like a vacation than an incarceration. He'd probably spent his days lying around reading books and working out in expensive sports facilities. The biggest punishment for him was that he wanted to be out here, growing his magic, furthering his agenda. Instead, he'd spent nearly half a year tied up in all the red tape Nyx could find.

"What can I say? I get a lot of visitors," Harker said with an easy shrug.

"I heard you've had some godly visitors."

My words shocked him to silence for a few moments, but he quickly recovered. "You're trying to trick me into giving away something."

I shot him my most innocent smile. "I would never do such a devious thing."

"You absolutely would do it. Sometimes I don't know if you're more innocent or wicked."

"Both," I told him.

He laughed. "Yeah. I think you might be right about that."

Nero had his eyes on the road, but I had no doubt he was watching our exchange. Harker was fun. It would have been a blast to have him as a buddy like Nerissa or Ivy. But the look Nero shot me was a reminder that I had to be careful with Harker, just as I had to be careful with Jace. Nero was my reality check, the counter to my habit of trying to save people from themselves. I wanted to see only the best in Harker—the good, the fun—but I should not forget that he served a god. And that god was trying to find Zane so he could force my brother into his service. The question of the day was whether the god had cut Harker loose when he'd failed to manipulate me into drinking the pure Nectar.

"We're coming up on the wall," Nero announced as he drove us toward the wall.

The soldiers standing up there rushed to open the gates, and we entered a vast tundra. Everything was white as far as the eye could see. The sunlight reflected off the tiny crystals of the sleek, white sheet of ice that covered the lands. This frozen place shouldn't have been able to exist so close to a desert and a mountain range of boiling volcanoes, but I'd given up questioning magic. After all, I'd recently experienced scorching heat in the dead of winter. Magic changed things. It made so many horrible, splendid things possible.

The truck shook a little as the wheels transformed into sled runners. We slid across the icy expanse, the soft scratch of ice whistling beneath us, carrying us along. There was a quiet peacefulness to this place.

But with every mile we ventured deeper into the Sea of Ice, I felt colder. An icy chill had taken root inside of me. It wasn't refreshing like the cool rush of winter tickling my cheeks. Dread, malice, pain, desire. The magic was calling out to me, whispering sweet temptations into my ears. It was like an ice cream sundae with lots of chocolate syrup. You knew it was bad for you, but you wanted it anyway.

Snowflakes fell softly, as cold and cruel as they were beautiful. As they turned, flipping between dark and light magic, they pulsed like stars in the night sky.

"It's coming from that mountain." Nero's voice was eerily quiet, hardly louder than the whistle of ice beneath our truck's runners.

I had to squint my eyes to make out the form of the white mountain camouflaged against the winter tundra. We were approaching fast.

"There's an opening," Harker said.

He was right. The hole in the mountain face wasn't large. There wasn't enough space for us to drive the truck through it, but it was big enough for us to enter by foot. Nero parked beside the mountain.

"I can feel Leila. She's close," Harker whispered as we walked through the opening.

A soft gasp escaped my mouth at the sight of the crystal cave inside the mountain. A light as bright as a thousand fire diamonds shone high above, bouncing off the icicles that hung from the ceiling like an enormous chandelier. That magical light sparkled off the smooth, purple walls and floors. A soft, sweet melody jingled in the distance.

A gate of stone slammed down, blocking the entrance. Soldiers popped out of the floor all around us, brandishing swords and guns. Hell's army had us completely surrounded.

CHAPTER SEVENTEEN
The Dark Force of Hell

THE DARK FORCE of Hell, the demons' army, preferred more armor than the Legion. The leather of their uniforms was thicker, heavier than ours. Some of them wore scale armor that shimmered with dark magic. The heavier materials didn't slow them down a bit. They charged at us, two dozen soldiers against our party of three, moving like lightning. Flames erupted on their blades. That same silver and gold glow I'd seen in so many Legion soldiers' eyes lit up their eyes too. Heaven and hell, light and dark, Nectar and Venom—our magic wasn't as different as most people thought.

I raised my sword to meet the Dark Force's advance. There were just so many of them, and my sword bounced uselessly off their hard armor. Nero and Harker darted between the soldiers, striking with brutal efficiency. They seemed to know just where to hit the armor to do the most damage. They'd clearly done this many times before.

Through the clashing steel and magic, I saw an angel shackled to the wall at the back of the cavern. Chains were locked around her ankles and wrists. Massive icicles punctured her wings—white and gold accented with orange that rivaled the most beautiful sunset I'd ever seen. It made my heart hurt to see the beautiful angel in such pain. The ceiling wept wet snowflakes, as though it couldn't bear to see her suffer like that either.

"Run to Colonel Starborn," Nero told me. "We'll hold off the Dark Force."

I nodded, then circled around the soldier he'd just engaged. I ran as fast as I could, dodging between enemy combatants hellbent on killing me. Nero and Harker covered my mad dash to Colonel Starborn. Spells streaked across the battlefield like berserk comets. My body shook every time one hit me, but I just kept pushing forward. Thanks to this last week of torturous training, my magic resistance was higher than ever before.

But would it be enough? The spells kept piling on, one after the other after the other. The magic was dragging me under. It was like moving through a pool of burning quicksand in the middle of a hurricane. Ignoring my frostbit fingers and fire-kissed toes, I kept running toward the shackled angel.

"Colonel Starborn," I said, stopping in front of her.

Like all angels, she was stunning. In fact, she was even more beautiful in person than she'd appeared in my visions. Her hair wasn't just orange like I'd thought before. It was the color of a sunset—mixed golden hues of orange, red, and pink. It fell like silk curtains to her shoulders, its glossy sheen penetrating the layers of sweat, dirt, and torture. Her eyes were closed, her long, thick eyelashes kissing her high cheekbones. Her feet were naked. She wore only a ripped, dirty tank top and shorts. Her body convulsed with ragged, persistent shivers, like the metal chains had carried the cold deep into her bones.

"Colonel Starborn," I repeated.

When she didn't respond, I grabbed hold of her shoulders and shook her. Jostled out of her nightmare, her eyelashes lifted. She looked at me with turquoise eyes that shone like a tropical ocean. I couldn't help but stare. No, make that gawk. She was stunning, almost as gorgeous as Nero. The dirty snow and deep tears that marred her clothing only made her more beautiful.

"I'm here from the Legion," I told her. "We've come to get you out of here."

Hope shone in her eyes. Such beautiful hope. I saw then that she'd all but given up on making it out of here. I reached for her chains.

Telekinetic magic slammed into me, throwing me to the ground. I jumped to my feet and met the icy blue stare of a dark angel. He stood between me and Colonel Starborn, his blood-red armor shimmering like satin in the firelight, his long black hair swirling in the magic breeze surrounding him.

"Get out of my way," I growled at him.

The dark angel laughed, such a beautiful, terrifying sound full of power and cruel intentions. He moved in a flash, his hard armor stretching impossibly with him. His fist slammed against my head. I stumbled back, barely evading his next punch. I drew my gun and fired, but the bullets bounced off his armor. It was magically protected. It would take magic to get through it, and I didn't have the power to make the bullets anything more than mundane. I aimed for his head. He knocked the gun out of my hand before I could shoot him. He swung another punch at me. I jumped back.

"Stop running, little girl," he taunted me. "Or are the Legion's soldiers too cowardly to stay and fight?"

Fight a dark angel? Yeah, I really didn't want to do that. He was faster, stronger, and had more magic than I did. It might be cowardly to flee, but it was stupid to fight. Not that I had much of a choice. It was either fight or die.

A flash of fire danced across my peripheral vision. I turned to see Nero toss me a flaming sword. I caught it and swung it around. The dark angel's sword met mine. And his was on fire too. Dark elemental magic raged like a firestorm across his blade.

"Windstriker," the dark angel growled, pushing his sword hard against mine to throw me off balance.

He drew a figure-eight pattern in the air with his sword. The flaming symbol pulsed once, then the gate to the cavern opened. Dozens more of the Dark Force's soldiers poured inside, rushing at Nero and Harker. The dark angel didn't give me a chance to contemplate their fate. He struck at me. Our blades clashed with a blinding bang. Holding onto my sword, choking on the stench of sulfur, I watched in horror as the flames jumped from his sword to mine. The fire slid down my blade with liquid ease. I bit back the pain as the fiery spell bit into my hand.

Surprise flashed across his face when I didn't drop my weapon. I took advantage of that brief moment of confusion and swung my sword. Powered by the elemental spell Nero had cast on the blade, it chipped a piece off the dark angel's armor. His beautiful face twisted into a vicious scowl. A telekinetic burst pulsed out of him, hitting me against the wall with the force of a high-speed train. Pain exploded from my ribcage, trickling down my left side.

"This is impossible," the dark angel said as I rose to my

feet and moved toward him.

I stuck a big smirk over the throbbing beat of agony inside of me. "I have a lot of practice wrestling angels."

"I am a dark angel."

My eyes darted to my flaming sword. The telekinetic blast had knocked it right out of my hands. It was now on the other side of the dark angel, too far out of my reach.

"Angel, dark angel." I shrugged. "Same game, different toys."

"You are a Legion soldier," he said with a hard face. Clearly, my attempts at humor didn't tickle his funny bone. "That blast should have knocked you out."

"And miss this party? No way." I wiped the blood from my nose. The impact had hurt like hell.

The dark angel moved like liquid steel. I avoided the brunt of his blow, but the tail end of the punch tore across my battered ribcage. I fell to my knees, coughing up blood.

"Impossible," he said again as I stood, his eyes wide. "You're weak against dark magic."

I grabbed my whip and attacked. The lightning-charged tail cut through the air and coiled around his leg. I gave it a solid tug, pulling him off balance. He hit the ground with a satisfying thump.

"And you are a dark angel," I told him. "Weak against light magic."

He was already on his feet. "You're resistant to dark magic." Gold flashed across his pale eyes. "There's darkness in you, not just light magic."

I swung the whip again. Fire followed on the tail of lightning, eating into his armor. Another crimson chunk of metal hit the ground with a resounding clunk. I tried to follow up with another attack, but the electric whip was out of juice. It had taken too much magic out of it to zap a dark angel. What just moments ago had been a roaring thunder, was now hardly more than a weak sizzle. I tossed the weapon aside. He struck at me with his sword, but his misshapen armor slowed him down—and lately I'd been practicing how to steal my opponents' weapons. I swung my pilfered sword at him, sprinkling him with tiny flames. A few of them landed on the exposed pieces of his undershirt, visible through the damaged armor.

"And you can wield dark magic," he said, calmly patting out the tiny flames on his shirt.

He was right. Only someone with dark magic could swing that sword without the flames going out. A slow, calculated grin spread across his lips. His hand flashed out, knocking my sword to the ground. He grabbed my wrist and pulled me toward him. My chest slammed into the wall of his armor, dealing a fresh dose of pain to my battered ribs. His arms locked around me like a cage, pinning my arms to my sides. He lowered his head to mine and drew in a deep breath.

"What the hell are you doing?" I demanded, kicking at him.

His feet moved quickly, deflecting my kicks. His hard heels came down on my boots. Now I couldn't move my feet either.

"Shh," he said, his voice a harsh whisper against my ear. "This will hurt less if you don't struggle."

Panic surged inside of me, panic born from the uncertainty of not knowing what he was going to do—and from the certainty of knowing that whatever it was, I wouldn't like it. Twin peaks of pain pierced my throat. The bastard had bitten me! I pushed against his hold, trying to shake him off, but I might as well have tried to move a mountain. Hot, volcanic agony shot through my veins like a river of acid. My blood boiled, my skin broke out in a sweat. I'd never experienced a torment like this. It felt like I was being burned alive from the inside.

And then it was over. The dark angel pulled back. "Incredible," he said, licking a drop of my blood from his lips. "Was it good for you too?" His icy eyes shone with unapologetic cruelty—and with something else. Victory. They shone with victory.

"Stay back, you psychopath," I snapped, snatching up his sword from the ground. The flames surged with a fury that matched my mood perfectly. I swung the blade at him, and the fire streaked through the air, screeching like a bird of prey.

"Incredible," he repeated, jumping back. His eyes darted to my throat. Silver slid over his icy irises. His tongue flicked out to slowly trace his lips.

"I will kill you with your own sword," I warned him.

I held onto that sword and resisted the urge to cover the two puncture marks on my neck. When Nero bit me, it felt good. No, better than good. It felt…right. I could sense my blood inside of him, merging with his own. Like our souls were blending together. When the dark angel bit me, it didn't feel good or right. It felt like an invasion, a violation, an unwelcome torture. It felt like he was ripping me open and tearing off a part of me. He wasn't becoming one with my blood. He was stealing it.

"There's no need for that," the dark angel said. "This fight is over."

Magic boomed like a cannon, and then he was gone. I looked up and found him flying above the battle, his dark silhouette growing smaller and smaller as he rose higher. An opening swirled at the top of the mountain. He flew through it, and it closed behind him.

I looked around. Dead soldiers were scattered across the icy floor. Harker was fighting what remained of the Dark Force. Up above, Nero wrestled with a second dark angel. I swung the dark angel's sword at Colonel Starborn's restraints, shattering the magic that bound her. The chains crumbled from her body, sprinkling to the ground like silver dust. I caught her as she fell. Holding onto the angel with one hand, and a sword in the other, I slowly made my way across the battlefield. The second dark angel swooped in, raining down magic upon us. I pulled us to the side, narrowly escaping a lightning bolt.

The dark angel came around for a second pass. Colonel Starborn was in bad shape. She couldn't even walk without assistance, let alone fight. I looked around for Nero. He'd been fighting the dark angel just a few moments ago. I found him blasting through a rocky cage on the other side of the cavern. The dark angel must have trapped him in there. Nero was too far away, and the dark angel was coming in fast. His comrade might have decided the battle was over, but he sure hadn't gotten the message. A firestorm raged over his head, building up to a devastating release.

A spark ignited, signaling the opening of the floodgates —or, in this case, the fire gates. A fiery waterfall poured down on us. We might make it—if we ran at full speed. But Colonel Starborn couldn't run, and I couldn't carry her out of here fast enough.

Silver flashed past me. Harker stood beside us, holding up an enormous shield. He must have taken it from one of the fallen Dark Force soldiers. Its dark magic consumed the dark angel's fire stream, but not without a price to pay. The shield had been made from dark magic, and Harker was a soldier of light magic. Blisters popped up across his hands, spreading down his arms every moment he held the shield. Pain cut across his face, but he gripped onto it with unyielding determination. He cared for Colonel Starborn, his former mentor. The look in his eyes told me he'd die for her too.

As upset as I was with him for betraying me, I wasn't going to let that happen. He was a good person. He was just horribly misguided. I grabbed the shield from his hands, holding it against the fire falls. Above, Nero tackled the dark angel, shutting off the fire stream. Harker collapsed to his knees beside Colonel Starborn.

"Your arms look awful," I told him.

"I'll live."

I sighed, tossing aside the shield. "How heroic, but now I have to carry both your asses across this cave."

"I like her," Colonel Starborn told Harker with a dry chuckle.

Harker glanced at me. "Yeah, so do I."

I looked up. Nero and the dark angel tumbled through the air, magic and feathers flying in every direction. I grabbed the other dark angel's flaming sword and drew a fiery figure-eight in front of me. The gate lifted, opening up the way out of this cursed mountain.

"How did you do that?" Harker asked in surprise.

"I just copied what the other dark angel did with this sword," I said. "We have to hurry. The gate won't stay open for long."

Harker continued to stare at me, even as I threw down the sword and lifted him over my shoulder. I balanced

Colonel Starborn over the other shoulder. My ribs screamed in protest, but I ignored the pain and kept moving toward the exit, one heavy step at a time. Before I'd joined the Legion and gained magic, carrying two soldiers would have been impossible. Half a year later, it was just painfully slow.

As we reached the gate, I glanced over my shoulder to check on Nero. He was running toward us, the unconscious dark angel swung over his shoulder. I didn't want to imagine what he'd had to do to knock out a dark angel. While I helped Harker and Colonel Starborn into our truck, Nero chained his prisoner up in the trunk. The gate had closed behind us, but it was opening again. Dark Force soldiers sped out in slender trucks of their own, chasing us as we drove away.

"Shoot to kill," Nero instructed Harker.

Harker aimed his gun out of the window. Twin shots of fire exploded out of the barrel. The magic bullets tore through the front wheels of the Dark Force truck behind us. The vehicle flipped over. Harker might not have been able to walk, but that hadn't affected his aim. He shot down the enemy vehicles with flaming bullets—and cold efficiency.

"Nero, that was Seth Battlestorm back there," Harker commented as our truck swerved around a hole the Dark Force had blown in the ice.

Nero's eyes briefly darted back to the unconscious dark angel in our trunk. "And Razeel Silverwing."

The way they spoke the dark angels' names was foreboding.

"Seth Battlestorm and Razeel Silverwing are hell's best reprogramming experts." Harker waved his hand, and a frozen wall shot out of the ground. It crashed down, slamming against the Dark Force's trucks, pushing them back across the ice.

"Reprogramming?" I asked. "Like brainwashing?"

Harker nodded. "The Dark Force uses them to capture and corrupt supernaturals and Legion soldiers. And, when they're feeling ambitious, an angel. Battlestorm and Silverwing are the strongest telepaths of all the dark angels. And they use that magic to warp their prisoners' minds."

"If they're powerful telepaths, that explains how they captured Colonel Starborn's mind in her dreams."

"Yes," Colonel Starborn said, stirring beside me.

I helped her sit up.

"I was overworked, up too late every night, digging too deep in magic that drained me," she said. "I thought I could handle it, but I couldn't. I should have realized what was going on, what these images of the Fire Mountains meant, why I felt compelled to go there. They controlled my dreams and planted that idea in my subconscious." Anger burned inside her eyes. "I left the castle. I put everyone in danger."

"It wasn't you," Harker told her as we drove under the wall. We were now safely on the right side of the world. "You thought you were dreaming when you left the castle."

She shook her head. "That's no excuse. I messed up, and I have to fix it. You need to bring me back to Storm Castle. Now. The other Dragons need me. Without me, the castle is not safe. The defenses are not secure. The magic is not balanced. I have to get back!"

I held her back before she tried to fly to the castle herself. She'd never make it there in this state.

"It's all right," I told her. "Captain Somerset is filling in as the Fire Dragon. She's keeping your element in sync—and the castle safe."

Colonel Starborn sighed. She looked relieved—and sad.

"What happened back there?" Harker asked her. "What did the Dark Force want with you? The usual, to turn you?"

"No, not the usual." She shook her head. "Not the usual at all. They didn't want to make me a dark angel. When angels go dark, they gain dark magic but lose their light magic. The Dark Forces wanted to turn me into an angel who could wield both light and dark magic."

"Such an angel, one with complete power over both light and dark, would be doubly powerful," Nero realized.

"Doubly powerful, and doubly resistant to light and dark magic," Colonel Starborn said.

Nero frowned. "They would be powerful soldiers and perfect spies."

"If you were in the Fire Mountains, you must have encountered the monsters there," she said.

"Encountered and killed," I told her.

"All of them?"

"Yes." I hadn't felt a single monster since we'd fried the horde against the base's barrier. "Were those the Dark Force's monsters?"

"The magic at the heart of the Fire Mountains is very potent. Powerful enough to turn regular monsters into perfectly balanced light-dark specimens," Colonel Starborn said. "The Dark Force was trying to do the same thing to me. It didn't go as they'd hoped."

"The dark magic didn't take because your light magic is too strong," Harker said.

"It didn't work because it's not possible," she retorted. "Monsters are one thing, but people are another. Our magic is considerably more complex, especially the magic of a Legion soldier. We possess both light and darkness inside of us in varying degrees, but no one can wield both light and dark magic. It's simply not possible. Nectar and Venom are jealous, volatile poisons. Only one can exist in a body at once."

"That's not entirely true," Harker said, glancing at me.

Colonel Starborn looked from him to me. "What do you mean?"

Harker shook his head. "Never mind. Just rest. You'll need your strength when you return to Storm Castle."

"I'm afraid to fall asleep…after what happened the last time I closed my eyes," she admitted, trembling.

Harker set his hand on her shoulder. "I will watch over you. No one will hurt you," he promised.

He spoke with such devotion, such loyalty. It reminded me of why I'd liked him. He loved her like a sister, and I had no doubt in my mind that he would do anything to save her, even if it meant challenging the gods themselves. I couldn't blame him for not extending that same loyalty to me. He'd only known me for a month when a god told him to give me a vial of Nectar that would kill me. No, I didn't blame him, but I didn't forgive him either.

CHAPTER EIGHTEEN
A Perfect Soldier

I SAT BESIDE Colonel Starborn's bed in the medical ward of Desert Rose's Legion base. Nero was off interrogating the dark angel Razeel Silverwing. I debated going back to the elemental magic training rooms but ultimately decided that Colonel Starborn needed me more than I needed another solid ass-kicking. The base's doctors had healed my fractured ribs, but the angel's injuries were far more extensive.

"Leda Pierce."

I looked at the angel wiping sleep from her eyes. "How did you sleep?"

"Better than I have in many weeks." She dipped her chin to me. "Thank you for the rescue."

"Thank you for not turning."

The last thing the world needed was another dark angel wreaking havoc on humanity—or a doubly powerful light-dark angel wreaking havoc on humanity. She might not have thought a Legion soldier could wield both light and dark magic, but I was living proof that it was possible. I'd held the dark angel's flaming sword, and it hadn't gone out.

I'd drunk both Nectar and Venom. There was dark magic in me too. Harker had been this close to telling Colonel Starborn about it, but he'd stopped himself. He hadn't betrayed me this time.

"How is Storm Castle? Is it well?" She wasn't asking about the castle. She wanted to know how Captain Somerset was doing.

"She is doing well," I told her.

A small smile broke the angel's lips.

"You were close."

"Yes, long ago. She was my student, like Harker. When her previous mentor died, I offered to train her. She was very good, a rising star. She had so much ambition." Colonel Starborn sighed. "But she didn't stay long, only a few months. We never formed the magical bond of student and teacher that I have with Harker."

"You regret that."

"Yes."

I'd always been so sure of what everyone was and what they weren't. I'd been so wrong. Sitting here, I was beginning to realize that angels could regret. They weren't as infallible as they pretended to be—and they felt more than they'd ever admit. And when they did feel something, those feelings were as strong as the magic that flowed through their blood. It only took one look at the pain burning in Colonel Starborn's eyes to realize how deep her feelings ran.

"We were close almost at once," she told me.

"But you grew apart."

"I pushed her away. Not consciously. I was just acting as I thought was right. Duty to the Legion above all else. I didn't consider that she was different, so new to the Legion.

She didn't know the ways of the angels. The ways of the Legion."

It always came down to the same issue.

"Do you know why there are so few angel matings?" she asked me.

"Too much Nectar in the human body changes its balance. Two people with powerful light magic cannot produce children, so an angel is always mated with a soldier of a lower level, someone the Legion's tests confirm to be a good magical match. Each person's body integrates the Nectar differently."

"Yes," she said. "Nero is rare, the child of two angels. One of a kind. Nero's parents' pairing worked because his father was dark enough, though they didn't realize this at the time. That darkness made them compatible. That made Nero's conception possible."

"The Legion wants to have as many angels as they can get," she continued. "So it decides whom its angels will marry. Pairings are made to create the highest chance of magic-rich children. A few years after I became an angel, when I was fertile for the first time, the Legion married me to another soldier in the hopes we would have a child." A look of sadness washed across her face.

"You didn't love him?" I guessed.

"Caleb was my best friend. I loved him like a brother. We'd been friends since we were initiated into the Legion together. We were both shocked when the magic tests showed us to be compatible, but we did our duty. We were married for many years without producing a child. Then I met Basanti. She knew about him, about our marriage. She said it didn't matter." Colonel Starborn frowned. "Until it did."

"What happened?"

"Do you know what happens when a female angel becomes fertile?"

I nodded, remembering Nerissa's speech about angel fertility. "It heightens the emotions of everyone around you."

"Basanti's emotions were very heightened when she attacked Caleb one evening in my apartment. We all said things we regretted." Resignation hardened her voice. "I went away with Caleb the next morning on our retreat. When I returned, Basanti informed me that she was leaving. She'd applied for a transfer to another office. This whole thing was too much for her. I tried to explain I was just fulfilling my duty as an angel, to make soldiers for the Legion, but she couldn't separate personal and professional. She even liked Caleb, but after that evening she couldn't stand to be around either of us. She felt betrayed. And every time she looked at us, she saw that betrayal. She couldn't be with me as long as I was married to him. Even after he married someone else, it was too late for us."

"I didn't know you could get out of a marriage the Legion arranged."

"It's hard for an angel to produce a child, especially a female angel."

That explained why most Legion brats had an angel father, not an angel mother.

"Even under perfect magic circumstances, even when everything is aligned, conception is very unlikely," she continued. "After many years of us not producing a child, the Legion decided we weren't compatible enough, that it wasn't meant to be. They allowed Caleb to marry someone else. I haven't been magically compatible with anyone else since, at least not enough to be paired."

Magic was incredibly complex. Merging magic was even more so. That's why angels rarely had children—and why the Dark Force hadn't been able to merge dark magic with Colonel Starborn's light magic.

"An angel's magic is very fixed," she said. "It's harder for us to level up our magic than it is for you. Each level takes more effort than the last."

I tried hard not to think about Nero's upcoming trials, the level ten ceremony. Damiel had said it would be like nothing he'd ever faced before.

"Angel magic is so set in its state," Colonel Starborn told me. "The dark angels knew what they were trying to do to me had never before been done, that it was most certainly impossible. They fully expected me to die."

But I had a light-dark balance. What did it mean?

"Why did the Dark Force take the risk?" I asked her. "Why go through all the effort to abduct an angel they expected to die?"

"They were tempted by the promise of a perfect soldier, I suppose. We've all been tempted at some point or another." Her eyes shifted upward in a thoughtful gaze.

"You?" I said in surprise.

She'd insisted the merging wasn't possible. And yet the wistful look in her eyes now told me she'd once tried to gain that power.

"Yes," she said, her voice strained with guilt. "Before the dark angels lured me out to the Fire Mountains that night, I was…dabbling."

Just like the other Dragons had said.

"I was trying to grow the castle's elemental power—and to do so, I experimented with dark magic. I thought if I could gain mastery over the entire spectrum of elemental magic, from light to dark, I could make Storm Castle more powerful than ever before. And with that power, we could change the world."

"And put the wild lands back to the way they were before the monsters invaded," I said.

"Among other things." She shook her head. "But none of my experiments to grow the castle's magic panned out. It was for the best. Tampering with light and dark magic can only lead to disaster. Just look at what happened to me. If I hadn't meddled, none of this would have happened. There never would have been monsters on the wrong side of the wall."

"What do you…" I stopped when I saw the look of unfiltered guilt on her face. "The Dark Force didn't create the monsters we found in the Fire Mountains, did they?"

"No."

"You did."

"Yes, I. So caught up in my experiments, in my crusade to master the full spectrum of magic, I created the monsters deep inside the Fire Mountains. That's why it was so easy for the dark angels to lure me out to the mountains. I'd already been spending so much time there. I was obsessed. I trained the monsters to guard my workshop. When they produced offspring with the same perfect light-dark balance, I saw it as an affirmation that I had succeeded, not as a warning to stop. I didn't even think about the consequences of so many monsters living on the wrong side of the wall."

"The Dark Force found out about what you were doing, didn't they?"

"When you reach for the powers of hell, hell reaches

back." She tried to sit up, wincing against the pain.

I set my hand on her. "You're not healed yet. You're lucky to be alive."

"But I am alive," she replied. "Because of you. And Nero. And Harker."

"Harker threw himself in the path of danger for you. That dark magic shield could have killed him," I said. "He really cares about you."

"He always tries to do the right thing."

I arched my brows. "But sometimes that's why he does exactly the wrong thing."

"Indeed," she agreed. "Some of that is my fault. I taught him about light magic, about being pious and good. I took it so seriously back then. After…"

"After what happened to Nero's parents," I finished for her.

Colonel Starborn blinked in surprise.

"Nero told me you were his mother's protege."

"Yes, I was. I blamed dark magic for what happened to Cadence. I thought it was evil, that duty was the most important thing in the world. Duty to the Legion, to the gods. I thought it was Cadence's disloyalty that was her downfall."

"Disloyalty?"

"Or more like her loyalty to Damiel. Her blind love for him. They knew the Legion was coming for him, that she would be assigned to hunt him down. He'd defied them."

"How?" I asked.

"By dabbling in dark magic."

Colonel Starborn had done the same. Would they try to kill her too if they found out? She didn't seem concerned. Maybe she realized I wouldn't betray her secret.

"Damiel was…different from us," she said. "He had a dark side. Cadence was so light, so pure. That's how she got the name Lightbringer when she became an angel. But she was always attracted to the darkness, to Damiel."

I heard Nero come in. I knew the sound of his gait. He could have muted his steps. The fact that he hadn't was not insignificant. He wanted us to know he was here. He was giving Colonel Starborn the choice to stop talking. She kept going.

"After Cadence's disappearance, I clung to duty, to my loyalty to the Legion. Those things defined me for many years, paving the way for me to become an angel. And it was those two things that I passed onto my disciple Harker. He took them to heart," she said. "At the time, I didn't realize the light was not so perfect after all."

"What happened?" I asked her.

"I saw Cadence."

I looked back to gauge Nero's reaction. He was very still, eerily quiet. He hadn't cleaned up since our trip to the Sea of Ice, and interrogating the dark angel hadn't helped with his terrifying, blood-stained appearance.

Colonel Starborn met his eyes. "I really saw her, Nero."

A hint of relief flashed across his face. He was finally starting to believe his mother was truly alive.

"I didn't see her in person," she amended quickly. "I saw her in my mind. She used our connection—and her telepathic magic—to reach out to me. I'd spent years blaming myself for helping her and Damiel escape. I thought he'd betrayed and killed her. When she spoke to me that day, she told me he'd never betrayed her. During the escape, they'd gotten separated, and she'd found herself in a new and wondrous place. A place where powerful magical beings protected her and other refugees."

"The Guardians," I said.

"So you've heard of them."

I looked at Nero. "We've heard the name, but we don't know what they do or who they really are."

"No one does. Not any of us out here anyway," replied Colonel Starborn.

"Out here?"

"Cadence told me the Guardians live in a dimension outside of our own. They speak to us in visions, in dreams. And sometimes people find their way to them. By searching, by being found, by mere chance. The Guardians found Cadence in the Western Wilderness. She was almost dead, her injuries severe. She'd just escaped captivity. Her captor had mutilated her wings to keep her in a cage, so she couldn't fly away."

Her captor. That was Raven, the man who'd been abhorrent even before he'd been turned into a vampire.

"The Guardians brought Cadence to their dimension. They healed her, bringing her back from the brink of death. She is with them even now."

"Damiel is looking for her," I said.

"She knows."

"Then why hasn't she left?"

"I don't know."

"I know," Nero muttered, his tone making his dislike for his father perfectly clear.

"When I talked to her, I got the feeling she wants to go to him, but she can't," Colonel Starborn told him.

"Why?" I asked.

She shook her head. "I don't know."

"Can you lead us to my mother?" Nero asked her.

"No. She is outside our dimension. She can contact me, but I can't find her. At least not under normal conditions." She bit down on her lip, her eyes lifting in contemplation. "When I was trapped in that dark nightmare being tortured, I reached out to anyone and everyone I cared about. Cadence must have heard me because she answered my call. She told me she was sending someone to get me out of there."

I looked at Nero. "The voice I heard in my head in the Fire Mountains, the voice who told me where the dark angels had taken Colonel Starborn, that must have been your mother trying to help us save her."

"That's something Cadence would do," Colonel Starborn said. "She was always so kind."

"If she has been alive all this time, why hasn't she reached out to me?" Nero asked her.

He looked so young, so vulnerable, so different from his usual hard, tough exterior. When I saw that vulnerability peek out from his armor, it made me want to throw my arms around him and give him a big hug.

"I don't know why she hasn't contacted you," replied Colonel Starborn. "We'll ask her when we find her."

"Yes. We will."

"I have a lot to say to her," she said. "Most of all, I have to apologize for doubting her."

"We all make mistakes," I told her. "What matters is not those mistakes, but what we do after them. That is what defines us, who we are, what we stand for."

"Yes. I need to stop the demons. I need to clean up the mess I've made, the mess the Dark Force has usurped for their own purposes."

"That's not what I meant. I know you will fight to the

end to stop the demons. I meant you and Captain Somerset. It's never too late to fix things." I could feel Nero's eyes on me.

"I don't think she wants to hear what I have to say," Colonel Starborn told me.

"I think she can be convinced. When I talked to her, she sounded like she regretted what happened between you two."

Hope lit up her eyes. "Really?"

"Really. You were both unwilling to back down, unwilling to accept the other without change. Love isn't conditional. It isn't about changing the other person. It is about accepting someone for who they are."

Colonel Starborn gave me a long, assessing look. "You are very wise for someone so young."

"I might know a thing or two about it."

She tried to sit up again, rising nearly an inch before she fell back down. "This is unacceptable," she stated with the cold ferocity of an angel.

"Give it time," I said.

"If only I had time. But the Dark Force is not done with us. I fear what they did to me was just the tip of the iceberg. I was so foolish."

"You were trying to grow the castle's magic and banish the monsters from this Earth. That wasn't foolish. It was very brave," I told her.

"It wasn't just about the castle and the monsters," she admitted.

"Oh?"

"I was looking for Cadence."

Nero watched her in silence.

"Before Cadence disappeared, she told me not to look

for her, but I just couldn't help myself," she continued. "I had to see her. I thought if I grew my magic, I could find her."

I could totally relate. After all, I'd joined the Legion to gain the magic I needed to find my brother.

"I thought if I could wield spells of dark and light, I could break the boundaries between realms and open a way to her," Colonel Starborn said. "But it didn't work out at all the way I'd hoped. I am the reason for all of this. My fiddling with the forces of magic attracted the attention of the Dark Force. It gave them the idea to blend magic. It allowed them to snatch me in my sleep, to control me because I'd opened my mind to their realm, their magic. This is all because of me."

"What is the Dark Force's next move?" I asked her. "What are they planning?"

"I don't know." She looked at Nero. "Has Silverwing shared anything with you?"

He frowned. "No, the dark angel has been less than forthcoming. Major Singh offered to interrogate him herself."

"She's ambitious," commented Colonel Starborn.

The Legion always assigned an angel to interrogate a dark angel. According to Major Horn, Major Singh had aspirations of becoming an angel, and breaking a dark angel was just the way to prove herself worthy of the promotion.

"Yes, she is," said Nero. "But Nyx has assigned Colonel Fireswift the task of breaking him."

"He has broken more dark angels than any other Interrogator."

"Yes. But he isn't an Interrogator anymore."

Colonel Starborn chuckled. "You two are still fighting?

It's been nearly two hundred years, Nero."

"As you know, Leila, immortals have long memories."

"I know," she sighed. "When will Colonel Fireswift arrive?"

"He won't. We're to bring the prisoner to him."

"I guess he couldn't take time away from his busy schedule of killing all my friends," I commented.

Colonel Starborn looked at me in surprise.

"Yeah, I don't get along with him either," I told her. "He's trying to promote as many Legion soldiers in New York as he can, and he doesn't care how many die in the process."

"He is better suited to interrogating than leading," she said. "I wonder why the First Angel didn't keep him as an Interrogator."

"Because the Legion doesn't have enough angels to go around," Nero said. "And if we don't find out what the Dark Force is doing and stop them, we might lose more angels to the demons."

"I think I can help you with that," Harker declared as he entered the room. He looked even worse than Nero. Blood was splattered like a crimson tattoo across his skin.

Nero gave him a long, hard look. "You have been interrogating the prisoner."

Harker did not deny it.

"I forbade you from going in there," Nero said, his voice hard and cold. "Silverwing is too powerful."

"Your concern is touching."

"That dark angel is one of the Dark Force's most powerful telepaths, Harker. He could have attacked your mind and confused you into releasing him."

Harker folded his arms across his chest. "I am stronger

than you think, Nero. And besides, I made sure he wasn't able to concentrate long enough to attack my mind."

"You had no right."

"Save the lecture for tomorrow. I've found out what the demons are really planning," Harker declared. He looked at Colonel Starborn. "This was never about turning you into a hybrid angel. This is bigger."

What could possibly be bigger than turning an angel... I gasped. "Storm Castle."

"You always were clever, Leda," Harker told me with an approving nod. "The Dark Force wants to gain control over Storm Castle. They have already turned the other three Dragons."

"When did this happen?" Colonel Starborn asked.

"Weeks ago."

"When I was too busy playing with magic to see what was going on right under my nose. Storm Castle and the Dragons were my responsibility. I was supposed to protect them." Anger flashed in her turquoise eyes. "I will not fail them again. And I will not allow the Dark Force to take control of Storm Castle."

Nero's eyes looked up from his phone. "Major Horn tells me the castle has gone silent."

"The Dark Force was after Storm Castle the whole time," Harker said.

"They just needed the fourth Dragon to gain control over the castle's magic," I added. "When they failed to turn you, they would have gone after—"

"Basanti." She jumped up so fast that she fell out of the bed.

Harker caught her before she hit the floor. "You can't go. You're still too weak."

222

She snapped her head around to look at Nero. "Get me healed. Fast. Use a Powershot."

"What is a Powershot?" I asked.

"A rapid healing technique used in war," Nero told me. "It gives you a few hours at full power with no pain, but it's temporary. When the magic wears out, you crash. And your pain returns with a vengeance."

"No." Harker's eyes were locked on Nero. They weren't angry, though; they were pleading with him. "It could kill her."

"Don't underestimate me," Colonel Starborn said.

"Your magic has just been through the blender. The dark angels have been chipping away at you for weeks. No matter how powerful you usually are, you know you aren't there now, Leila."

"It doesn't matter. I will hold on for as long as we need to stop Battlestorm's army from taking the castle," she said. "There's no time for this, Harker. The other three Dragons are under the Dark Force's control. If the castle has gone silent, chances are good Battlestorm is already there, torturing Basanti. We have to get there before they turn her and gain control over the castle and all its magic."

"She's right," Nero told him, magic glowing on his hands.

Harker tried to put himself between Nero and Colonel Starborn, but his feet wouldn't move. Nero had locked them to the ground. It was a telekinetic trick I'd seen him use before. Harker pushed against the invisible magic holding him in place.

"Stop." Colonel Starborn's voice snapped with command.

Harker stopped, as if controlled by magic.

"We have to do this," she told him. "You know that. Our first duty is to this world and the people in it. We stand between them and destruction. We are the protectors of the weak. If the Dark Force controls Storm Castle, they could create storms that rage across the whole world, devastating cities and bringing down the wall that keeps out the monsters. We must stop them, and our best chance of doing that is with me at full power."

Harker's sense of duty to the Legion battled it out with his desire to protect his mentor. I saw it in his eyes. It must have been tough for him. He lived and breathed his duty to the Legion, but he loved Colonel Starborn more than anything else. She was the sister he would die for. But she wasn't asking him to die for her. That wouldn't help anyone. What we needed right now was all of us at full strength, fighting the Dark Force to take back our castle.

Harker met her eyes with a vicious smile. "Let's send the Dark Force back to hell where they belong."

CHAPTER NINETEEN
Battlestorm

A STORM BREWED over the Dragons' Castle—and we were driving right for it. Nero, Harker, Colonel Starborn, and I sat in the truck. Major Singh had come along too. Apparently, kicking Dark Force ass was a hobby of hers.

Colonel Starborn sat beside me, pumped up on the quick-fix magic that injured soldiers used to survive gruesome battles. She kept squeezing her fists, as though she couldn't wait to plow through the Dark Force, rescue Basanti, and reclaim her castle—not necessarily in that order.

The storm was spreading across Desert Rose, the Sky Plains, and the Wetlands. The fact that it hadn't yet hit the Fire Mountains gave me hope that Captain Somerset was still holding out.

"Hold on," Nero warned us as he swerved the truck to the right to avoid a massive lightning bolt.

I looked up at a purple sky streaked with gold. More lightning bolts slammed down, bigger and brighter than their smaller cousins I'd faced in the Dragons' obstacle courses, big enough to cut right through our truck. The earth shook beneath our wheels. Fissures split the ground, growing into rifts. A raging river flooded the cracked earth like a stampede of a thousand stallions. It froze as it grew, moving like a hyperactive glacier across the land. Nero turned the truck onto it, riding the ice wave toward the castle.

"He's crazy," I told Colonel Starborn through the frosty fog swaddling us like a diamond blanket.

"But that's why you love him, isn't it?" she said in a low whisper, so quiet I could hardly hear her over the raging storm. I didn't think Nero, Harker, or Major Singh could hear her from the front seat.

"I…"

"He loves you too, you know," she told me.

I blinked.

"He wouldn't risk Nyx's wrath for just anyone. I'm enormously impressed you convinced Nero Toe-the-Line Windstriker to disobey orders and galavant across the Black Plains with you." She chuckled.

"Nero didn't disobey any orders. We just happened to be after the same thing. And going in the same direction. Which we did in an orderly and dignified manner without galavanting of any kind."

"As befits a soldier of the Legion."

"Exactly."

She snorted. "I take it Nyx didn't buy that load of bullshit either."

"How do you figure that?"

"She made Nero leave New York."

"She's promoting him."

"Nyx could have promoted him *and* kept him in New York."

She had a point.

"The First Angel doesn't like to shake things up," Colonel Starborn told me. "She won't reassign an angel unless she believes there's a problem."

I guess that made me the problem.

"Nero doesn't see you as a problem," she told me.

"Are you reading my thoughts?"

"Would you believe me if I said no?"

"No."

The truck quivered as we broke through into the eye of the storm. But a whole other storm was brewing here. The road to the castle was saturated in dark magic.

"The Dark Force's soldiers are inside," Nero said, stopping the truck. "The mountain is too exposed. If we try to climb up, they'll shoot us down before we reach the top. We'll take the lower entrance." He pressed his hand against the mountain. The rocks groaned, parting to reveal an opening.

"There's a lower entrance." A pitiful laugh broke my lips, and I shook my head. "Why did I even bother climbing the mountain?"

"Because it builds character, Pandora," Harker said with a smile, slapping me on the back.

We entered a tunnel only to be ambushed by Dark Force soldiers. Major Singh cracked the icy tail of her whip in the air. Beside her, Nero's telekinetic tug pulled the soldiers in, and she froze them with a snap of her whip. Tug and snap, tug and snap—they worked in perfect unison.

"Don't feel bad," Harker told me as the last enemy soldier fell. "They've had decades to train and fight together."

I resisted the urge to knock him upside the head. We'd

probably need him to defeat Battlestorm's forces and take back our castle.

"Has anyone ever told you that you're a real—" Pain exploded in my neck, pouring out in pulsing, burning waves from the exact spot Battlestorm had bitten me.

"What's wrong?" Harker asked me, genuine concern crinkling his brow.

"I can feel him," I choked out. The pain had spread to my head. Right now, I was fighting the mother of all migraines.

"Who?"

"Battlestorm."

Harker's gaze dropped to my neck. "He bit you."

Nero was suddenly beside us. "Who bit you?" he asked me, his hand locking around my arm.

"Battlestorm. Back in the mountain on the Sea of Ice."

"Why didn't you tell me?" His eyes burned with cold fire.

I met those eyes. "Because I knew how you'd react."

"I'm going to kill that dark angel," Nero swore.

"Yep, just like that."

"This is serious, Leda."

"No shit, Nero. Whatever he did to me, it hurts like hell."

"That's the Venom," Colonel Starborn told me.

"Venom?"

"In his fangs. Legion soldiers have a small dose of Nectar in their blood and their bite. Dark Force soldiers are the same, except with Venom," she explained as we entered the stairwell. "Don't worry, the amount of Venom in even a dark angel's bite is really, really tiny. Battlestorm bit me too when he was trying to turn me. It stings for a while until the Nectar in your body destroys the Venom."

Icicles fell from the spiral stairwell's high ceiling. Nero waved his hand in a smooth, overhead arc, drawing a burning rainbow on top of us. The icicles dissolved into steam when they hit the rainbow.

"The Sea Dragon," Nero said, waving at Major Singh. "We're going after her. Be right back."

Without another word, he punched through a wall of frost, running down a chilly hallway with Major Singh in search of the rogue Dragon.

The rest of us kept climbing stairs.

"It's not getting better," I told Colonel Starborn two floors later. "It's getting worse."

"Oh."

"Oh? What does *that* mean?"

"It means your body isn't fighting the Venom, and you're probably going to die."

You could always trust an angel to be brutally honest.

"I'm not going to die," I told her, biting back the pain.

"How do you figure that?"

"It's not convenient for me to die right now."

She laughed.

"Plus, I've had some experience with Venom," I added.

"What kind of experience?"

"At my last promotion ceremony, someone laced my Nectar with Venom."

"What?" she gasped in shock. "Who did this? *How* did they do it?"

"I don't know." I pressed my hand to my throbbing neck. "I think… I think the pain is growing stronger the closer I get to Battlestorm."

"So you can track him?" Harker asked.

"Yes. He's in the Fire Tower," I said.

Colonel Starborn and Harker exchanged loaded looks.

"We should wait for Nero," she said.

"But we're not going to," he replied.

"No. We're not. I can feel Basanti's mind breaking. We can't afford to wait. We move on Battlestorm now."

We found Seth Battlestorm at the top of the Fire Tower. Captain Somerset was chained to the wall in front of him. Her uniform was in tatters, her dark braid unraveling, her body a timeline of cuts and bruises. Tiny tremors shook her shoulders, rippling down her torso to her arms and legs. Her jaw was clenched in stubborn defiance. She was still fighting Battlestorm—and whatever he was doing to her.

"Stop," the dark angel said, turning around slowly to face us. His dark eyes lit up with silver and gold when he saw me. "You." His tongue traced the tip of his left fang. "I'll deal with you soon enough. After I'm done with her." His gaze shifted to his prisoner.

Fire erupted across Colonel Starborn's blade.

"Put that out, Leila," Battlestorm said impatiently. "You're too late. The Venom will consume her."

"She's stronger than you think."

"No, she's not. The change is killing her. She won't make it. Not unless I stop now." He shot the angel a saccharine smile.

"What do you want?" she demanded, her voice simmering with barely-contained violence.

"I propose a trade. If you surrender yourself to me—and to the change—I'll cure your scorned lover."

"Don't do it, Leila," Captain Somerset croaked out.

Colonel Starborn's eyes shifted from her to the dark angel. Love was overriding reason. She was going to do it. Why? She must have realized that Battlestorm was going to kill Captain Somerset either way.

"We don't make deals with the forces of darkness," Harker stated, stepping in front of his mentor.

"What a shame."

The dark angel pulled out a syringe and jammed it into Captain Somerset's arm. She began to convulse.

"What was that?" I demanded.

He smiled at me. "Pure Venom."

In other words, a death sentence. Pure Venom would kill a Dark Force soldier in minutes. Captain Somerset, a soldier of light magic, didn't even have that long. As Colonel Starborn and I rushed to her, Harker shot past us. His face contorted with raw anguish, he tackled Battlestorm. He was going to avenge his friend. He thought she was already dead. But I wasn't ready to give up on her.

"It's spreading fast," I said, watching the Venom blacken her veins. I remembered how Nero had drained his mark from me by drinking my changed blood, just as you would drain poison. "We have to drink the Venom out of her."

Colonel Starborn waved her hand, dissolving the chains to dust. She reached for Captain Somerset's arm.

"No, not you." I cut her off. "You have too much light magic. The Venom will kill you."

I didn't hesitate. There wasn't any time for second thoughts. I grabbed Captain Somerset's convulsing arm with both my hands and sank my fangs into the black vein. I drained the Venom from her. When my mouth was full, I pulled back just enough to spit out the contaminated blood, then I went back to drain more. I repeated the motion three times before the black tint faded from her veins.

"I drained most of the Venom from her, but a few drops remain that I can't get," I told Colonel Starborn. "Can you use your magic to cleanse the remaining Venom from her blood?"

She set her glowing hands on the small punctures I'd left on Captain Somerset's arm. "I will try."

I coughed.

"Are you all right?"

"Fine," I said.

I'd tried to spit out all of the Venom, but some of it had already slid down my throat. It had a sweet taste, not quite like Nectar. Different. But delicious. It was a potent punch to my system, jolting me awake. I felt so alive.

"Are you sure?" Colonel Starborn asked as I swayed to the side.

My hands were shaking. My body was having trouble dealing with the power rush. My legs gave out from under me. My knees hit the floor. Colonel Starborn moved to help me.

"No," I snapped. "Not me. You have to keep healing Captain Somerset. If you stop, she won't survive."

"You'll die, you know." She kept her glowing hands on Captain Somerset's arm.

I rose slowly to my feet. "I've survived Venom before. I can handle a few drops." A convulsion shot down my body from tip to toe. I caught myself on a stone pillar to stay upright.

"A few drops of pure Venom will kill an angel."

"Then it's a good thing I'm no angel," I replied. "I have my fair share of darkness."

Despite my nonchalant smile, I wasn't feeling all that confident. My vision was blurring. The Venom was pulling me under. Beside me, Colonel Starborn was healing Captain Somerset as fast as she could, pouring all her magic into destroying the Venom I hadn't been able to drain.

Harker was still fighting Battlestorm, but things weren't looking good for him. The Sea, Sky, and Earth Dragons burst through the door, Nero and Major Singh hot on their tails. Had they chased the three Dragons all the way here?

The Sky Dragon spun around and hurled a lightning bolt. The Sea Dragon cast an icy spike, and the Earth Dragon cooked up a bouquet of Soul-eater Vines. The Dragons' elemental salad exploded at Nero and Major Singh's feet, releasing a magical miasma of light and dark magic. Pieces of furniture shot in every direction.

"They did it," I said, steadying my steps as I moved away from the pillar. "The Dark Force created soldiers who could wield both light and dark magic."

Nero and Major Singh jumped to their feet, brushing the remnants of the elemental explosion off their leather uniforms. The magic shockwave had thrown Harker clear across the room. I reached down and pulled him to his feet —then I pushed him toward Colonel Starborn and Captain Somerset.

"Protect them," I told him.

The explosion had also ignited the Venom inside of me. With every step that I took toward Battlestorm, I was growing stronger. I could feel the dark magic cascading through my body. I drew my guns and fired at him. Leg, arm, wing, stomach. Dark magic ignited on the bullets, tearing through his armor. Dark angels were strong against dark magic, but they were not immune. Nor were they immune to bullets.

I shot him in the wing again because that spot seemed to hurt him the most. He snarled in pain, and his wing went limp. He countered with a psychic blast that knocked me against the wall. My back bounced off the bricks, and my face hit the floor. Woozy, lightheaded, I peeled myself off the ground and shot him again. The dark angel roared in pain, then launched himself into the air, flying away with one crooked wing. The three Dragons covered his ragged retreat with another elemental cocktail. Spells boomed and bellowed across the full spectrum. Light and dark melded together. A storm was building, boosted by the castle's magic.

"That's enough," I growled under my breath. I ran at the three Dragons, taking the brunt of their assault head-on. The wall of magic hit me, and I blacked out.

"Leda."

Something was tapping against my cheek. I batted it away.

"What were you thinking?" Nero demanded. He sounded upset.

I opened my eyes to stare up into his face. He looked upset too.

"Explain yourself."

I rubbed my head, wincing when I found a sizable bump there. "I was protecting you from the blast."

"Excuse me?"

"Of course you're excused."

"What?"

"I forgive you."

His eyebrows drew together. "For what?"

"For wearing yellow socks."

"She's delirious," Harker commented.

I tried to sit up. When that didn't work, I decided lying on the floor was the next best thing. I began to close my eyes.

Nero shook my shoulders.

"That's annoying," I told him.

"You need to stay conscious."

"You can't tell me what to do." My eyelids were so heavy.

"Of course I can."

"Says who?"

"Says me. And the rank on my uniform."

I squinted up at him. "Then take off your uniform."

Captain Somerset laughed. "I think she's hitting on you, Nero. She must be feeling better."

"Or worse."

The cold bite in that voice brought my mind back to the interrogation I'd witnessed last week—and the viciously intelligent Interrogator who had manipulated a witch into signing away her life to the Legion. It was like a splash of cold water.

I tried to sit up again. This time, it actually worked. Captain Somerset and Major Singh stood on either side of Nero. Harker stood with Colonel Starborn. We were all still in the Fire Tower. The three Dragons lay dead on the floor.

"How long was I out?" I asked. "What happened?"

"Roughly two minutes, and we killed the corrupted

Dragons," Major Singh told me.

I looked out the window. "If you killed the Dragons, why is the storm raging stronger than ever?"

"We weren't fast enough," said Colonel Starborn. "Their spell has reached the edge of the Elemental Expanse. Soon, it will ravage the world, pushing across sky, water, and land. Moving faster than any living thing or machine can go. It will devastate the Earth's cities and short-circuit the wall protecting civilization from the plains of monsters."

"How is this possible?" I asked. "They didn't have a Fire Dragon to help them."

"They didn't need one. With their magic doubled, they had more than enough power to cast the storm."

"So we're talking about hurricanes, tornados, earthquakes, and thunderstorms without the volcanic ash and fire falling from the sky?"

"Basically."

"Splendid," I said grimly. "How do we stop it?"

"We can't."

I rose to my feet. The room shook—and not from the Dragons' storm. I blinked a few times.

"What do you think you're doing?" Nero demanded.

"Standing. Looking up at all of you is hurting my neck."

"You have a head injury."

"I'll have an even bigger one if the castle falls on my head."

Nero shook his head slowly, clearly baffled by my superior logic.

"I'll heal her," Harker offered.

"No." Nero moved into his path. "I'll do it."

He set his palms on either side of my face. A warmth

pulsed out from his hands, and the throbbing ache in my head dulled. I caught Nero as he staggered to the side. My vision once again clear, I noticed how battered he looked—how battered they all looked.

"What happened to you?" I asked them.

"Taking out the Dragons proved to be more difficult than anticipated," Colonel Starborn told me.

"You all look half-dead."

"That would be an accurate description of how I feel," Harker said.

No wonder no one had tried to heal me earlier. They didn't have much magic left in them. How much had fixing my head just cost Nero? He stood tall and battle-ready beside me. He was putting on a good show. Only the intermittent flicker of pain in his eyes gave him away.

I turned at the rustle of movement from the staircase. Soren and Nerissa were coming up the steps. They looked like they'd just fought their way through hell.

"What happened to you?" I asked them.

"Earlier today, the Dragons summoned everyone in the castle to a ceremony in the throne room," Soren said.

"As soon as we got there, the ground sank into the dungeons, trapping us down there," Nerissa added as several of the castle's staff came up the stairs behind them. One of them was the master magic smith, just the man I needed.

"I need to borrow the Lightning Spear," I told him.

"You want to borrow an immortal weapon?"

"I want to borrow *that* immortal weapon."

"Why?"

"I need something that can absorb a lot of magic." I waved at the storm raging outside.

He shook his head. "The storm is too powerful."

"You said the rod was indestructible," I reminded him.

"It is, but even it has limits as to how much magic it can absorb. Once it's full, it will spit the magic back out. The concentrated blasts of magic will devastate the Elemental Expanse, which will in turn throw the world's weather out of balance."

"What if we had a second battery to absorb the storm's magic?"

"We don't have anything nearly as powerful as the Lightning Spear."

"That's not true. We have a magic castle," I told him.

"You want the castle to absorb the excess magic?"

"Yes. Will it work?"

He considered the idea. "I believe so. In defense mode, the castle can absorb large amounts of both light and dark magic." He looked at Colonel Starborn. "But I must caution you, the castle might not survive this. It's never before faced the likes of that storm."

"We have no choice," I told Colonel Starborn. "We have to risk it. If this storm spreads, it will devastate the Earth. The world's cities and walls won't survive. The Lightning Spear and Storm Castle are all that stand between the storm and the coming of the second apocalypse."

"Bring us the Lightning Spear," she ordered the master smith.

"Get everyone out of the castle," I told the castle staff standing at the top of the stairs.

They all looked at Colonel Starborn.

"Do it," she said. "And hurry."

They ran down the stairs as the master magic smith

came up, carrying the Lightning Spear. Wow, he sure moved fast.

"Mount it at the highest point on the castle, and it will serve like a lightning rod for magic." He handed me the rod. "You'll need to access the controls to switch the castle to defense mode so it absorbs the magic the rod channels. There's a control panel on the roof of every tower."

"Thanks," I said, moving toward the roof access ladder on the balcony.

Nero caught my hand before I stepped outside. "There's a massive storm brewing up there. You won't survive it."

"My blended magic makes me the person most likely to survive a storm of light and dark magic." At least long enough to place the rod and switch on the castle's defenses.

I expected him to stand in my way. Instead, he let go of my hand. "I'm going with you."

"Glad to have you, Colonel," I said with a crooked smile.

"Get moving!" Nero barked at everyone still in the tower, then followed me onto the balcony.

Needle-hard rain pricked my face as I climbed, one hand pulling me up the ladder, the other gripping tightly to the Lightning Spear. By the time we reached the roof, my clothes were soaked through to my underwear.

"I'm going to lock the rod in place!" I shouted over the hurricane winds battering my body, trying to throw me off the heavily slanted roof. "As soon as it's in, you need to switch the castle into defense mode to absorb the storm!"

A bolt of lightning crashed against the roof. Red tiles shot in every direction, spilling off the tower. My foot slipped under the force of the avalanche, and I began to fall.

Nero caught my leg—and I caught the Lightning Spear. He pulled me back up, and I slammed against the solid wall of his chest.

"Careful, Pandora," he whispered into my ear. His breath was warm, driving out the chill the storm had beaten into my bones. "Don't fall off."

My heart thumped against his. "I'm not planning on it."

"Good."

I lifted my hand to brush a wet strand of hair from his face—then stopped. There was no time for this now. I gave him a half-smile, then climbed up to the peak of the tower and snapped the Lightning Spear into place. I slowly moved back down to Nero. He typed in a few codes to switch the castle into defense mode. Then we hurried down the ladder.

We'd made it nearly to the spiral staircase when a heavy boom shook the castle, blowing a hole in the tower. The wind sucked us out into the storm. Caught in a funnel, I saw the battered face of the Fire Tower. The roof had been blown clear off, but the Lightning Spear was still locked into the castle's support beams. Magic crackled on the rod and poured down the metal vein. It was working! The castle was absorbing the storm.

Lightning flashed across the sky. The wind yawned, and I dropped several feet in the air. I kicked my feet, trying to find something to grab onto, anything. I crashed into the Sky Tower. The wind carried me across the roof. I tried to grab onto the tiles, but they broke apart in my hands. I dropped off the edge of the tower.

Arms locked around me, catching my fall. I looked up into the face of an angel.

"Nero," I said, my heart racing, my body shaking. I'd nearly fallen to my death.

"It's ok. I've got you."

I dropped my head to his chest, trying to steady my ragged breathing. "Yes." I sighed in relief. "You do."

A bolt of lightning slammed against us. We fell, twirling out of control toward the ground.

CHAPTER TWENTY
Dragon's Storm

I MUST HAVE blacked out for a few seconds because I couldn't remember hitting the ground. Black and yellow spots danced in front of my eyes, flickering in time to my pulse. I rose slowly, looking around. I was just outside the castle gate. All around me, smoke rose from the castle, masking most of its structure—assuming there was anything left of its structure. I shook out my limbs, surprised to find that nothing was broken—and that I was alive. Nero must have broken my fall.

Nero! Dozens of Legion soldiers had clustered in front of the gate. Nero wasn't one of them. No, wait. A body lay facedown amongst broken bricks and other debris, his black leather uniform torn, his short blond hair streaked with crimson. At the sight of all the blood, I hurried toward him, swaying with each step. Dropping to my knees, I grabbed his shoulder and flipped him over.

It wasn't Nero. It was the Sky Dragon. His lifeless eyes stared off into nothingness.

"Leda."

I jumped in surprise at the sound of Nero's voice. I

looked back to find him standing over me.

"You thought I'd crashed?" His eyes shone with smug amusement.

I just stared at him like an idiot.

"Leda?"

I jumped up and threw my arms around him. "Of course you didn't crash. An angel always lands on his feet." Hysterical laughter shook my chest.

His brows drew together, perplexed. "Are you all right?"

"No."

"You have another head injury." He brushed his fingers through my hair, looking for a wound.

He wouldn't find one. I wasn't suffering from a concussion. I was suffering from an overdose of Venom—and a case of total euphoria. I was still alive. Nero was alive.

Something high above crashed down. It sounded like rocks hitting harder rocks. I looked past the clearing smoke. The sight was very sobering. Larger parts of the castle's structure had collapsed.

"Did everyone get out?" I asked.

"Yes," Colonel Starborn said, walking up to us. "Except the corrupted Dragons." She glanced down at the Sky Dragon's body.

Captain Somerset was beside her. "Together the Lightning Spear and Storm Castle absorbed the storm." She patted me on the back. "Your plan worked."

"But at great cost." I gave the castle a mournful look. "There's nothing left of it."

"I think you'll find my castle's tougher than you think," replied Colonel Starborn.

"I'm going to take a look." Nero set his hand on my cheek. "Don't go anywhere."

"Where exactly would I go?"

He favored me with a hard smile. "I'm sure you could find some calamity to dive headfirst into."

"I'll try to contain myself," I said drily.

"Good."

He launched into the air, flying over the castle. The glossy feathers of his black, blue, and green wings shone against the dissipating storm clouds.

Colonel Starborn and Captain Somerset left me to check on the wounded. They looked pretty wounded themselves, but they weren't letting that bother them.

"I'm glad he survived," Harker said, stopping next to me. His eyes tracked Nero's flight. "He is my best friend, like a brother to me. Even after all that's happened."

His voice rang with sincerity. Colonel Starborn was right about him. He really was a good person. He wanted to do the right thing, but sometimes his ambition got in the way.

Nero landed in front of us. "The castle is salvageable. The main structure and two of the four towers are still stable. The rest can be rebuilt, though it will take some time to weave the magic back into the stones. Time and the care of four Dragons."

"So it's decided," Captain Somerset declared.

We all looked at her.

"We're having a party in the throne room tonight." She wrapped one arm around Harker and the other around Nero, leading them toward the open gates. "We narrowly averted the end of human civilization. It's time to celebrate life."

Inside, the throne room looked—well, awful, but it was still standing. And Nero seemed to think it wouldn't fall on our heads.

"I'll have this place ready in a couple of hours," Colonel Starborn said, plopping onto her throne. It looked like her quick-fix healing solution was finally wearing off.

"This place looks like a war zone, and she is barely conscious," I whispered to Nero as Colonel Starborn groggily waved the castle's soldiers over to her. "How is she going to make it ready for a party by tonight?"

"Never underestimate the stubbornness of angels."

I smirked at him. "Don't worry. There's no danger of that, Colonel."

Snowflakes fell softly from a stormy ceiling of pink, orange, and blue magic swirls. Fire lanterns hung in the air over the grand hall, their orange lights flickering off the trees and flowers that had spontaneously popped out of the stone floor. Appetizer platters sat atop a ring of giant mushrooms growing around a majestic waterlily fountain. Beside the fountain, on a raised wood stage, glowed four elemental magic sculptures, one at each corner. A red flame, a gold lightning bolt, a green tree, and a blue water drop—the symbols mimicked the same ones on the Dragons' thrones.

As far as party decorations went, Colonel Starborn had outdone anything and everything I'd ever seen. Everyone at the castle was in attendance, decked out in silk and satin, platinum and gemstones. In addition to celebrating our thwarting the end of the world as we knew it, tonight was the promotion ceremony for the six level-four candidates.

Like so many times before, I was spending the final moments before the ceremony at the bar, drinking magic cocktails with Captain Somerset. The soldiers of the Legion sure drank a lot. What did that say about our lives? I suppose it said that we needed something to help us forget all the horrors we'd seen—and to remember that we were alive. Every battle we survived was a victory, something worth celebrating.

"How are you feeling?" I asked her.

"Alive. Thanks to you." She smiled at me. "I might have been only half-conscious, but Leila told me about how you drank the Venom out of me."

I returned the smile. "Just doing my job to keep you alive, Captain Somerset."

"No, what you did went far beyond a soldier's duty. You acted like a true friend. And you're going to call me Basanti."

"Are you sure? It might go straight to my head. I might become all disobedient and unruly," I teased her, smirking.

She snorted. "I suppose that's a risk I'm willing to take." She lifted her glass. "Friends?"

"Friends." I clinked my glass against hers. "So, as a friend, I should tell you that Colonel Starborn is still in love with you."

She narrowed her eyes at me. "You don't waste time, do you?"

"In helping my friends? No, I really don't. You should have seen the anguish on her face when she was trying to purge the remaining Venom from your body with her magic. And you should have heard the regret in her voice when she spoke of what happened between you two."

"The crazy thing is I'm not actually surprised that you managed to convince an angel you'd only just met to pour her heart out to you."

"What can I say? I have a way with angels. Except Colonel Fireswift." A cold chill shivered down my spine. "And it might have helped that I'd just helped save her from the Dark Force. People tend to get real sentimental when you save their life. That experience makes them reassess what's really important to them. And who is important to them." I looked at Basanti over my glass.

"I saw what you did there."

"You should talk to her," I said. "Angels can be overbearing—don't I know it—but they're not as inhuman as they pretend to be."

"And we're not as human as we like to think," she sighed.

"Yes." I sighed too.

"I hear you've developed a very angel habit."

"Which one? Taking myself too seriously?"

She laughed. "Deciding what's best for people. Leila said you pushed her away before she could drink the Venom out of me."

"She's an angel with very strong light magic. She wouldn't have survived the Venom."

"And Nero told me how you went behind his back, asking Nyx to send Harker here."

"It was our best shot at saving Colonel Starborn. And you know how stubborn Nero is. He wouldn't have made the call."

"So you made it for him," she said. "Sound familiar?"

"I was acting like Nero."

"You were acting like an angel. Come to think of it, you've *always* acted like an angel. You'd been at the Legion for hardly a month when you drove alone across the Black Plains to save Nero."

And before that, I'd joined the Legion without telling my family. I'd decided how we were going to save Zane. I'd decided what was best. Gods, she was right. I'd always been like this, even before I'd sipped the gods' Nectar.

"It's not a bad quality. Not in you," she told me, setting her hand on my shoulder. "It's precisely that trait which compels you to selflessly throw yourself in danger to save others. It's what makes you a hero."

"Thanks. That sounds a lot better than an overbearing, stubborn, bossy pants angel."

"Talking about me?" Colonel Starborn said, sweeping up to the bar with angelic grace.

Basanti smirked at her. "Of course."

"Good," she replied to Basanti's immense amusement.

Colonel Starborn looked at me. "The ceremony will begin in a few moments."

I swallowed hard.

"You're ready," she said. "I saw how you fought against the Dark Force—twice."

"I just can't help but remember what happened at my last ceremony."

"How you were poisoned with Venom," she said, nodding. "I wouldn't worry over that. You already survived the Venom last night. It's just good old Nectar this time around."

I didn't point out that Nectar was also a poison. We all knew it.

"Well," I said, rising from my barstool. "I guess I'd better go splash cold water on my face or something."

They waved to me, then turned toward each other. I left them to it. They had a century of heartbreak to mend, and I really hoped they could do it. I moved across the room, looking for a friendly face. I found Major Singh instead. She was standing under a blossoming cherry tree, speaking with Nero. They weren't even flirting, but that didn't stop a surge of anger from boiling up inside of me. I felt an irresistible, irrational urge to impale her pretty body on that pretty tree.

"Leda," Nerissa said, catching my arm.

Soren moved in front of me, subtly blocking me before I made a scene. So this was an intervention.

"You look ready for a fight," he said. "Didn't you get enough of those lately?"

"Maybe just one more." I tried to move around him.

Nerissa closed the opening. "Rumor has it the Major is a biter."

I slid my tongue over my fangs. "So am I."

Their honest laughter soothed the anger in me. My head cleared enough to realize that attacking Major Singh would not end well. My newfound sanity also allowed me to see what I hadn't before: Nerissa and Soren with their arms wrapped around each other.

"I take it a lot happened while I was away from the castle?"

"Yes. The Dragons showed their true faces and trapped us all in the dungeon," Nerissa said.

That's not what I'd meant, and the mischievous spark in her eyes told me she knew it.

"It's a real medieval dungeon down there," Soren added. "We'd almost escaped when Colonel Windstriker and Major Singh smashed through the final wall, chasing the Sea Dragon."

"He's a real dynamite angel," Nerissa said to me, wiggling her eyebrows.

It was an open invitation to share the details of what had happened between us—which was nothing thus far—but the chiming of the bell saved me from utterly disappointing her. The promotion ceremony was starting. As Colonel Starborn made her opening speech, Jace sidled up to me.

"It looks like you got to have all the fun and glory again, Leda," he said, his expression equal parts humor and resignation, with a hint of jealousy.

"You got your share of glory too. You and the others drove the soldiers of the Dark Force out of Storm Castle."

"That was but a brief battle."

I smiled slyly. "A testament to your prowess on the battlefield."

"Yes, I was part of the five-minute battle in which I and a hundred other soldiers drove out the Dark Force. On the other hand, you rescued an angel from dark angels, defeated the three corrupted Dragons, and saved the world from a storm that would have ended life as we know it."

I didn't mention that I'd been unconscious for the defeat of the three Dragons. I didn't think it would make a difference to him.

"It's not nearly as glorious as it sounds," I said.

"Leda, I was trapped in a dungeon for most of the day," he said drily. "Next to that, making sandwiches sounds downright glorious."

"Well, if it's any consolation, your sister was also trapped in that dungeon."

He laughed. "Actually, yes, that is some consolation. Better yet, Kendra was knocked out by stray magic when Colonel Windstriker blasted through the dungeon. She missed the whole fight against the Dark Force. Our father will be *thrilled* to hear that. He might even torment her instead of me for a change."

"I'm getting the feeling you don't like your sister very much."

"I hate her. And I love her." He shrugged. "It's complicated."

"Jace Fireswift," Colonel Starborn called out.

Jace walked up to the stage. Alec and the two soldiers from Los Angeles stood beside the waterlily fountain. They'd survived the Nectar. Jace survived too. I held my breath when Nerissa went up there, but her magic also proved strong enough. It was down to just me.

"Leda Pierce," Colonel Starborn's clear voice cut through the room.

I climbed the three steps to the stage, lifting the skirt of my gown so I wouldn't trip on it in front of all these people. Someone—probably Alec Morrows—whistled in appreciation. Admittedly, it made me feel a little better. I stopped in front of Colonel Starborn.

"Sip now of the gods' Nectar," she recited, handing me the gold goblet. "Consume the magic of their fourth gift. Let it fill you, making you strong for the days to come."

"For the days to come," the crowd repeated in unison.

I lifted the cup to my mouth, hesitating for a moment before I downed the contents in a single go. The Nectar slid across my tongue, igniting sweet sensations on its way down my throat. My breath caught, my heart stunted—frozen in the moment a cold rush of magic gushed into my bloodstream. I could feel my light and dark magic circle around each other like two warriors before a fight. The Nectar and Venom inside of me were trying to reconcile, to balance.

My heart restarted, my lungs came alive, and I drew in a deep, gasping breath. Slowly, the chill melted off my body, dissolving before the burning river cascading through me, knocking my magic up a notch. The magical euphoria, that drunk-on-Nectar feeling, kicked in. I saw everything so clearly—and in that moment, I saw Nero too.

I walked over to him with renewed purpose, thinking of Basanti and Colonel Starborn, of how one moment of anger and fear could lead to a lifetime of regret. Well, not me. I wasn't going to regret anything. Not ever.

"Nero," I said as I came to a stop in front of him. Rising to my toes, I grabbed the back of his neck and pulled him against me for a long, deep kiss.

Then I pulled back just as quickly. I could feel people staring at us, but I didn't care. I turned into him, wrapping my arm around his back. My hand settled on his hip. Major Singh looked at us, uncharacteristically perplexed. I met her stare, willing her to step back. Anger flared in her eyes when she realized that I'd compelled her.

I leaned forward. "Your dress is on fire," I whispered to her with a wink.

Then I led Nero from the room, leaving the Major to deal with the burning train of her slinky evening gown.

"I don't actually know where I'm going," I admitted to Nero after a few steps down the hallway. "I just wanted to make an exit."

"And you certainly did. That was remarkable."

I chuckled. "Yeah, setting her clothes on fire was fun."

"Not that," he told me. "Your presence. You made someone of a higher magic level back down."

"I'm not sure how I did it. Pure force of will, I guess."

"The Nectar and Venom in you have made you

powerful. Each ability is enhanced. But that wasn't enough. The power we witnessed back there was something else. A mating bond." A joyful spark lit up his eyes—joy with just the right amount of smugness.

"I was…" I struggled for words.

"Murderous, possessive." His brows lifted. "Bitchy."

"All of the above," I said. "And for no reason. These feelings have been gnawing at me ever since I saw her at the Desert Rose base."

"Now you know how I feel all the time."

"You're not bitchy. Gruff, maybe," I joked.

"What you did back there was the sexiest thing I've ever seen. You showed everyone in that room that you are mine and I am yours."

"Surely not everyone was watching," I whispered against his throat. I could feel his heart beating, his pulse throbbing against my lips. I wanted to show everyone that he was, without a shadow of a doubt, entirely mine.

"I can assure you that every eye in that room was on you. Mine included."

The look in his eyes, the surge of feeling, the raw need burning in them—it was too much. My fangs descended, sinking into his throat, drinking deep. His sweet blood spilled into my mouth, flashing through my veins in hard, hot pulses.

He groaned in protest when I pulled back. Smiling, I brushed the hair from my throat.

"Drink from me," I said. No, *demanded*.

A silver-blue sheen lighting up his green eyes, he dipped his mouth to my neck. His bite was a hot splash of pleasure. Every draw of his mouth synced to my breaths, to my pulse. I could feel myself inside of him, making him mine.

He pulled away, chuckling.

"What?" I asked.

He leaned in, his lips so close I could taste them. "So you've made your decision."

"What decision?"

I shivered as his mouth brushed against my neck one more time. "You are an angel through and through, Leda. You always have been. All that's missing are the wings."

I blinked. His words echoed my thoughts from before.

"If this is about me calling Nyx without asking you—"

"That and so much more."

"I don't understand."

He smirked at me. "You marked me."

"What?" I gasped.

"Just now, when we exchanged blood. You drank in my blood, then returned it to me with your magic marked into it."

"I…"

His chest shook with laughter.

"How is that even possible?" I snapped in frustration. "I can't mark people. I'm not an angel."

"Perhaps not, but you have an angel soul."

"What does that mean?"

"I don't know. It's like some part of you is an angel. I felt that part calling out to me when you marked me. You are an angel inside, Leda. You just don't have the magic yet."

"That's completely backwards. It's the magic that makes someone an angel."

He shrugged. "I can't explain it."

"And it's angel magic that allows them to mark

someone. I read it in your book," I continued. "Without that magic, you can't mark someone."

"I didn't say it made sense."

I sighed.

"Your magic has grown so much in just a few days," he said. "You might not have all of our abilities, but thanks to the Venom and Nectar, you control both light and dark magic for the abilities you do have. Perhaps it was that which gave you enough magic to mark me."

This was all so confusing. "What am I?"

"I don't know." He set his hands on my face. "But we will find out, I promise you."

I let out a strained laugh. "I've been so worried about losing my humanity. But it seems I was never really human at all."

"You're disappointed."

"No." Smiling, I touched my forehead to his. "I'm not. Really. Nothing has changed. I am the same person I always was. That means...I don't have to be human to have humanity. I... It seems things aren't as black and white as I've been making them out to be. I don't have to lose something to become an angel. I can gain something. Someone." I gave him a sheepish look. "Are you mad I marked you?"

"No," he replied without hesitation. "In fact, I have to amend my previous statement. *That* was the sexiest thing I've ever seen. You were positively stunning. So possessive." His hands dropped to my shoulders, sliding down my back. "So vengeful." His lips parted in a sensual smile. "So Lethal." His words kissed my face. "But I bet you could push yourself harder."

"To be like you?" I gasped as his hand caught on the

front zipper of my dress.

"You are just like me." He slid the zipper halfway down. "Just as raw."

My breasts swelled against the fabric of my top. Another half inch down with that zipper, and they'd pop right out. This is what I got for not wearing a bra.

"You will make a magnificent angel, Leda." He closed his eyes, savoring the thought.

"So you came here to push me hard?"

"Yes." His voice was like liquid silk—like the silk burning against my nipples.

He pushed me against the wall. Steam hissed. I realized we'd somehow stumbled halfway across the castle to the Tranquility Pools, the same place Nero had found me after flying here through the storm.

"And to save the world, of course." He kissed me gently.

But I didn't want him to be gentle—not now. "Aren't you busy enough with your own promotion training without worrying about me?" I asked.

"I always worry about you."

I arched my back.

His gazed dipped to my chest. "But I must admit that my intentions were not entirely selfless."

"Oh?"

"They were at least fifty percent selfless."

I caught his lip between my teeth, drawing it out slowly. A deliciously dark groan rumbled in his chest.

"Fine," he said, his voice strained, like he was having trouble holding back the darkness. "At least twenty percent selfless. I need something from you."

I peeled back his collar to kiss his neck, teasing his pulsing vein with my mouth. "I need something from you too."

I slid the zipper all the way down. My dress slid off my body like a waterfall, leaving me in nothing but my panties and a pair of high heels.

"Pandora," he said, his voice a hard, needy rumble, like sandpaper on silk. "I'm trying to be serious."

I stepped over my dress. "I'm very serious."

He cast a long look down the length of my body. Temptation flared in his eyes. "I need to talk."

"Talk." I peeled back my hair, baring my neck to him. "I'm listening."

His hands flashed out, locking onto my arms. I gasped in delight as he turned me around roughly. My back slammed into the hard wall of his chest.

"I missed you so much," I said.

His mouth trailed kisses across my shoulder. "I missed you too. When I came to the castle, I wasn't sure you'd be happy to see me."

"I was."

His hand traced the outside of my breast, brushing down my ribcage. I could feel the hard prick of his fangs against my neck, pushing just lightly enough to not break the skin.

"After what happened in New York, I thought I'd lost you."

"You didn't," I said, glancing back at him. "You have me, Nero."

All the doors to the room clicked shut.

"Good," he said, his eyes burning with dark desire.

He moved like lightning. He lifted me off the floor—and tossed me into the pool.

I surfaced, spitting out water. "That was *not* what I had

in mind."

He was already in the pool, facing me. And there wasn't a shred of clothing on him. Water streamed down his chest like diamond tears. I shivered.

Nero slid his hand across the water's surface. Heat spread out from his glowing fingers, warming the pool. "Better?"

"Moderately."

"You're so hard to please."

"I seem to remember a certain angel who was never satisfied with my performance."

"You would have preferred me to go easy on you?"

"Oh, did you think this was about you?" I smirked at him. "I was actually talking about Colonel Fireswift."

His mouth hardened.

"Sorry, I couldn't resist." I rose to my tiptoes and kissed him on the cheek. "Of course I meant you, Colonel Hardass."

"I'm not always dissatisfied."

"Only most of the time."

"I'm trying to push you to be something more, something greater. I warned you from the beginning that the road you were on would be difficult, that I would have to push you hard. And that you might hate me for it."

"I don't hate you, Nero. I could never hate you."

A sweat broke out on my face. The pool wasn't just warm now; it was scorching hot. A week ago, the heat would have been too much for me. Now, with the magic of Dragon's Storm flowing through my veins, it actually felt pretty good. It soaked into my muscles, melting the tension out of me, soothing me.

I closed my eyes. "So why have you really come here?

What is your not-entirely-selfless reason?" I asked him, dipping deeper into the water, allowing the heat to permeate my body.

"I couldn't be away from you."

The bubbling water beat against me, a slow, deep massage.

"You're trying to make me more accessible to suggestion," I said.

"Leda, we both know it doesn't take much to make you accessible to my suggestions."

Liquid ribbons streamed between my legs, each kiss searing my soft flesh. My body pulsed with an aching, growing need.

"If all I wanted from you was sex, I would have had you many times over already." His voice was dangerously soft.

My breath caught in my throat. "Confident, aren't you?"

"I'm merely speaking plainly."

"So what else do you want from me?"

"I need your help."

Water streamed over my shoulders, cascading down my breasts. My back arched, my legs parted, and I moaned in wanton desperation.

"Nero." His name was a demand, my voice a hard and ragged rasp, my body a throbbing pulse of agonizing need.

The side ties of my panties burst open. The lacy garment peeled away from me, floating up to the water's surface. The pool bubbled higher, harder, faster. More liquid ribbons flashed out, thrusting between my thighs. Like a bolt of lightning, the pressure inside of me exploded. My mind shattered, my body convulsed, and sweet ecstasy spilled over me.

"Gods, Leda. You will be the death of me." Nero was breathing heavily, his shoulders shaking with the aftershocks of his own release.

I slumped against him, shaking, quivering. My pulse was pounding in my ears. Magic ignited in my blood. His magic, mine, both of us merging together as one. One blood, one magic. He wrapped his arms around me in a protective, tender embrace. He dipped his mouth to mine, kissing me softly. I'd never known an angel could be so gentle. So sweet.

He chuckled, his chest humming against mine. "If you could read my thoughts, you'd hardly call me sweet. And I'm not done with you yet."

I smirked back at him. "Bring it on."

He lifted me into his arms and carried me out of the pool, laying me onto a lounge chair. He sat down beside me, his naked hip burning against my quickly-chilling skin. I shivered.

"You're cold."

He waved his hand in the air, and the large umbrella lamp over us began to glow red. Heat bathed our bare bodies. He gazed down upon me, his eyes dilated with magic. His hand stroked along my side, his mouth trailing, kissing every spot his fingers touched. His lips brushed my scar, and I cringed, drawing away.

"Does it hurt?" he asked, concern warming his eyes.

"No, not anymore. I…" I glanced down at the hand I'd used to cover my scar. "I'm just self-conscious about it," I admitted.

"Don't be. It is a mark of honor. You survived the kiss of an immortal weapon." He peeled my hand off the scar. "This scar is a window into your soul, Leda. It is a testament to how strong you are, to your compassion, to how you will always do the right thing, no matter the cost." He kissed the ripple of imperfect skin burned into my stomach. "It is as beautiful as you are. Just like every part of you."

"Even my quirks? My incorrigible snark? My penchant for undignified, dirty fighting?"

"Yes." He took my hand between his, kissing my fingertips. "Every single one of them."

I smiled. "Ok, I admit it. I'm a sucker for your charm. I'll do it."

"Anything?" The look in his eyes made me blush.

"You said you needed my help," I reminded him.

"Yes. I do." His lips caressed my shoulder. "I will soon undertake the trials to level ten, challenges set by the gods themselves. Every promotion until now was about proving that I could embrace my new power, that I could use it. This is different. This time, I will need to prove I can survive without my magic, by my will alone."

"I don't understand."

"They will strip me of my magic."

"I didn't know that was possible."

"There is a potion, a temporary magic inhibitor," he told me. "It will strip me of my powers one by one as the trials become more difficult. By the end, my magic will be gone. I'll have to succeed by my wits and will alone. And with one weapon."

"A magic sword?"

"Not a weapon like that. I may choose one person to be my support in this. One person to be my ally." His hand traced the curve of my spine, sliding over my bottom to settle on my hip. "I choose you."

"Shouldn't you choose someone with more power?"

"Magic is irrelevant. Yours will be stripped too for this trial. What matters is the power within."

"So you want me there with you because I'm stubborn and hard-headed."

He laughed. "I want you there with me because I trust you more than anyone."

Warmth—content and happy—spilled out from my heart.

We've been playing this game for too long, Nero's voice spoke inside my head. *Do you trust me, Leda?*

"Yes."

Smiling, he climbed on top of me, his hand gently parting my legs. Heat blossomed inside of me. I felt myself opening up, ripening, wanting him with an intensity that bordered on madness. The insides of my thighs were slick and hot. A hollow, empty ache throbbed deep inside of me. He slid lower, a gasp breaking my lips as he thrust inside of me. A feeling of intense fullness filled that emptiness.

"I've wanted you for so long," he told me.

My fingers dug into the hard muscle of his back, pulling him in closer. I wrapped my legs around his waist. "I've wanted you…" I groaned as he began to move faster, harder. "…too."

"Will you be my partner in the trials?"

An inferno raged inside of me, building and burning. Heat pulsed through my body in dizzying, feverish waves. The hot-white kiss of his fangs pierced my skin, and I nearly came again.

"You know I will, Nero. You've always been there for me. I'll always be there for you."

"Will you be my partner in life? Mine, my lover, the

keeper of my heart?" The raw vulnerability in his voice nearly made me cry.

"Yes. I'm all yours."

Satisfaction spread across his face, lighting up his eyes. Gold and silver flashed across a sea of green, like a tropical lightning storm at sea.

His next thrust came so hard that the lounge chair groaned in protest beneath us. "Say it again."

A soft whimper tore out of me. "I'm all yours."

"And I am all yours." He traced his finger down his neck. "Show me."

I sank my fangs into his throat, and as the sweet nectar of his blood filled my mouth, he bit me too. Pain collided with pleasure in an explosion that sent a shock wave rippling through my whole body. A deep growl tore out of Nero, his face twisting in pure rapture. His body still shaking, he folded his arms around me.

"Show you like that?" I asked with a shy smile, my heart hammering in my chest.

"Yes, Pandora." He kissed my forehead. "Just like that."

CHAPTER TWENTY-ONE
Lightbringer

MY DREAMS CAME in jumbled flashes of battlefields and armies, of angels and monsters. The nauseating carousel of broken images spun me around and spat me out in the desert.

I ran barefoot, in stumbled steps across the scorching sand. The white-hot sun beat down on me, burning against the wet sweat that drenched my dehydrated body. My tired, broken wings dragged a trail of blood behind me. I was dirty, wounded, thirsty. My hair hung limp and lifeless on my back. My tongue felt like sandpaper.

A fierce, primal roar tore across the empty expanse, and a monster leapt out from behind a forest of cacti. A sand wolf. It was only the size of a large dog, but in my current state—weak, weaponless, and half-dead—it was more than enough to finish me off. It bounded toward me on pale blond paws, its mouth opening in anticipation of dinner. I didn't have enough power left in me to do magic, so I had to let it get close. As the monster sprang into the air to tackle me, I stepped out of the way. It flew right past me. I tackled it before it could come around for another pass, snapping its neck in a single merciful stroke. It fell to the ground, never knowing what hit it.

I spread the sand wolf across my lap, my fangs descending from my dry, swollen gums. I bit down on the fat vein in the wolf's leg and quickly drained its blood dry. The creature had been starving just like I was—and its impatience had gotten the better of it.

A chorus of howls pierced the quiet air. I rose quickly, tossing aside the dead wolf. Its pack was close by, at least twenty wolves by the sounds of it. Too many to fight. Fear rattled against my many years of Legion training, intensified by my pain and starvation.

"Cadence Lightbringer."

I spun around. Two angels stood before me, cast in the harsh glare of the sun. I squinted to see them more clearly. They were beautiful, both with long, luscious hair that shimmered with magic. The male angel wore a suit of bright armor. It reflected so much of the sun's light that I had to look away. His companion wore a light dress and a pair of boots. A bow was slung across her back. The angels' wings were a delightful tapestry of perfect color combinations, and their eyes…their eyes were strangely calm. At peace. So unlike an angel.

"Who are you?" I asked, wiping the beast's blood from my lips.

I knew every angel and dark angel, but I didn't recognize either of them. I might have thought they were new, but their magic felt older than mine. They possessed a power immune to the ebb and flow of time, to the world's changing tides.

"We've come to help you, Cadence," the female angel said, waving her hand in a smooth circle.

A glow brighter than the sun broke through a rift in the air. Magic swirled around it, a perfectly balanced dance of light and dark.

"Who are you?" I asked.

"We are the Guardians," she said.

The name sounded vaguely familiar. If only my head hadn't hurt so much, maybe I could remember where I'd heard it before.

"We're the defenders of magic in its true, pure form," the male angel added. "Before gods and demons split magic into light and dark. Before they tore the Earth apart."

His comrade shot me a sympathetic smile. "You have lost so much to the unnatural division of dark and light. The Legion of Angels ordered you to kill your beloved because he was 'too dark'."

Memories bombarded me, every bad thing that had ever happened to me compacted into a dense, five-second burst. Fighting Damiel. The Legion forcing my hand. The demons attacking, their Dark Force surrounding me. My son, my sweet boy I had to leave behind so he wouldn't grow up powerless. Without joining the Legion, without drinking the gods' Nectar, he wouldn't become an angel.

"Is it better to be a slave with wings than a slave on the ground?" the female angel posed.

Before I could ponder the question, the rift flashed, swallowing us in a blanket of silver light.

I drew in a deep breath. Cool air flooded my lungs—cool air that smelled of summer flowers. Soft grass tickled my cheek. I opened my eyes to find I was lying in a sunny field.

Roses and sunflowers quivered in the gentle wind. The desert was gone, nothing but a distant memory. Even my lips had lost their dry, cracked texture.

"Where am I?" I wondered aloud.

"At the Sanctuary," replied a light and breezy voice.

I pushed myself up, surprised when my arms didn't collapse under me. I felt stronger than I had in a long time. A young, beautiful girl with blonde curls and big, blue eyes sat on a rock beside me, her hands folded primly over her pink flower-pattern dress. She didn't look older than ten.

"Giselle and Taron brought you here."

"The angels?"

"Yes."

"How long have I been here?" I asked.

"Ten days."

"I've been asleep for ten days?"

"Yes. Your injuries were severe. My brother kept you in a sleeping state to speed along your recovery."

"Your brother?"

"Our healer."

I fluttered my fingers and toes, testing them. There wasn't even a flicker of pain, a small miracle considering the near-death state I'd been in before the angels had found me. The healer had done a remarkable job. I was in perfect health. But had Damiel fared as well? And Nero? Had the Legion learned of what we'd done? I had to find them, to make sure they were all right. I turned, looking for anything that resembled an exit.

"You can't go," the girl said. "It's not safe out there."

"Giselle and Taron left."

"They've passed the test."

"What test?"

She reached into the picnic basket at her feet and pulled out a gold goblet. It looked a lot like the one the Legion used in their promotion ceremonies.

She giggled. "They got the idea from the Guardians."

She'd read my mind.

"I'm a telepath." She set the goblet into my hands. "If you want to leave, you must drink."

I stared at the thick liquid swirling inside the cup like melted silver. "What will it do?"

"It will balance your magic. The Legion sent you down a narrow path, giving you access to only light magic. That is just a piece of magic. Wouldn't you like to experience true magic?"

I had to admit the idea was intriguing. "If I pass this test, I can leave this place? I can go find my family?"

"In time," she replied. "This is just the first test. The road to magical enlightenment is a long one. Those who reach the end may go back to their own world. If they wish."

"And do they?" I asked. "Ever want to go back?"

She smiled. "No one ever has."

I stared into the silver liquid. I would pass these Guardians' tests. I would find my way back to Damiel and Nero. With that decided, I drank from the goblet. The liquid wasn't as smooth as it appeared. A bitter flavor burned across my tongue. The fire spread out, flashing through my veins like a forest fire. My blood was boiling, my body quaking in agony. Tremors tore through me, sending me to my knees.

The little girl was dancing in front of me, her fluffy pink skirt twirling like a gigantic spinning peony. She spun, the world spun, and I blacked out.

I sat perched on the glowing wall over Purgatory, magic masking my body. If someone were to stare up at my exact spot, they wouldn't see me. They would see only a shimmer of moonlit mist rising from the wall. Taron was crouched beside me, his blue wings tucked against his back. My ever-vigilant babysitter.

"We've been waiting for nearly an hour," I said. "Nothing is happening down there."

"Evelina is never wrong."

Maybe not, but her foresights also didn't come with a timestamp. We could be sitting here for another hour—or for another week.

A door swung open, and a vampire dressed in leather pants and a silk shirt burst out of the Witch's Watering Hole. He sprinted down the street, heading for the wall. A woman in a tank top and summer shorts hustled after him, her long braid streaming after her like a comet. Her hair almost seemed to glow in the moonlight.

She was running like her life depended on it—but the vampire was faster. He was already scrambling up the wall. The hunter drew her gun and shot him.

"This isn't her first time," I commented as he fell off the wall.

Taron ignored the woman, his eyes following the man who'd just emerged from the shadows. "He's the one we're looking for."

I watched the vampire kick both their asses. "What do you want me to do?"

"Just watch. We need to be sure."

The Guardians had an uncanny habit of telling you only as much as you needed to accomplish the tasks they set you—and not a tiny snippet more. After nearly two hundred years with them, I still didn't like it, though I couldn't find fault with what they were trying to accomplish.

Taron said we were after the man, but I found myself more intrigued by his female companion. Her moves weren't elegant—in fact, she looked like a street fighter—yet there was a raw beauty in her tenacious spirit. And no one could deny she was resourceful. She fought with anything and everything she could find. I chuckled when she wrapped an old sweater around a rock and slammed it against the vampire's head.

"What do you think of her?" I asked Taron.

"She's undisciplined and has no magic. We're here for her brother, not her."

But I couldn't shake this feeling that there was something…different about her. For one, I'd never met anyone with hair that glowed like that, even if it was only an intermittent glow. It seemed to react to her mood. Strong emotions were the trigger.

The vampire stood over her, his boot pressed against her head. He stopped, then stumbled back, clutching his head, crying out in pain. The woman's companion stood behind him, chanting furiously.

"He's a telepath," I said. "We came here to snatch a telepath."

"Yes."

Of course they hadn't told me. I wasn't one of them yet, not even after all these years. Not until I took the final sip of Life. That's what they called the silver liquid that balanced your magic, giving you control over the full spectrum of light and dark magic. It took a long time to balance an angel, especially an angel with predominantly light magic. At the Legion, my light magic had been a blessing that helped me survive the gods' Nectar; with the Guardians, it was a hindrance.

"You knew he would expose his powers," I said. "That's what Evelina saw in her visions."

He said nothing. He didn't have to. I knew I was right. The telepath had exposed himself just as Evelina had foreseen, and now we had to take him with us. If we didn't, the Legion or the Dark Force would. And neither army was kind to its telepathic guests. *Guests.* That's what we'd called them at the Legion. In truth, they were treated like slaves.

Down on the street, the telepath fell under the vampire's wild rampage. The woman sprang to her feet to save him. She tore the shutter off a nearby house and thrust it through the vampire's stomach.

I looked at Taron. "Still not interested in saving her?"

He blinked in surprise. "I don't believe she requires saving." His face grew serious, recovering from his temporary shock. "We'll move in when he's alone. Or at least not with his sister."

I nodded. If we tried to take him when she was around, I had no doubt she'd fight us. She didn't stand a chance against two angels, of course, but she'd fight just the same. And she'd die. That would be a real waste.

CHAPTER TWENTY-TWO
Sanctuary

CADENCE'S MEMORIES FLASHED through my head like fireworks. As the last one faded, I found myself in a familiar field. Sunflowers and roses blossomed in front of cozy huts. Streams of butterflies danced across the blue sky, their iridescent wings sparkling in the sunlight. This was the peaceful sanctuary where the Guardians had brought Cadence. But she wasn't the only one they'd brought here.

"Leda."

I turned at the sound of my brother's voice, not even trying to contain the silly smile on my face. "Zane!" I tackled him into a big hug.

"Ow." He rubbed his arms. "You've gotten strong."

"Or you've gone soft." I smirked at him. "How can you even get hurt in a dream?"

"Only you are dreaming. I'm using my magic to connect to your mind."

I hugged him again, more gently this time. "I'm so glad to see you. I've missed you so much."

He shot me a sheepish, charming grin. His trademark smile. "I've missed you too."

"So you're hanging out with the Guardians."

"Yeah." He ruffled up his hair. "They're helping me, Leda. I'm growing my magic, balancing it. It's like a whole new world."

"I was worried about you. We all were."

"I'm sorry. I wanted to contact you before, but I wasn't strong enough. And neither were you. Your magic has grown so much. That's how I could connect to you."

"You," I realized. "You were the voice in the Fire Mountains that showed me Leila Starborn."

"I might have given your dreams a little nudge before that too."

"All those drowning-in-lava dreams were because of *you*?" I frowned at him. "You had me totally freaked out. I was sure the gods' fourth gift was going to kill me."

He winced. "Sorry. I was trying to send you to the Fire Mountains. It took me a while to figure out how to communicate with you."

"The phantom voice in the Fire Mountains was very ominous."

"Thanks. I'm quite proud of it. That and when I gave Nero a cameo in your dreams."

"*That* was you too? I thought it was just my subconscious playing tricks on me. Instead, it was you playing tricks on me. Or were you playing matchmaker?"

"Not me. Cadence."

"Nero's mother was trying to get us together?" I gasped.

"She says you have spirit."

"Did she say it with a straight face?"

He snorted. "She likes you, Leda. She asked me to connect to you, to show you what happened to Leila. And she asked me to show you her memories of how we each got here." He lowered his voice, as though afraid to be overheard. "She said you and Nero deserved to know."

"The Guardians don't want us to know," I guessed.

"It's complicated. Our Sanctuary is a special place. It's a commitment to peace and living outside the black and white world of conflict. Everyone who enters here must purify their souls and magic." He spoke with reverence. He clearly respected the Guardians.

"It sounds splendid, Zane. Really it does," I said. "But your family misses you too."

"I want to see you all again. I just can't leave yet, not until my magic is balanced. If I leave now, I'll have to start all over again."

"But if you don't leave now, you might never see us again. I saw Cadence's memories, remember? She's been at this for two hundred years, and she still hasn't passed their tests. You aren't immortal."

"Cadence is an angel. She has so much light in her that the process of balancing her magic takes much longer. I'll be faster, I promise."

"I just wish I could see you." I touched his face. "For real. Just to see that you're ok. I joined the Legion of Angels so I'd have the magic I needed to find you."

"I know. The Guardians have been watching you."

"They told you that?" I asked, skeptical. The Guardians didn't strike me as the sharing type.

"I might have eavesdropped a little."

I beamed at him. "You scoundrel."

"I fear my soul isn't yet pure."

"Well, if you're going to be bad, might as well do it all the way."

He sighed. "Why do I have the feeling you're going to

get me into trouble?"

Maybe because I'd been getting him into trouble since we were kids.

"Sneak out. Come on. Just long enough to visit home," I pleaded. "You'll be back before the Guardians know it."

"As I said, trouble. Aren't soldiers supposed to behave?"

"Where did you get a crazy idea like that?"

"I must have read it in a magazine."

"Paranormal Teen?" I kept my face perfectly neutral. Not even an eyebrow twitch. Nero would have been so proud.

"Sorry, we don't get that one here." He winked at me.

"You can stock up when we get back home."

"I can't leave, Leda. The Guardians are helping me grow my magic. I'm doing things I only dreamt of before. If I leave, not only will I lose all that, the gods and demons will hunt me down. I'm not strong enough to fight them." He grinned. "Not just yet."

He was right. It hurt to admit it, but that was the part of my plan I'd never really worked out. Even if I gained the power to find Zane, how would I protect him from those who wanted to use him?

"Then I'll come to you," I said quickly. I had to see with my own eyes that he was all right.

"I don't know the ways in and out of the Sanctuary. Only the Guardians do."

We'd just see about that.

"I want to speak to these Guardians," I told him. "You said they've been watching me? So that means it's just a matter of screaming up at the sky and they'll come running?"

"From what I overheard, you are exactly where the

Guardians think you should be: out there, leveling up your magic."

"That doesn't make any sense," I said. "I can't be where the Guardians want me to be. They believe in balanced magic, and I'm a soldier in the gods' army of light."

"And yet you've gained both light and dark magic," he pointed out. "It seems to be working out exactly to plan."

"Maybe," I said, frowning. I didn't enjoy being a pawn in someone else's game, no matter how benevolent they were.

"I guess they'll contact you when they see fit."

Good or evil, all authority bodies were exactly the same. They decided and you waited.

"Listen to me, Zane." I set my hands on his face. "I'm going to find you. I'll break into this paradise if need be."

"You sure do know how to make friends, don't you, Leda?"

"From heaven to hell to Earth and everywhere in between."

The field was fading. So was Zane.

"Say hi to Calli and the girls for me," he said. His voice sounded so distant now.

"I will," I promised.

And then I woke up.

I opened my eyes, staring up at the sun shining in through the stained glass windows, where scenes of angels fighting monsters sparkled with heavenly beauty. Beside me on the lounge chair, Nero leaned against one arm in a pose that nicely accentuated the supple, muscular curvature of his body. Ok, I'll admit it. I stared. Ogled even. Last night I'd seen, touched, and tasted every part of him—and I was ready to do it all over again. He met my stare with a self-satisfied smirk.

"Good morning," he said, kissing me softly.

His body was like an inferno against mine. A blanket covered us from the waist down, trapping in the scorching heat. He must have pulled it over us sometime during the night. A balmy breeze tickled my skin. It smelled delightfully rich, like dark chocolate and a slowly burning fire. And there was something else in there—a thick, intoxicating scent. No, a musk. And it was coming from me. Nero's mark.

"Your mark is stronger than mine," I pouted.

His mouth dipped to my neck, his kiss jolting my body fully awake. "When you're an angel, yours will be stronger."

I caressed his cheek. He was so unbelievably gorgeous. And he was all mine.

"Do you want me to mark you when I'm an angel?" I asked coyly.

"Nothing would give me greater pleasure, Leda." The look in his eyes could chase away any storm. "I find myself impatient for you to be an angel. A female angel's mark is uniquely powerful."

"It might be a while."

His hand traced slowly down my back. "I am counting on your precocious nature."

I laughed. No, *giggled*. Gods, I was in so deep.

He drew me in closer, holding me tightly to him, like he never wanted to let go.

"Having...trouble...breathing," I gasped.

Amusement slid over his face. "You can hold your

breath for over five minutes. I looked up your training scores. Now that you possess the power of Dragon's Storm, it must be at least double that." He loosened his grip anyway.

"It still feels weird to not breathe."

That wasn't the only thing that felt different. When I'd set out to join the Legion, I'd done it to save Zane. I'd known my body and magic would go through changes. But I hadn't expected to fall in love with an angel.

Nero watched me closely. "Do you have any regrets?"

Either he'd read my thoughts, or read them on my face.

"None," I told him, smiling. A tear slid down my cheek.

"Are you sure?" He didn't let go, but his hold eased enough that I could have broken free.

I pulled him in closer instead. "My life wasn't supposed to be like this. I was supposed to be a bounty hunter, staying as far from the Legion as humanly possible. I was supposed to save my family, not the world." I drew in a deep breath I didn't need, but it felt good nonetheless. "But I can do both. You showed me that. You weren't just always there when I needed you; you were what I needed. So, no, I don't regret anything, Nero. Not a single thing. Because it all led me to you."

His eyes widened, his lips parted. "I love you," he whispered into my mouth.

My heart burned with emotion. "I love you too."

Happiness flashed in his eyes. "I felt like my heart was frozen, stalled, until you came."

Angels didn't give their hearts easily. They had many lovers, but only one true love. A love eternal. I didn't flee from the pressure of knowing I was the only one he would ever love; I embraced it. I loved the way his eyes lit up when he looked at me. It was the same look I'd seen in Damiel's eyes when he'd spoken of Cadence. She was his one true love. I'd always known it in my mind, but in this moment, I knew it with every part of me.

"There's something you need to know," I said.

And then I told him of my dreams—of Zane and Cadence and the Guardians.

"My mother and your brother are in the same place," he said when I was done.

"Yes. The same place I saw in my mind after our first blood exchange. If your mother is there, you can use Ghost's Whisper to connect to her, to find her. Then we can go to them."

"I tried that after Damiel told us she's alive. I felt nothing."

That explained why he'd been convinced Damiel was lying.

"Until she visited me in my dreams last night," he said.

"Really? What did she say?"

"That you're pretty."

I blushed. "You're making that up."

"No, I'm not. She told me I shouldn't be afraid to give my heart to someone who deserved it." The long, penetrating look he gave me melted me from the inside out. "And she told me not to look for her just yet. When I awoke, I tried to connect to her again, but I felt nothing." He frowned. "She's blocking me."

"You are powerful. You could break through and find her."

"The battering ram approach?"

"Absolutely. It is the way of the angels, isn't it? Brute

force."

He chuckled lightly. "You still have a lot to learn about being an angel, Pandora."

"Like how battle debris is not a recognized weapon?" I said silkily.

"You haven't transgressed in that regard recently, have you?"

"Of course not. That would be totally uncivilized."

"Are you mocking me, or have you truly learned your lesson?"

"All of the above?"

He snorted.

I wet my lips. "You're welcome to try to teach me that lesson again."

His hands gripped my hips roughly. His voice was a low, vicious growl. "Was that a challenge?"

"That depends. Do you accept?"

"Yes."

"Good."

He brushed my hair from my face. "When you become an angel, you'll mark me. That will allow us to merge our magic." He kissed me once on the lips. "Then we'll have the power we need to find them, whether or not the Guardians want us to." His hand traced the inside of my thigh.

I squirmed beneath him.

Nero's phone made a noise.

"What is that?" I asked.

"Nothing."

It made another noise.

"It sounds angry," I commented.

"I assure you that a phone is incapable of sounding angry."

His mouth came down on mine, his kiss ravaging, his hunger consuming. I forgot all about his phone—until it began to ring.

Growling against my mouth, Nero grabbed the offending device roughly from the side table. "What is it?" he demanded gruffly.

"What's the matter, Colonel? Did you wake up on the wrong side of the bed?" Nyx's amused voice sang out from the other end.

Nero's face sobered. "My apologies, First Angel."

"Indeed." She still sounded amused. "With the situation at Storm Castle resolved, I expected you back in Los Angeles already. Your next assignment is waiting. And I know you'll like it."

"Of course."

"Unless you have something better to *do*?" she said, mischief in her voice.

I could have sworn she'd put emphasis on the last word. *She knows about us,* I mouthed to Nero.

His face was impassive. "I will leave right away."

Her laughter sang across the phone line like sleigh bells. "You can finish cuddling first, Colonel. Say hi to your Pandora for me." Then she hung up.

"I told you she knew," I said as he set his phone down.

When I tried to stand, his arms tightened around me, holding me in place.

"Don't you have a mission?" I reminded him. "I'd hate to be the reason you got in trouble. Again."

"You heard the First Angel." His hand brushed across my forehead, his touch remarkably tender for someone who had me pinned down. "She officially ordered me to finish cuddling first."

"I wouldn't call that an order so much as permission," I laughed.

"Leda, you'll find that with angels, those two things are often one and the same."

One of my hands was still free. I traced it down his chest, lower and lower.

He captured it inside of his. "I don't think we have time for *that*."

I arched my eyebrows. "Oh, I don't know. I'm up for the challenge if you are, Colonel."

Half an hour later, we were scrambling to find our clothes. My ride back to New York was leaving soon, and I couldn't find my underwear. Nero pointed up at the lamp hanging over our chair. The tiny piece of lace dangled daintily from one of the metal arms.

"Well, at least you aren't wearing my panties around your neck," I said.

His mouth twisted into a sexy smile. "I considered it, but pink really isn't my color."

Chuckling, I grabbed my panties from the lamp. Thankfully, they were dry. Nero must have fished them out of the pool last night and hung them up.

"Thank you," I said, leaning in to give him a quick smile.

"For what?"

"For being so thoughtful."

He didn't say anything. When it came to Nero Windstriker, actions really did speak louder than words.

I grabbed his uniform off the ground. "Get dressed, Colonel. If you go out there naked, you will create a stampede. And I don't want anyone ogling my angel."

We parted ways at the door to the Tranquility Pools. Nero had a few matters to sort out before he left Storm Castle, and I had to sort out some decent clothes. I had no intention of giving my comrades front row seats to the underside of my skirt as we climbed down the mountain, no matter how much Alec Morrows would have approved.

After a quick change, I left my room in the Sea Tower for the last time and headed back down toward the throne room. Along the way, I caught Nerissa and Soren leaving the same bedroom. When she walked up beside me, I gave her a sly smirk.

"You're one to talk," she told me as Soren made a side trip to the armory. "Everyone in the whole castle heard what was going on between you and Colonel Windstriker all last night. And this morning."

My cheeks burned. Damn supernatural hearing.

"I didn't say a thing about you and Soren," I said innocently.

"But you wanted to."

"Some of us can control ourselves," I teased her.

She took that as an invitation to gossip. "Speaking of controlling, Major Singh and Harker went to bed together last night. They were obviously venting their frustration."

I laughed. "Good for Harker."

"I didn't think Interrogators were his type. Though they do have all the good toys." Her eyes lifted in thought, as though she were speaking from personal experience.

I gaped at her.

"I had a fling with an Interrogator once," she told me.

"Where is Harker?"

Back in prison perhaps. I wasn't sure how I felt about that.

We passed Basanti and Colonel Starborn.

"They sure look cuddly," Nerissa commented in a low whisper.

The word reminded me of what Nyx had said to Nero —and what we'd done after he'd hung up the phone.

Basanti smiled at her angel, then fell into step beside us. Nerissa had barely opened her mouth, when Basanti lifted her finger.

"No gossip." It was a warning—with implied dire consequences for noncompliance.

Nerissa pretended to look angelic. The effect was slightly spoiled by her total lack of innocence—and the fact that angels weren't innocent either.

"You know who else hooked up last night?" Basanti asked us. Apparently, the 'no gossip' rule only applied to her own love life.

"Who?" Nerissa's eyes lit up. She was practically chomping at the bit to know.

"You'll never guess," Basanti taunted her.

"Stop torturing me and just spit it out."

As we passed through the Dragons' throne room, Basanti glanced at Jace's sister Kendra, then her eyes slid over over to Alec. He was winking at her from across the room, which she was pointedly ignoring. We all laughed. Kendra Fireswift and Alec Morrows. Now *that* I hadn't seen coming.

We passed through the gates and stepped outside. The air was fresh, cool but not cold. Like a morning mist after an early spring rainfall. Everyone else who was heading back to New York joined us.

Nero was standing outside. Wow, he sure knew how to take care of business. How had he beaten me here? I paused in front of him. As I met his eyes, I found myself completely unable to hold back the dopey expression spreading across my face. Basanti slapped us each on the back on her way to the ledge. Everyone else exchanged winks and knowing looks, then followed her over the edge.

"Need a lift down the mountain?" Nero asked when we were alone.

"I think I can handle it, but thanks for the offer." Why couldn't I stop grinning? "It's very chivalrous of you." I leaned in to kiss him.

Cooing noises rose from the rocks. I stepped over to the edge and looked down to find my buddies hiding just out of sight. The dirty little spies.

"Get moving, or I'll find a spectacularly unpleasant mission for you all."

The mountain magnified Nero's voice. It seemed to come from everywhere at once. Everyone suddenly made a race for the bottom.

Chuckling, I turned to drape my arms over his shoulders. "I guess this is goodbye again."

"I'll visit you soon," he promised, stroking his hand down my face. "We have a lot to discuss."

"Ok, but when we move in together, I call dibs on the right side of the bed. On that one point I won't budge," I joked.

He grew very still. Oh, shit. I'd already scared him away.

"I was kidding," I said quickly to cover my own ineptitude. Why had I never learned to be a grownup?

"You like to do that." He captured my mouth,

devouring the inside with a slow, deep kiss that left me gasping for breath. "Try to be good, Pandora," he whispered against my lips, then pulled away.

Dark wings spread out of his back, appearing by magic. He threw me a long, languid look. And then he was gone, flying off toward his next adventure. I wasn't sad. Even though he was high above in the sky, I felt him here with me, like he'd left a part of him behind. I hurried down the mountain, wings in my heart.

CHAPTER TWENTY-THREE
Back in New York

IT WAS SUNNY in New York when we arrived in the city. Spring was truly in full bloom. Yesterday's storm had cleansed the streets, washing away the dirty slush.

"Home sweet home," Basanti said as the two of us entered the Legion's large New York building. We'd just stopped by Damiel's apartment to check on him—and to tell him what I'd learned about Cadence.

"You miss her already, don't you?" I asked.

"Yes."

"Why didn't you stay longer?"

"I could have stayed. Leila offered to make me a Dragon."

"Why didn't you say yes? You looked very cuddly."

Basanti threatened to barbecue me with her stare. "I need time. Believe it or not, Pandora, it actually takes more than one night to get over a century of bad feelings between us."

"But what a night it was," I said wistfully. "What was in those drinks?"

She looked rather wistful herself. "Nectar probably."

"Probably."

"I'm glad you and Nero could work things out," she told me.

"Thanks."

"This is going to be a big deal, you know."

"That I had sex with an angel?"

"That an angel marked you. Especially since it's Nero."

"You can smell that, can you?"

"He wasn't subtle," she said. "The whole Legion must know by now."

"That's just because Nerissa got back before we did, and she's probably told everyone."

"You're not wrong about that."

I wasn't embarrassed. I was too happy to care what anyone thought about Nero marking me as his. Besides, I'd marked him as mine too.

"Well, this will certainly be entertaining," Basanti declared. "I can't wait to see how Colonel Fireswift reacts."

"Didn't you hear?" Ivy said excitedly as she and Drake ran past us in the hall. "Colonel Fireswift is gone!"

"He's gone back to his own office in Chicago," Drake added.

"Party tonight!" Ivy squealed.

"Everyone's headed down to the canteen to meet the new angel in charge. He's arriving soon," Drake told us.

Basanti and I looked at each other, then ran to catch up to them. Colonel Fireswift was gone! Now *that* was something to celebrate.

"It looks like your news took a backseat to this," Basanti said.

"Oh, no. Everyone is still talking about that," Ivy assured us, grinning. "Personally, I'm hoping the new angel in charge is the old angel in charge."

Nero come back? I wished for that too, even knowing it was impossible. It couldn't be. He was headed back to LA.

But what if it were possible? What if Nyx had given him his old job back? She'd mentioned a new assignment for him, an assignment he'd like. I couldn't imagine anything he'd enjoy more than to be back here with us.

My phone hummed. I answered on the first ring.

"Leda," Nero's voice said. The background buzz sounded familiar. Were those the same cheers I heard echoing through these halls?

"Where are you?" I asked with tentative optimism.

"Back in New York. Headed for Demeter. I was hoping you would join me for lunch."

My heart was thumping so fast in my chest, it couldn't be good for my health. "Definitely."

"Then I'll see you soon." He hung up.

I'd reached the canteen. A thick crowd blocked the way in. I slipped past them, propelled by my excitement to see Nero again. I could feel him close, so close now. I had to see him. To sit at the table with him and tell him my silly jokes. To fall asleep in his arms every night. To wake up with him every morning. To even have him kick my ass in training, day after day after day. Just to be together.

We'd only been apart for a few hours, but those hours had made me realize that was what I wanted. The joke I'd made about living together, it suddenly wasn't so funny. Maybe it was too fast. Maybe this mating thing was making me crazy. But that's what I wanted. And I was going to tell him just that.

As I moved toward the main table, I reminded myself that I couldn't throw myself in his arms and kiss him in front of everyone. The Legion still had its decorum, its rules and procedures. I would be perfectly dignified. I would *not* sit on his lap and feed him fries while making dorky cutesy noises.

My steps hastened. I was racing now, so excited to see him. Screw decorum. It was so seriously overrated. I looked at the main table. Nero wasn't there. No one was. Everyone had gathered in the center of the room, where the tables had been cleared away to make room for a platform. High above this spot, the points of the gigantic star in the glass ceiling slid apart. Warm, golden light spilled inside. A black and blond shape shot down, landing on the platform in a crouch. Slowly, his dark wings spread open, black with bright brilliant blue accents.

My heart sank when I realized it wasn't Nero at all. The angel rose from the ground. Shock trailed surprise when I saw his face. It was Harker. Harker was an angel now.

"Legion soldiers of New York," he said. "By order of the First Angel, I am taking command of this facility."

Author's Note

If you want to be notified when I have a new release, head on over to my website to sign up for my mailing list at http://www.ellasummers.com/newsletter. Your e-mail address will never be shared, and you can unsubscribe at any time.

If you enjoyed *Dragon's Storm*, I'd really appreciate if you could spread the word. One of the best ways of doing that is by leaving a review wherever you purchased this book. Thank you for your invaluable support!

The fifth book in the *Legion of Angels* series will be coming soon.

About the Author

Ella Summers has been writing stories for as long as she could read; she's been coming up with tall tales even longer than that. One of her early year masterpieces was a story about a pigtailed princess and her dragon sidekick. Nowadays, she still writes fantasy. She likes books with lots of action, adventure, and romance. When she is not busy writing or spending time with her two young children, she makes the world safe by fighting robots.

Ella is the international bestselling author of the paranormal and fantasy series *Legion of Angels*, *Dragon Born*, and *Sorcery and Science*.

www.ellasummers.com

Made in the USA
San Bernardino, CA
27 May 2017